Phoenix Rising, Lemuria Down

Phoenix Rising, Lemuria Down

A Novel

Rod Drought

Book cover and interior design by David Ter-Avanesyan/Ter33Design LLC
Edited by Marcy Dermansky
Marketer: Kristen O'Connell

The Library of Congress has catalogued as follows:
Drought, Rod.
Phoenix Rising, Lemuria Down: a novel-Rod Drought-1st ed.
1.Identity and belonging-fiction • 2. Coming of age-fiction
3. Satire and parody-fiction

ISBN: 979-8-218-64879-4

ebook ISBN: 979-8-218-65836-6

Poetry by Rod Drought

The Song We Left Behind
Wake of the Desert Belle
The Adventurers and other poems
Love and Chaos
Spawn from Eden

Poetry Anthology edited by Rod Drought

Ukraine: The Night and the Fire

*For Molly and Micah and
all the birds with broken wings.*

Book One:
Phoenix Rising

Chapter One

The bird changed everything.

The fledging squirmed helplessly outside our apartment on the smeared grime of the Go Away welcome mat. It was the third day in a row: a feeble, newly hatched bird laid at my feet. Purple and black with ridiculously ineffective pin feathers, the baby bird's eyes shut, too new to see. Its beak repeatedly opened and closed on the miraculous chance something worth eating would enter its tiny maw.

Like the previous two, I almost stepped on it before, braving the roasting Phoenix sun for my mid-morning walk across Van Buren enroute to Circle K. Squinting upward, I could not find the nest from which it had fallen. It was not like I cared for any of these birds. I was mystified. In the six years I lived at The Oasis Apartments, I had never experienced this. The Oasis was anything but an oasis. It was your typical run-down apartment complex in Phoenix, lots of brick, swamp cooler air conditioning and heat, all the units having the pleasant funk of stale tobacco and mildew. Its sixty units stacked two stories with outside stairwells wrapped around what was in its' prime a little desert paradise with grass, state-of-the-art pool, hot tub, and exotic palms. The Oasis' main problem was the property was state-of-the-art in nineteen-seventy-three.

What was left of The Oasis centerpiece was a yellowed frond tilted palm that would probably fall and take out a couple of apartments the next monsoon season haboob. The only green part left of The Oasis was stagnant pool water, cited by the city for its' fine and efficient mosquito sanctuary. The centerpiece when my roommate and old high school friend, Thad Torti and I moved in, was called a green zone. At one point there was grass and three other palms. The loosening on pet restrictions and lazy tenants, who let their poodles, mutts, pit bulls piss and poop everywhere, became what Thad and I fondly named, a brown zone.

Now The Oasis apartments fostered mosquitos and bats that feasted on the bloodsuckers. This was why I could not understand why baby birds were dropping on my welcome mat. The first two birds I simply stepped over to get my ration of slushy and hot dog for the day leaving them for the stray cats to devour. I was not an epicure. I would wake around 10am and take the short walk to Circle K for breakfast. Sometimes Thad would walk with me to pick up Churros and coffee. He mostly skipped breakfast, opting for pizza late in the day. I would take a slice or two while we were getting stoned. Before the bird, it was the best that I could do. I thought I was content.

I was about to step over the bird like I had done before with the others, but instead, I paused. It might have been the early April heat wave that affected my thinking. I felt it burning my pale skin already. I shunned the outdoors, so for an Arizona native, I looked quite odd. Not many people in Arizona look like bleached ghosts.

This time I did not look away. The bird panted rapidly, writhing in direct sunlight; it would not survive. The first-floor walkway was already scalding hot. A faint, smoldering ember of pity glowed inside me. I tried to ignore it, like I tried to bury my lousy childhood, my miserable mother. Sometimes memories bubbled up, came to a boil making me worthless or I should say, more worthless than normal.

Pity for the bird bubbled to the surface. Probably because the night before Thad and me, getting blitzed, dredged up YouTube videos of me, Cody Redman, when I was a fledging kid toy promoter star with my costar father. Thad found the first episode of The Cody Redd Show. It was a terrible first effort on our part. My dad and I played with some action figurines from a short-lived cartoon called The Fossil Family. It was a pre-historic family, a rip off Flintstones. The toys were produced by the Peter Dinky's Funhouse toy company. Somehow, people found my father, Rusty Redman, and I amusing. Despite our clownish first episode, my mother, the brainchild of the program, eventually made millions exploiting us. She was a brilliant and cunning woman.

Thad played the first episode just "for a laugh" except the joke was on me. We were both high, but I did not think it funny. Thad was often a big asshole. He was usually fine, sarcastic in a fun way when stoned but other times, not so much. After a few minutes of being laughed at, I retreated to my room to sulk. I thought of going to Chick-A-Dees to talk to Grace, a forty-five-year-old ex-stripper converted to bartender that befriended me but decided against it. There was a good chance she would tell me to grow a pair and quit being a pussy. Instead, I put in some earplugs so I would not hear Thad's cackle—he really does cackle when he laughs—and turned in early.

Maybe that's why I couldn't look away. I felt sorry for the bird. I muttered "shit," went back inside to search for an ersatz bird container. The apartment was dark. My eyes had to readjust after exposure to the sun. I stumbled toward the kitchenette, a bothersome name for the space where a stove, fridge and sink were wedged. Our adorable kitchenette could not fit two people without rubbing against each other.

We had intentionally made the apartment dark taping newspaper on the front and rear windows to block sunlight. There was little interest in budgeting what money we had to buy actual curtains. After my eyes adjusted to the usual gloom, I searched the kitchenette, finding only three empty pizza boxes, too large and narrow for the chick. I checked the garbage can for a small container. By some miracle Thad took out the trash. Nothing.

I kept my room free of debris. No possible bird container there. The cramped living room only had a half empty, melted slushie drink which I wanted to finish later. I walked into the miniature landfill that was Thad's room, confident I would find a suitable container.

Thad was sleeping. His PC with huge processor tower was humming like an expensive white noise machine. His computer was his life. When not ridiculing our dubious friend, Jeffery Lesmour, he could be found screwing around on his PC. He made a sport of hacking into systems, annoying innocent people. As far as I knew he never stole from anyone or sold information; his primary fun was interjecting strange images and cleverly edited videos in inappropriate places. He was my age, twenty-six, but had the maturity of a thirteen-year-old. I considered myself more mature than Thad. I'd say I had the maturity level of a socially repressed nineteen-year-old.

Door open, I found him curled on his bedroom floor snoring. Thad was too cheap to buy an actual bed frame or box spring and mattress. Instead he bought some blankets from a nearby Target and a memory foam pillow that seemed to be suffering from Alzheimer's. It had a permanent indent where his head rest. He slept on the floor in a fetal position on top of the blankets and then a few over him for good measure. It made me think of an article I read about why dogs walk in circles before they lay down. In the wild they circle to either flatten grass to lay on or distribute leaves and brush for comfort. I dubbed Thad's bedding his sleeping nest.

I stepped into his room. He snored lightly, looking almost likable while his eyes were closed. Long, twisted locks of mouse brown hair became tangled and matted when he did not make the effort to comb. His pouty, thin lips when awake pressed together while attempting to think, now relaxed resting for a day of witty invectives. He seemed serene when asleep compared to waking life after too many hours of computer glare, his bloodshot brown, eyes tortured by cigarette and weed smoke. I often wondered if his addiction to PC activities was what made him an irritable wise ass. Thad seemed at times to be carrying a grudge. For what, I did not know.

Among the takeout bags of America's greatest fast-food joints strewn across his floor, I found a Chinese restaurant box of fossilized white rice. I picked it up, dumping the loose rice on the floor. I would have to get a spoon to wedge out the rest. I thought it was an adequate box for the bird.

"What do you want, tubby?"

Thad was awake, peering at me with one bloodshot eye, his sleeping serenity fading fast. His latest pet name for me was tubby because of the paunch I developed from a diet of hot dogs.

"I didn't mean to wake you at the crack of noon," I said. "I got what I was looking for. Go back to sleep."

"No hot dogs this morning? You on a strict diet of putrid rice? Careful, you might waste away to something."

"There is a baby bird outside. I'm using the box to put it in."

Thad opened his other eye and stared at me. He kicked a pillow from between his crotch, sat up, slouched, scratched his shaggy mane.

"Baby bird and stale rice, wow, you are a regular Gordon Ramsey."

"I am trying to save the bird. I need a box to carry it."

"When did you get all Mother Theresa on me? Where are you taking it?"

Thad smiled. He sensed my discomfort, revealing concern for a bird. We often had conversations of how we did not give a crap about anything or anyone. He enjoyed exposing my vulnerability. I had not thought about what I should do with the bird once I put it in the box. My main intent was to get it out of the sun.

"I don't know. Maybe take it to a veterinarian," I said.

Thad rolled his eyes and pushed himself from the floor. He sat in his swivel chair and fired up his computer.

"They would probably feed it to a snake," he said.

He found a site called Birds of a Feather in Tempe that adopted injured birds to heal, feed and reintroduce into the wild. I took my phone out of my pocket and did a Waze search of the address. It was a fifteen-minute drive from The Oasis. I asked Thad if he wanted to come.

"Hell no," he replied.

In the kitchenette I scraped the hardened rice from the take-out container. Outside again, I carefully rolled the bird, still alive, into the box with my bare hands. I wondered whether it was wise to touch a bird with bare hands. It could be carrying deadly viral things. I decided it could not be worse than what I let cultivate in the food rot of our apartment. The bird trembled when I touched it, emitting two tiny screeches. Maybe it thought I was going to eat it after all.

Bird in box, I went to the carport where I parked my old Honda Civic. It had seen better days. I bought it with money I had left in my bank account when I turned sixteen. My parents left me a week before my sixteenth birthday. I moved into Thad's parents' house. They felt sorry for me because my parents did not say goodbye or tell me where they were going. They literally left in the dead of night. The police conducted an investigation. They had theories. They thought they were running from the law but couldn't understand why they left me behind. I knew the real reason. I was no longer profitable to them, so they split. I could accept that from my mother, she was a heartless, manipulative narcissist but I was surprised my father left without at least saying goodbye. I thought he loved me in his own, ineffectual way. I was wrong. My family trended wildly on social media for two weeks. A month after they left, I got a letter from our family lawyer stating a trust fund was established for me in the event of their disappearance. That's when I began to believe they did die which would explain why I never heard from my father. Maybe Marvin K. Putz got even with them. When I called the lawyer he said he knew nothing other than that I would get a monthly allowance of $1,500 dollars until I turned forty. I was outraged my mother's idea of compensation for depriving me of a normal childhood amounted to such a paltry sum. She made plenty of money from The Cody Redd Show which she parleyed into real estate investments, and no doubt other deals I was ignorant of.

At the time, I thought it was rather hopeful of them to think I would want to live. For weeks, months, I felt like dying. The whole farce of our happy family came crashing down when our YouTube empire collapsed. Mother had deducted it was no longer cost effective to have me as a child. I knew what was coming because I overheard a conversation between my parents the night of my thirteenth birthday party. They thought I was asleep, but at the top of the stairs I heard them caught up in an argument. Mother was spit balling the idea that they should have one more kid, so they could develop another YouTube child selling toy revenue stream. My father, in his typical malleable protest, disagreed.

"Darling, you must remember our agreement that I was to play the part of Cody's father until he grew out of toy promotions. In return, you would help me in my acting career afterward."

To this day, I find it insane my father thought he was *playing* the part of my dad. He was my biological father. But he had his "dream" of becoming a famous actor since taking his first acting class in college, where he met my mother. My mother, the greatest manipulator I have ever known, exploited my father for years. She strung him along like an animal trainer with yummy, little morsels enticing him to sit still and be a good fake father on YouTube. While acting as his agent, she threw him tiny bits, getting him booked on soap opera cameos or TV commercials or some summer theater group gig. She would tell him; "We are parents and must focus on Cody's career and future first," while all along, she played with us like the thousands of plastic toys I played with, hawked and outgrew.

My old Civic looked terrible but ran great. It was cherry red at one point but the Arizona sun and constant bombardment of bird poo from the carport nests at The Oasis parking lot eliminated its once lustrous hew. The left front fender and bumper was partially shredded due to one of my few excursions out. Three years ago, Thad and I decided on a minor road trip that turned into an ill-fated day drinking episode. We drove one Sunday afternoon to revisit our hometown Fountain Hills where we grew up and the Cody Redd Show was shot. We wanted to drive by our childhood homes but never reached them. Unwittingly, we happened to choose one of the town's massive art fair weekends where tens of thousands of people infested it looking for cultural enlighten-ment and kettle corn. We got as far as The Alamo Saloon, opting to drink with locals until sundown. I recklessly drove buzzed all the way back to The Oasis nodding off as I rolled into the covered parking space. Thad passed out halfway home and had a rude awakening when I scraped the steel pylon of the carport. We were lucky it wasn't worse.

I wedged the bird in the takeout box in the console cup holder, turned the key to the Honda and switched on the AC. It was a miracle the AC still worked. I wanted to keep the bird cool because it had been out in the sun. I later found out that was a dumb idea. Young birds need to stay warm.

On the way to Birds of a Feather I turned on the radio and listened to KJZZ, the local NPR station. I liked NPR. It rarely had any celebrity news unless it was an interview with some actor or musician that actually used their brain. When I was a celebrity I was bewildered why anyone wanted to know what I thought or what I liked. I was just a kid. What did I know?

I listened to a feature story on Lemuria Down. The grand experiment of creating a model utopian society was about to start. It was the brainchild of the mysterious Darby Summers, a worldwide real estate mogul and business entrepreneur. Years earlier, she made a grand announcement. She secured the rights to a submerged, extinct volcanic formation off Kauai, Hawaii. Her goal was to build an island that would support a community of two thousand people. She wanted to create a model utopian society by dredging and filling around the submerged volcano's base to build an island for the future home of specially selected individuals. People from all walks of life were being recruited to participate in her experiment.

I listened with mild interest and a tinge of disdain. The island construction was completed. A hired board of social psychologists and city planners were in the process of selecting from hundreds of thousands of applicants the perfect people to be part of a model society. I was skeptical of the whole concept.

Birds of a Feather sat in a residential area. It was an older house on a big, wooded lot. A copper sign at the entrance of the circular driveway read: The James and Betty McKeever

Memorial Birds of a Feather Sanctuary. There was a small plague by the front door. It told the story of the McKeever's life-long passion for birds. For over thirty years, they took birds into their home to rehabilitate eventually making it a full-time sanctuary bringing in volunteers and organizing fund drives. James McKeever passed in 2012, Betty in 2017. They willed their home to Tempe on the stipulation that Birds of a Feather remained in the community to help their feathered friends. I had no idea it was there.

Holding the bird in the Chinese take-out box, I entered the sanctuary through an ornate Spanish Mission style front door. It was a large ranch house with Saltillo tiles. The reception area was set up in what used to be the living room. Stand-up wall partitions normally seen in office settings blocked the view into the rest of the house. In the center of this walled off area was an old mahogany desk with numerous drawers bursting with files. I could only see one bird in the room, a scruffy canary in a cage suspended by a brass stand with a looped hook, but the muffled sound of many birds chirping and squawking echoed from the back of the house.

No one was manning the desk. A tarnished copper bell with a wood handle and a sign that read "please ring for assistance" was next to an old rotary dial phone. I tapped the bell alarmed by its' loud ring. A female voice called out, "be right there." I waited, examining a picture on the wall of an aged couple with parakeets perched on their hands; both wore very thick lensed glasses. They looked alike. I figured it was the McKeevers. Later I learned they were brother and sister.

"Can I help you?"

Startled, I nearly dropped the bird in the box. Poor fucking thing. I did not see or hear her walk in because I was engrossed studying the pictures of the McKeevers. I turned quickly and gasped. She was the most beautiful girl I ever saw. She had smooth, caramel colored skin, gleaming black hair, and dark sparkling eyes, long, upturned eye lashes and this sweet, delicately featured face. Her only imperfection was a small scar just below her hairline. The scar was a slightly raised bump a few shades lighter than her skin tone. Her hair was in a bun which only accentuated her graceful neck and two small diamond studs in each earlobe. She was wearing khakis and a tight emerald-green shirt with a name tag that read Sierra Gonzales above her left breast. I stammered, forgetting why I was there.

I gawked blankly at her beauty. She looked at me with raised eyebrows; head tilted up. I felt like an idiot. She noticed the take-out box I held. Her expression of questioning turned sour.

"What's in the box?" she asked.

"Ah, it's a bird. I found it."

She moved quickly from behind the desk, took the box from me and opened it.

"What is the matter with you? There is rice stuck on this bird. This container is filthy!"

"I, I'm sorry."

She stopped and looked at me. Her face softened.

"I am sorry for being rude," she said. "It pisses me off how little people know about birds. But you are doing a good thing. Come with me."

I followed her to a back room. Shades were drawn, but I could make out in the darkened room several small clear plastic boxes with holes on a shelf. There was cloth bedding and young birds in most of the boxes. The birds began to chirp. The girl put the takeout box on a tall examination table then quickly pulled on latex gloves. She grabbed a pair of scissors and cut down the sides of the box over another white cloth.

"I found it by my apartment door. It was in direct sunlight on the sidewalk. I put on my AC in the car to cool it down."

She stopped what she was doing. Her jaw tightened.

"They need to be kept warm, not cold. Did you touch this bird with your bare hands?"

I nodded, feeling like an adolescent boy after his mother caught him in the act of masturbation. She sighed, telling me to wash my hands in the bathroom. I apologized again and did as I was told. When I came back, she had the little bird under a bare light bulb, gently picking several grains of rice off its body. I felt lazy and stupid for not thoroughly ridding the box of rice. When she was satisfied that the nestlings' body was free of rice, she took an empty plastic box from the shelf, put the bird in its' new home, then placed the box back to its rightful spot.

"With any luck, it will live. You should never handle a bird with bare hands. You could get sick. The bird could die."

I nodded, trying not to gape at her beauty. I had an urge to hug her. I could not remember the last time I was with someone that cared a damn about anything. For years, it was just me and Thad and a couple of our old, warped friends from school. It felt good to witness a caring person. I wanted to hold her like a kid holds a favorite stuffed animal. I saw her looking intently at me.

"You look familiar. Do I know you?" she asked.

This happened too many times, which was one of the reasons I had chosen to live as a recluse. It had been a long time since someone her age recognized me as the one-time wunderkind star of the YouTube universe. I hoped she would let it go. When people recognize me as Cody Redd, they are either happy to be in the presence of a low-grade celebrity or repulsed by the scandal perpetrated by my mother. I wanted neither recognition. I wanted to forget my earlier life existed.

"Nope. We have not met."

"What's your name?"

Thad helped hide my identity by legally changing my name to Cody Green. At the time, we thought it was clever to have it like my real name. We were smoking a lot of dope then. Plus, he was used to calling me Cody. Looking back, my new name should have been radically different. It should have been something cool like Everett Ryder. I thought of the name Everett Ryder only after I legally changed to Cody Green. People often figured out who I really was because of the similarity to my real name. It came off as a clue. I told her my fake name. Her beautiful, dark eyes got wide in astonishment. She got the clue.

"Oh my God, you are Cody Redd! I used to watch you all the time!"

I smiled, pleased she was excited to meet me instead of upset about what my mother did. The Cody Redd Show in its' heyday was a big deal. For three years we were the most viewed children's

YouTube show. Images of my father and I appeared on toy packaging, and we even had our own cereal that tasted like shit, not a strong selling point. Toward the end, my mother signed as a Hail Mary, a toy promotion deal with owner of Happy Timez Toyz, Melvin K. Putz. By then The Cody Redd Show was fading in popularity. I was thirteen trying to pretend I was much younger, playing with toys, along with my father. Nobody was buying it, but my mother convinced Melvin K. Putz that she was going to upgrade our franchise and grow his toy industry exponentially. Shortly after signing, she and my father ran off with the money, from the deal, over three million dollars, leaving me behind to face the media onslaught. At first, people thought I was part of the scam. When my parents could not be found, rumors spread that they met an untimely end. Then Putz disappeared, too. There were whispers that Sal Martino, owner of Peter Dinky's Fun Factory, the original revenue stream for our show, wasted all three of them especially since he eventually bought out Happy Timez Toyz from the Melvin K. Putz estate. It has been over ten years since my parents and Putz were last seen.

"Busted," I said. "I try to stay incognito these days."

Her smile faded. She frowned, a look of pity. She was lovely.

"What happened to you was terrible. You did not deserve such treatment, kicked from your nest without learning to fly."

I was uncomfortable when someone took pity on me for childhood trauma; this time I was not. My heart raced. I wanted to take her hand.

"My name is Sierra, but you already know that" she said pointing to the name plate on her shirt. "Would you like a tour of the sanctuary?"

She took me through the kitchen out a sliding glass door where all the muted chirping and squawking came. There was a sizable aviary in the back of the property where dozens of birds fluttered from many perches. To the side was a smaller aviary of birds that were unable to fly, recovering from injuries. I saw parakeets, parrots, and a large cockatoo. In various cages under the shade of the covered patio there were grackles, a crow, a bright, red cardinal, and others I could not identify. Their many calls drew me in, all a part of a chorus in a language I did not understand.

"The McKeevers were brother and sister. They passed and now volunteers carry on their legacy. All of these birds were found in the wild. The exotic ones were abandoned by pet owners. We try to find non-native birds good homes. The wild ones that are injured or young fallen from nests are nursed back to health and released. Some you see have a broken wing or other disability. We must keep them because they would die in the wild."

"Can I volunteer?" I asked impulsively.

I had to volunteer. It wasn't because I suddenly was overcome with compassion for orphaned birds. I wanted to be with Sierra. I wanted to be like a hummingbird to her hummingbird feeder, continually dip into the sweet nectar of her spirit. I was afraid if I asked her out, she would say no and be done with me. I took the coward's path. If I pretended an interest in birds, maybe in time she would say yes.

Sierra flashed a dazzling smile.

"It takes a lot of training," she cautioned. "I am studying to be a veterinarian. The sanctuary doesn't bring people in unless they know what they are doing, but if you want I can teach you how to feed the bird you brought. You can be one of its caretakers."

I agreed, especially since she offered to train me. Her willingness to personally train might be an indicator she liked me. I filled out a volunteer form writing my real name, Cody Redman, on the form since she was impressed I was once famous. What a fool I was. Before I left, she wrote on the back of a Birds of a Feather business card the hours she volunteered and told me I could come then. She walked me to the door.

"One more thing," she said. "You get to name your bird. Anyone that takes care of a new arrival gets to name it. It is too young to determine its sex so pick a gender neutral name."

I thought for an appropriate bird name. One came to mind.

"Phoenix," I said.

"Good one!" she giggled.

Chapter Two

After ascending the lofty heights of my encounter with Sierra, I returned to the dismal swale of The Oasis. My good spirits of meeting the girl of my dreams were immediately dashed when I stepped into our apartment. Thad's absurd sidekick, Jeffery Lesmour had paid a visit. The two were hunkered down on the living room couch engaged in heady competition. They played MLB The Show on a PlayStation.

Neither of them were huge baseball fans, but they liked to create franchises and players. They thought it was funny to give a franchise a ridiculous name and create ugly uniforms, ugly players with suggestive names like Dick Head or Big Dawg Pyle, etc. Thad's franchise was named the Chicago Hitmen and their uniforms looked like old gangster, pinstripe suits. Lesmour named his team the Death Valley Butchers. Its logo was a lumberjack with streams of blood coming from his mouth and two axes crossed above his head. They purposely made players incredibly bad at hitting, pitching, and fielding so when they tried to control them a comedy of errors would ensue. Of course, they smoked weed while doing this and laughed hysterically as the blunders mounted. I admit it was funny at first but when they played into early morning laughing and shouting non-stop it got old. They were always stoned.

Neither acknowledged me, too engrossed. Lesmour always bought cheap beer for their marathons. I took one out of the fridge and popped the lid, taking a swig from the can. It tasted like carbonated aluminum. At least it was cold. I read the label. It was called Fringe Lite and had a poorly conceived graphic of a horsehead with its teeth showing. I assumed the graphic "artist" that created this image was trying to depict a horse in mid whinny. The horse looked more like it was in the final stages of rabies. I do not know why there was a horsehead on the can.

"Hey nature boy," Thad asked me. "Did you find a home for the bird?"

I slumped on a black bean bag chair near the couch.

"Yep, they took the bird in. I volunteered to take care of it."

I braced myself for verbal abuse. It was not common practice in our slovenly household to display any amount of responsibility. We were not supposed to care about anything, so I knew my caring for a bird or pretending to care for a bird to be with Sierra would pose a threat to my roommate. I dared not mention my interest in Sierra. I would eventually but not when Lesmour was within earshot. He would chip in with some bullshit about a conquest he had in an attempt to prove his virility. Lesmour was a devout follower of one upmanship. Most of his stories were self-serving lies.

"You take care of a bird?" Thad laughed. "You can barely comb your hair!"

Lesmour laughed. I felt like smacking Thad's toady. I always felt like smacking him. Thad knew Lesmour from a brief semester stay at Scottsdale Community College. They met while taking a video production course and did nothing except tape each other getting drunk at various parks. They were kicked out of school when they posted a video of them giving beer to monkeys at the Phoenix Zoo.

"What do you know?" I said. "You are not exactly a high functioning adult."

"Yeah, Thad, you are more like a semi-functioning dolt!" Lesmour laughed at his own joke.

To know Lesmour was to despise him. He was short, squat, talked in a hurried whisper-lisp and possessed a constant fat-lipped smirk. When smiling, he bared these little rat-like teeth. He drank coffee all day long even if it was cold and the milk was curdled. People treated him like garbage because he was either bragging or complaining. His head was round. We had given him a dozen nicknames through the years pertaining to its shape ending up with pumpkin head as the definitive one.

Thad threw a crusty, ornamental couch cushion at his bulbous head. Lesmour complained bitterly saying it was "really cruel" that Thad committed such a heinous act. Thad ignored his whining. It was best to ignore Lesmour until he was needed.

"Hey, old chum," Thad said. "The takeout should be ready. I bought, so you fly."

Lesmour grumbled that he gets no respect. This was true. Dutifully, he got up to leave. I hoped they ordered enough food for me.

"Oh, and can you get more beer, sweetheart? We are running low."

Lesmour scowled. "Why do I always have to get the beer," he said, but left on his mission. He knew the rules.

"Is it really worth keeping him around?" I asked.

"To quote another great leader, he is a "useful idiot." Now tell me about this bird you have such an interest in."

Despite his appearance and personality, Thad was perceptive and clever. He knew me well and knew it was unlikely I was so altruistic as to be interested in the wellbeing of a baby bird. His bushy eyebrows raised in feigned concern; his eyes glittered with snide glee.

I took a deep breath and told him about Sierra, the beautiful, warm, enchanting creature that totally took me off guard. I confessed I was not interested in the bird. I was captivated by her and wanted to be near her any way possible. I was surprised that Thad did not laugh. Instead, he was silent for a moment before he spoke.

"Wow, my buddy has a crush. Good for you. So, what's the plan; get to know her while taking care of the bird, then ask her out?"

It seemed like a viable way to ask her to out. I was relieved that Thad had not mocked me. "Yep," I said.

"Excellent, especially seeing as you have no game. It is your only best chance to get laid. Take her out, get her drunk, get her in the sack."

Thad's moment of acting like a compassionate friend subsided. He chuckled at his base assessment of how I should proceed. I felt nervous and overwhelmed thinking about dating, going out and the Holy Grail of relationship, having sex. It all seemed impossible to me. I tried to date occasionally. I sometimes met girls at odd part-time jobs I picked up but always failed. It was an unwitting act of self-sabotage. I could never get close to anyone because the two people that were supposed to love me, did not. I only trusted Thad because he was with me before and after they left. I was hopeful about Sierra, though. She showed compassion for broken birds. I wanted to try.

"Thanks, buddy," I said with a touch of sarcasm.

We celebrated that my heart was able to beat for a pretty girl by having a couple of gummy bear edibles, washing them down with the last two cans of Fringe beer. Thad advised me to go online, order new clothes, get a decent haircut, solid ideas. I generally schedule a barber visit when my morning bed hairdo resembled Albert Einstein's. Most of my t-shirts either had food stains or small holes, rips frayed thin from use.

Lesmour came back with the Mexican take away. It was from Sloppy Jose's, a little hole in the wall a block from us. The restaurant didn't look like much, two dine-in tables, geared mostly for take away, but the food was great. I always got shrimp tacos with extra cilantro. Thad knew this.

Like a good, little foot soldier, Lesmour also brought a fresh six pack. It was yet another beer I never heard of called Lon O' Land. Its label depicted a javalina rooting a prickly pear cactus with a psychedelic sky for a background. Thad asked him which discount rack he found the beer. Lesmour went immediately on the defensive.

"You guys never buy beer and then I get shit when I buy it. If you chipped in maybe I would buy better beer."

"You are such a cheap bastard," Thad said. "Aren't you making big bucks? Can't you splurge for your friends occasionally?"

Lesmour claimed a week before he was promoted to captain

a pontoon boat on Saguaro Lake, north of Fountain Hills. It is a manmade reservoir that is utilized for sport and site seeing tours of the surrounding red rock peaks and desert flora and fauna. Still, it was a job. Thad and I always assumed his stories were fabrications at best. Years ago he blabbed an entire summer that he and Alice Cooper were tight. Thad found out later through a mutual friend that Lesmour "met" Alice when he was bussing tables in a Scottsdale restaurant. He cleared the table Cooper, and his wife sat and then asked for his autograph. The owner of the restaurant noticed Lesmour badgering a bemused Cooper. The owner was not amused. It almost got Lesmour fired but Cooper was kind enough to intervene and tell the owner to spare the round headed boy, he meant no harm.

The validity of whether Lesmour had a real job or not was entertaining conversation while we ate. He became increasingly agitated because we doubted him and suggested he prove his wealth by buying us stuff, which of course he refused. Thad and I laughed while Lesmour turned red in the face. Good times.

Then Thad turned the tables on me and told Lesmour more about my "crush."

"That's great, Cody," Lesmour said, "I had to let this hot girl go. She was too clingy."

Thad feigned concern.

"That's so sad, Jeff, I thought Sparky and you were a great couple."

Sparky was Lesmour's ferret. His fat lips pursed then his infamous scowl flashed.

"That's really cruel! Sparky was a pet, and he died! I had a real girlfriend!"

The sun's slow descent deposited simmering heat in sidewalks and all things concrete. It continued to seep inside our poorly insulated apartment. The food was good, the beer bad but cold. The edibles were kicking in. The couple of tokes we shared from the dispensary lightened the mood as night fell. Thad announced he must work on his novel. He told Lesmour it was time to leave. Lesmour never left on his own.

Thad's novel was a con. He told his parents the reason he chose to be unemployed was to devote his waking hours on a novel that would certainly rival James Joyce' Ulysses. He asked if they would financially support him while he toiled on his great work of art. His sweet and gullible parents agreed. They would do anything for their son, the exact opposite of mine, come to think of it. They agreed to pay his share of our rent and even gave him a living expense while he worked on the book. He hadn't a job for two years.

After the first several months, even they became suspicious and insisted they meet every other week with Thad providing a copy of the novel's progress. Even though after high school Thad did two semesters at A.S.U. toward a literary degree, rather than write anything on his own, he developed a unique template and algorithm where he could search other published novels, steal phrases, passages and have them re-worded so it was not a literal rip-off of an original work. He created another program that researched popular literary characters which created amalgam characters on its' own that he punched into his novel template.

I commented it would be easier if he just wrote an original work or resort to AI rather than putting in countless hours building a cheat system. He said he did write twenty pages at first but found it boring. His deception was more fun.

Telling Lesmour he must devote his time to writing was an effective way to get rid our annoying bro. Lesmour respected this request as if it was a sacred act. I often wondered if Lesmour really knew he was getting shoed out the door because Thad had grown weary of him. Our round headed friend never challenged the rejection. Lesmour possibly thought it better than being told to get the hell out.

Lesmour left, Thad did retire to his room to actually work on his novel. He had given his parents the first two hundred pages. He had yet to come up with a title. As he exited I asked him what the book was about. He said, "I don't know. I haven't read it."

I took the last bottle of Lon O' Land beer to my room. I kept thinking about Sierra. I was thrilled to feel such an attraction but also confused. The more I thought about her, the more I wanted to be with her. A tap I closed years ago had burst due to back pressure. Desire was drowning me. For years, my only desire was to be left alone. Now Sierra flooded my mind.

I never had a real girlfriend. In the later years of The Cody Redd Show, my mother arranged this sick little scenario where I met another YouTube child star named Lila. She was my age and promoted toys, just like me. My dad left to do summer stock theater, playing a bit part my mother got him. By then the show was losing viewership because I was no longer a kid. Mother thought it would be a good idea if Lila and I combined forces to promote toys that were gender neutral by delving into a retro look at family games like Monopoly or Life.

I was thirteen and had just begun to notice girls, their legs, the way they talked, acted and clothes they wore. Lila was a pretty girl. She was Asian American, straight dark, hair, almond eyes, and a truly happy smile. We shot three episodes at our house. When the cameras were on everything was fine, but when there was a break and we hung out in my tree house, eating lunch or general chilling, I could not keep my eyes off her.

One afternoon after lunch, we climbed the ladder to my treehouse. It was hot out, but the treehouse was air conditioned. It even had running water and a mini fridge. My parents had gotten rich off me, so they spoiled me rotten in that respect. Still in make-up, Lila was reading a book. I was working on a Lego set, at least trying to work on it. Lila had on this blue floral ruffle top. The neckline hung low, and I could see her breasts which were already full.

It was quiet. I felt a sort of heightened tension in the air. Then Lila spoke, without looking from her book.

"Stop staring."

My face was on fire. I looked away.

"Sorry."

She averted her eyes from the book and seemed a little taken aback. I think because she noticed that my head blushed into a fire hydrant.

"No worries. It's just not polite to stare."

I muttered sorry again and looked down at my Legos, pretending to get back to work on a Star Wars Jedi fighter. I couldn't focus on the task. Now, it felt like I was being stared at. I looked up. She smiled, playfully twirled a lock of hair between her fingers.

"You can touch them if you want."

I didn't know what to say. My mouth dropped open in astonishment. Several seconds passed. She spoke again after I appeared to have been turned mute.

"It's ok, Cody. I don't mind. I let other boys touch them. Besides, I like you."

She stood, so did I. She drew close. I reached slowly and gently cupped my hands on her breasts. My palms covered the fabric of her top, but my fingers touched the soft, cool of her exposed skin.

"Now you have to kiss me," she said.

My first kiss. Looking back, I almost cry thinking how innocent and breathtaking it was.

For the next week, it became our afternoon delight. We shot some lame toy playing episode in the morning then would go "play" in my treehouse. The Legos were pushed aside. Sometimes, she would read me Harry Potter but mostly we kissed until our lips got sore. Every day she allowed me to touch her breasts. Twice, she took her top off and I my shirt. That is as far as it went. By the end of the week, the shoot was done. Lila and her mother flew back to San Diego. I never saw her again. I e-mailed and messaged her, but she never replied.

I cried every night for two weeks. My father came in one of those nights and asked what was wrong. I wouldn't tell him, but he put two and two together.

"Do you miss, Lila?"

Head buried in pillow, I nodded and said that she did not return my texts. He was silent for a long time.

"Women can be like that."

He patted my head and left.

That was my only girlfriend. In junior and senior high, I was laughed at for being that "creepy" YouTube kid. Then, when my parents split, I had totally given up on people and having a normal life. My parents didn't love me. Why would anybody else?

From then on it was Thad and me. Thad dated briefly in college but whenever he brought a girl home they were repulsed by our living conditions and never returned. We both gave up.

I finished the beer, watched a documentary on the wild west, but was not tired. I was terrified of even attempting to have a relationship with Sierra. I was inexperienced and socially inept. Why would she want me? I decided I would let Phoenix die. I opened my laptop and looked at naked girls on a free porn site. I thought I would jerk off, but then I thought about Phoenix, covered in rice.

I was not going to fall asleep this way.

I closed the laptop, grabbing my car keys and made the quick drive to Chick-A-Dees to see my ex-stripper friend, Grace. Two years ago, Thad and I went there for the first time, out of boredom we said, a joke. Chick-A-Dees had the reputation as the seediest strip club in Maricopa County. We had never been there, neither of us were into that, but we wanted to see how bad it was. We were not disappointed.

Two cars more beaten up than mine parked in Chick-A-Dees lot as I pulled in. Littered about were empty bottles of rut gut liquor in wrinkled paper bags and crushed cigarette packs. The name was in neon lights on the square brick and mortar building with barred windows. The front door handle was loose, missing a couple of screws like any patron that thought it was a good idea to frequent the place. Grace was behind the bar, her back leaning against it watching the Diamondback game.

She looked older than her age. She had the face and demeanor of someone who lived a hard life. Her teeth were yellowed from nicotine and coffee, one incisor chipped. She quit stripping when she began to sag then worked behind the bar. Long, stringy grey-brown hair touched her shoulders. She rarely wore a bra saying she got bigger tips that way.

I met her when Thad and I did our initial field trip to Chick-A-Dees. Thad insisted on seating at the end of the stage to get a good look at the dancers. At first I joined him but felt uncomfortable when girls asked if I wanted a lap dance. I didn't have any cash for tips, so I sat at the bar and ordered a drink. Grace was sullen at first, but I made a joke about Thad looking like a dog having a T-bone waved in his face which caused her to laugh. I liked her laugh. It was boisterous, an explosion of joy.

After a few drinks I told her my life sob story, then felt silly after she said she was raised by her uncle because her parents were "fall down drunks." Her uncle repeatedly raped her until she ran away, living with a slightly less abusive boyfriend. She got a job at Chick-A-Dees and that was that.

Grace gave a short laugh and made me a vodka cranberry. I rarely had hard liquor. I ordered it the first time we met because I wanted something strong, nervous about being in the strip club. Some hip hop song was playing while a girl in loose fitting lingerie danced without interest in her craft. Two withered dudes sat at the end of the bar engaged in a solemn discussion their backs facing the dancer. Now, I was forever stuck drinking vodka cranberries.

Grace once told me it was a popular disco club in its' day named Fascinations but along with the death of disco, it slowly devolved into a strip club. On either side of the stage two golden bird like cages remained where featured disco dancers did their moves. On crowded nights strippers still used the cages inviting patrons to pay money to "set them free" and thereby removing all their clothes. The cages reminded me of the bird sanctuary which reminded me of Sierra. I wanted to forget Sierra.

"Hey Red, how's it hangin'?"

"Big news, Grace, I like a girl." I had told myself I wasn't going to think about her and that was the first thing I said. With raised eyebrows Grace mocked surprise at my news.

"Holy shit! Will miracles never cease! You won't be needing me anymore!" she laughed.

So for the second time that day, I told her about the bird, Sierra, and the unexpected discovery I still had a beating heart. I also told her I was clueless on how to proceed.

"Red, don't worry about it, take the plunge. She obviously likes you. Didn't she invite you to take care of the bird?"

"Yeah, but she offers that to everyone who brings one in."

"Right, numb nuts, but didn't she say she personally will train you?"

"Okay but then what? I just ask her out?"

"Of course, genius, go ahead and ask her! Find out what she

likes. For example, you know I like basketball, so if it was me you were asking out, you would take me to a Suns game. It's not rocket science. Stop being a coward, you gotta take the plunge. Get your feet wet! You never know until you try."

"Is that why you don't go out with anyone, you're scared?" I felt defensive about being called a coward. I stupidly thought to turn the tables on Grace.

"Hell no, I ain't scared. I am just sick and tired of it, same old shit, different day," Grace said. "I don't mind what I have. I am going to adopt a cat, maybe two. I can be one of those crazy old cat ladies. Listen, you are still a kid, you got to live a little or you'll die inside. I can see already you are different, how you talk about this girl, how awake you are. You used to look like a zombie. You don't look like that anymore. Get to know her, ask her out, use breath mints and if you go out drinkin', try not to puke on her!"

She laughed her atomic bomb laugh. The two guys at the end of the bar turned and the stripper stopped her dance of boredom, shouting to Grace, "What's so funny?"

Grace waved her off and made me a second drink, saying it was on her.

"Tell me how it goes down," she said. "In case you can't get here..."

Grace tore off some receipt paper and wrote down her phone number. I was touched by her interest and enthusiasm. I know nothing about people or life, but I do know when someone who is abrasive or rough around the edges does you a solid, it means much more than your regular nice person. I entered Grace's number into my phone so I wouldn't lose it.

I finished the second drink, left Grace a big tip, then placed some bills on the stage for the dancer who shouted as I left that I was sweet. On the ride back, I had the windows down. The air was cooler. April in Phoenix was like that. Some hot days followed by cool nights. It took time for the concrete and hard packed earth to retain the heat. I hoped to gain the courage to ask Sierra out before the nights became hot, thinking we could do something outside like walk the botanical garden.

Chapter Three

Each day Sierra volunteered at Birds of a Feather, I dutifully woke and drove to Tempe to feed my adoptive bird, Phoenix. Sierra said it's wing was broken and probably would not heel enough to survive in the wild. She also said Phoenix was a male Starling. She could tell by his bright yellow bill and orange gape. She said males are fun as adults because of the variety of sounds they make and their iridescent plumage. I told her I was glad Phoenix was a boy because I identify better with males. It made her laugh. Her laugh was like birdsong itself, bright, full of cheer. I was grateful Phoenix hadn't died.

"So true, Cody," she teased. "You can manly bond with your seven-ounce friend."

I quickly learned how much care was involved in saving a baby bird. Phoenix must always be warm and clean. Any time he pooped, the fecal sack had to be removed. Any formula from the syringe feeder that spilled from his ravenous mouth must be wiped from the cloth nest. At first, he had to be fed every two to three hours. I volunteered on the days when Sierra was there, Monday, Wednesday and Friday afternoons. I also assisted her in the care of other resident birds and the general upkeep of the sanctuary. I got to meet a few volunteers; Trevor, a teenager wishing to get community service hours for high school grad-uation, also a fifty-year-old widow named Martha, originally from Virginia spoke a honey like drawl. She found comfort and company volunteering after she lost her husband to cancer and her children flew off to college, a true empty nester. Then there was Gus, a tall, thin elderly man who was kind and personable, loved to tell stories about the old days. He was from Connecticut but moved here for business reasons. Now retired, he was trying to fill his days.

My favorite bird (besides Phoenix) was a cockatiel named after the Sesame Street character Oscar the Grouch. He was a stray found in Mesa. Oscar became a full-time resident at the sanctuary much to the delight of visitors and staff. He could only speak one phrase, but it fit with anything you could possibly say to him. That phrase being "Aw, shut up!"

One day, Sierra and I ushered a class of fourth grade kids on a school trip. Oscar was the highlight and finale of the tour. He was on his usual roost while Sierra spoke in glowing terms about his brains and beauty. She rambled on until she could tell the kids were getting restless.

"I am sorry, class," she said, "I get long winded talking about Oscar, he is such a wonderful bird. Oscar, do you have anything to add?"

On cue, Oscar said: "Aw, shut up!"

The kids squealed with laughter.

Every day with Sierra was pure joy. She looked at everything positively. I had to keep my gloomy nature in check so as not to turn her off. The second week she surprised me with a small, gift-wrapped box. I opened it and found a Bird's of a Feather name badge with my real name, Cody Redman, on it. I fought back tears when she took it from me and pinned it on my shirt. It felt good to be wanted and accepted even though I was concerned my real name was once again in the public eye. She seemed to sense my trepidation.

"Don't hide who you are, Cody Redman. You are a good guy that had a lot of bad."

Time passed swiftly. Phoenix grew. In two weeks, he gained weight, strength, and size. He developed glossy black feathers with iridescent purple-blue shades. Sierra said if he was healthy with two good wings he would have flown the nest by now. Instead we transferred him to the smaller aviary on the side of the yard for permanently injured birds.

It was easy being with Sierra although the more time I spent with her, the more I tormented myself trying to build up nerve to ask her out. Between feeding and caring for the Birds of a Feather clientele, I got to know her. She was not big into crowds. She preferred walking in parks rather than being in festivals. Her favorite eating out activity was wine and a good cheeseboard. Sierra, to my surprise, also mentioned she had never visited Fountain Hills. She admired online pictures of the park that circled Fountain Lake and the giant fountain centerpiece that attracted many tourists. I saw the opportunity. Both Thad and Grace thought Sierra was sending me signals.

I asked her out at Birds of a Feather. We were eating Thai take away at the backyard picnic table under a shady tree. She mentioned that Sunday she had nothing to do. She was caught up on her studies and her family were out of town visiting relatives in Tucson.

"I don't have anything going on, either," I said. I never did. "Maybe we can go to Fountain Hills, walk around the fountain, catch sundown. It shouldn't be too hot at sundown with all the grass and water. There is a wine bar with outside seating. It has misters. You can see the fountain go off," it felt like I was giving a sales pitch. I was trying too hard.

"Sure," Sierra said. "I would like that."

I was taken aback how nonchalantly she accepted. Sierra didn't skip a beat, deftly using chopsticks to navigate Pad Thai noodles to her mouth. I was a slob and could barely manage eating with fork or spoon without staining my shirts. She was so casual in reply I wanted to verify this was not a friend hookup but an actual date. I knew trying to affirm it would be awkward.

"What time will you pick me up?" she asked.

I was about to tell her, but Gus interrupted. He was gone a few days taking care of "personal business" as he put it. He normally volunteered in the afternoon. Gus startled us both. We did not hear him approach. The tall, lanky old man was beginning his shift.

"Where should I start, boss?"

He called Sierra boss, said it with a wry smile. It was cute, like a private joke. She did the scheduling but was not a manager. Then he saw me and stared at my new volunteer badge. Sierra had given it to me while he was gone.

"You are stepping up in the world, young man but I see they got your last name wrong."

Sierra joked that I was under the witness protection program, Cody Redman was my real name, not Cody Green. Gus shook his head and feigned concern.

"Oooh, kid. It is not good to be found in this town. I hear there are a lot of tuff birds around."

Gus was joking but I had an uneasy feeling about the way he said it. He winked and jerked his head toward the varied tough birds in the sanctuary backyard, gave a low whistle then walked off.

The rest of the week, before our date, I did my best to clean up my act. Rather than order clothes online, I went to Tempe Marketplace, an outdoor mall, and bought a blue button-down shirt, tan cargo shorts, and a pair of black leather sandals. Grace approved, said I looked cute. I then took my weathered heap of a Honda to the car wash, hoping it would remain intact in its pass through the rollers and high-powered dryer. It survived, still dented, and stank on the inside but clean and crumb free. I bought an air freshener that I hung from the rearview. The inside now smelled like old takeaway food and fake pine. At least the outside was free of splattered bird poo.

I went to a Greek barber shop down the street and got a trim while the barber tried to engage me in a political conversation. I remained neutral because he was holding a sharp implement. On the way back to The Oasis, I stopped at Chick-A-Dees to have a vodka cranberry to quell the tightening knot in my stomach. Grace advised me to buy a shot bottle of Fireball and have it right before picking her up. I got one at a liquor store next to the strip club. At The Oasis, Thad saw the result of my haircut commenting

I looked almost human. I put on my new clothes, combed my hair a dozen times even though it didn't need it then downed the shot. It was sweet and burning. The knot loosened.

I picked her up at seven. Sierra and her family lived in a block construction home in the old part of Phoenix. The yard was sparse with white gravel and three large barrel cactus. It had a car port with two cars and a pickup truck with Jaime's Lawn Service magnet signage on the door.

Sierra came out of the house as soon as I pulled up, locked the front door, and hurried to my car. Her black diamond hair was not pinned up like at work. It flowed past her shoulders. She wore white sandals with little colored studs, tight fitting white shorts, a crimson halter top exposing midriff. I knew I had to make a point of not staring, but I thought it would be impossible.

"You look great," I told her. I felt my blush.

"You clean up well," she teased. "So tour guide, tell me about Fountain Hills."

On the drive, I told her Fountain Hills was conceived by a guy that helped plan Disneyland and another who was from the McCullough family of chainsaw fame. Their idea was to build a little oasis in the desert, but they needed an attraction. That's how they came up with creating the tallest continuous running fountain surrounded by a lake. It worked. Initial investors and developers were helicoptered in to see the fountain in all its glory rising upwards of five-hundred-sixty feet. At the time of construction it was the world's tallest fountain but now several others eclipse it.

"I was just a baby when my parents moved there," I told Sierra, "By the fountain there was a luncheonette and an octagonal shaped real estate office. Now it has restaurants, a gift shop, nail salon, and expensive apartments above the shops."

"I am excited to see the birthplace of the Cody Redd Show," she teased again. Sierra liked to tease me. Grace said that was a good sign.

"Nice. You get to see the birthplace of my mother's profiteering," I smiled. I said it like it didn't hurt me anymore even though it did.

She lightly touched my shoulder, "That is the past. You have a bright future ahead."

By the time we got to Fountain Park, the sun was hugging the distant mountains creating ribbons of purple and pink clouds. The sun dipping below the horizon in late spring and summer cooled the air especially near grass and water. Our walk around the fountain would be tolerable. We parked by a statue that residents and tourists called the iron horse. It was a statue of a horse made from things you could find in either a junkyard or a pricey antique shop, washbasins, sewing machine, old cutlery improvised its' tail, barbed wire for the mane. Sierra was impressed.

She inspected the ingenuity of the piece telling me several members of her family were painters and sculptors, but her passion was science and nature.

"You seem to enjoy volunteering at the sanctuary, maybe you should take classes relating to the natural world."

"I guess I could," I said, "I would have to get a job to help pay for tuition."

She turned and smiled, "Go for it," she said, holding her stare, before walking toward the fountain.

We walked past the row of restaurants and stores to the circular paved path that went around fountain lake. In the center of the lake was the famous fountain. It shot a powerful torrent every hour on the hour. When I was young I imagined the base with its sleek silver curved metal bands from which the jetted water rose were the ribs of an alien spacecraft. In the middle of the base a giant nozzle and bank of lights created a shining, watery beacon at night.

"When does it rise?" Sierra asked playfully several times, like a child waiting for Christmas. I pretended to be annoyed which only made her ask more. It was a fun game we played as we took in statuary of Teddy Roosevelt, frogs, dogs, children and gazed in the fading light at numerous native plants with signage of their names in English and Latin. Then, water gushed from the fountain, climbing higher and higher like a NASA rocket gaining the velocity needed to combat gravity. Sierra was speechless. I was jaded. I witnessed the fountain rising a thousand times, but I enjoyed watching Sierra admire the scene. Her big, dimpled grin beamed brighter than the gushing water. Head tilting back, her sleek black hair nearly touched her butt. I wanted to kiss her; tell her she was more beautiful than the fountain framed in a sky crowded with stars.

"It is so wonderful," she said.

"When we first moved here, I would always ask my parents to stop whenever we passed the fountain when it was up. Like anything else, it became ordinary. Thad used to say this quote he heard somewhere, familiarity breeds contempt. Living here, shooting the show, my parents, all left a bad taste in my mouth.

Did you know Sheriff Joe lives here? When we were in high school Thad called him a Nazi during the Thanksgiving Day Parade. He was on a stupid float waving at people and throwing candy to kids."

Sierra's dimples disappeared. She stared at me in disbelief. I ruined the moment.

"Don't you know you are supposed to keep things light on a first date, Cody Redman?"

I felt foolish but delighted she acknowledged we were on an official date.

"I am sorry about the Sheriff Joe reference."

Sheriff Joe Arpaio was dubbed at one time, "America's toughest Sheriff" for putting prisoners in tents in the desert and feeding them bologna sandwiches while making them wear pink underwear. He later was convicted of racial profiling Latino neighborhoods to terrify and send back to Mexico. It was stupid of me to say considering Sierra was a Daca recipient. I hope she understood that I did not approve of Sheriff Joe, that I did not think that way.

"Mentioning him does not bother me," she said. "There are good and bad people everywhere."

She started to walk. I followed.

"I was admiring the beauty of this place. You went dark mentioning your experience. Did you bring me here to tell me how horrible it was for you? That is not so fun. Besides your experiences alone do not make this a bad place. You make it a bad place with your thoughts. My parents and I nearly died coming to America. They love Mexico but they could not live there, there was no hope. They wanted to give me a better life. Do you see the scar on my forehead?"

She stopped and positioned herself so the light from the fountain shone on her forehead. She put her finger to the faded scar. I noticed it before but thought it impolite to ask.

"We had to get through a barbed wire fence. We were chased by border patrol. I was gouged by the wire, and it left a scar. I was just a baby. We lived with my uncle and aunt; my parents worked constantly and made a life here. It was hard. At times my parents were treated kindly but other times treated like garbage. Now my father owns a landscaping service, my mother works in a school cafeteria. It is still hard but a better life than they had before. It is not the land or the place that hurts you. It is your experiences and how you chose to look at them."

We were passing the line of stores and restaurants. Out the back of the wine bistro and the restaurants were tables full of people in spirited conversation. A man and woman duet were playing guitars and singing: What a Wonderful World. I thought of suggesting we get a table but hesitated, not knowing if it was proper to cut off the conversation. We were both silent passing the gaiety. The silence bothered me. I spoke up.

"I'm sorry. I am cynical. I don't like that about myself."

"Replace the bad times with good," Sierra said. "We can make this a good time and that will replace some of the bad you lived here."

"It's just that . . .," I glanced at her. I knew what I was going to say was not positive or "fun", but I could not help myself. I had to get it out. Besides Grace, I felt she was the only one in the world that would listen.

She sighed, exasperated.

"Alright. We are going to walk around this circle one more time. Say what you want but then," she stopped and pointed directly at me, "leave it behind! Then we are going to sit down, drink wine and eat cheese!"

She poked me in the chest a few times for emphasis which caused me to laugh. We continued our walk as I dumped my past woes on her. Nice guy.

"The way I see it," I said "My parents set me up to distrust everything. My family was not really a family. It was a business arrangement. Because of them, everything I see is a fabricated, disingenuous creation. Fountain Hills is a fake oasis in a desert, a mirage created in part by a designer of Disneyland. The horse in the parking lot is made from stuff we no longer use. That contrived utopian society they are building off Hawaii, sends chills down my spine. The internet, texting, social platforms, dehumanizing. Thad is making a novel but not really writing it, it is all as real as those crummy toys I unwittingly sold when I was a kid . . ."

I railed for nearly the entire loop but ran out of steam when we drew close again to the merry throng of drinkers and eaters. Sierra had her head down the entire walk, listening intently. She said nothing as the sound of people living it up grew in volume. I had one more thing to say, a question, I was burning to ask Sierra. I stuck out my neck hoping she would not chop it off.

"Why do you like me?"

She smiled ever so slight. I felt my heartbeat in my throat.

"My momma tells me I was empathic when I was young. I would cry if another child cried. She also says I can see the soul of others. I think that is true. I see the soul of the birds we care for. I look into their eyes and there it is. When I was young, I remember watching you on YouTube. There was something about your eyes. I could sense your hidden sadness. When you brought Phoenix to the sanctuary, I saw your soul. You have a deep, beautiful soul, Cody, but your wings are broken. You must learn to fly with broken wings. Time to stop whining."

We were at the patio entrance to the bistro.

"Enough walking in circles. Are you willing to fly?"

I nodded. She took my hand.

"Time to wine!"

Chapter Four

On my way home after driving Sierra to her house, I reviewed every detail of our first official date. Our walk around Fountain Park, the wine and cheese shared at the bistro, how our conversation became more animated with each sip, laughter, actual real laughter, it was all extraordinarily normal and natural. I kept thinking the night appeared like a scene from a movie about two happy people engaged in an evening out except it was so well done, it was believable. The most unbelievable part was having me in the scene. It was out of character for me to gently touch her arm when we shared a laugh. It was out of character when I held her hand on the walk to my car, out of character when I kissed her. The final touch was walking Sierra to her front door, kissing her deeply, not wanting to stop. We held each other for a long time, then she pushed me away and said, "Go before we do something rash."

I wondered if this was how real life was, if this was falling in love. It was wonderful, astonishing. I wondered if this was what it was like to be a man.

Back at The Oasis, I was glad to see Thad wasn't home. I did not want to be exposed to any of his sarcastic comments about my date and ruin the dream-like high I was on. I slumped on the couch and sipped a beer, even though it did not go well with the cabernet Sierra, and I shared. I wanted to celebrate my good fortune. I kept thinking how pretty and sweet she was. Did she really think my soul was deep? Why?

The door swung open. In stepped Thad. He was cleaned up, combed, shaved, and wearing khaki shorts with Birkenstock sandals, a brown button-down shirt, and a bolo tie. It was his summer dinner attire, meant to convince his parents he was a serious artist working on the next great American novel. His parents swallowed his masquerade whole.

"How'd it go, Romeo?"

"Great."

I tried to give him as little ammo as possible, but knew it was useless. He would find a way to needle me.

"Come on, details, details. I want details!"

I gave him as brief a description as possible hoping it would satisfy. I made the mistake of mentioning Sierra saying I had a deep soul. I could not help myself. He chortled.

"You have a deep soul? That's rich. I think she's been hanging around with those birds too much."

I made a beeline to my room. I wanted to smash my beer on his head.

"You don't know shit, asshole," I said.

"Hey buddy," he said. I stopped and stared at him. "I do know shit. You have no idea the shit I know."

I paused, grasping the door handle to my room confused by his cryptic statement. Rather than ask what he meant, I retreated to my own space rather than get sucked in by his snide pessimism. I thought of Sierra, who told me to avoid such negativity.

I closed the door to my room. Grace worked the day shift, so I called her. I knew she would be more supportive than Thad. She would restore the good vibes he had managed to squash within minutes. I put on iTunes to create some sound space and privacy. Thad would find it difficult eavesdropping on my conversation if I had a musical backdrop. Grace answered my call on the first ring. I heard in the background she had the Coyotes game on.

"Heya, buddy. Did ya have your big date?"

I shared the entire evening. Grace listened with little comment interjecting encouragement at key moments, things like; awesome, wow, you rock, and laughing her big, hearty laugh, happy for me.

"That's fantastic, bud. Keep it up, don't change a thing. Just listen to what she says and be yourself, be honest. She sounds like a great girl!"

Grace raised my spirits. I had trouble quieting my mind too excited about what the future would bring.

Chapter Five

The following weeks were by far the happiest time of my life. We went on dates when she was not attending night classes or studying, to a speak easy in Gilbert, movies, coffee shops, walks at sunset and a weekend day trip to Jerome, a funky old northern mining town turned artist community. I started working part time at Door Dash and registered for two biology courses at Scottsdale Community College for the fall semester.

After each date Thad asked me, "did you get any?"

I lied saying yes and remained vague wanting to not taint the time we shared. We did not sleep together or consummate our love. It was difficult to arrange. She living with her parents and siblings and my apartment with Thad made privacy impossible. We talked briefly of splurging for a room at a resort. Sierra hesitated because she would have to lie to her parents, possibly contriving a story she was staying at a party overnight on campus. Her family were devout Catholics and did not believe in sex before marriage. Finally we agreed to wait until her fall break. Her parents were visiting relatives in Puerto Penasco, Mexico. Sierra had already told them she wasn't going.

One night, I had a strange dream that Sierra and I were at the house my parents and I lived in during the Cody Redd Show days.

Phoenix, my adopted bird was in the dream, too, but his wing was not broken and was flying loose in the house. Sierra told me I had to catch him, or he might fly out a window and be gone forever. We chased him upstairs and downstairs a couple of times then Sierra was gone. I could not find her.

I ran downstairs, out the front door to see if she had left. I felt a rush of air near my head, heard the sound of flapping wings. Phoenix flew past me into the clouds. I looked at my arms and saw they were growing feathers. I held them out to my side. They became wings.

I woke from the dream to a light tapping on our apartment door. I checked my phone. It was 8am. My bedroom was already uncomfortably warm. I put on shorts and t-shirt then opened the door thinking a maintenance man had come to either spray for cockroaches or fix our leaking toilet valve. When I opened the door I was stunned to see the visitor.

"Good morning, kid, mind if I come in?"

It was Gus, my elderly co-worker volunteer from Birds of a Feather. He seemed embarrassed and annoyed at the same time. He wore a baggy, grey jacket buttoned at the top, black shirt, red tie, black, shiny, leather shoes and dress pants. It looked as if he came from a funeral. At the sanctuary he liked wearing Hawaiian shirts, light, casual clothes. I had no idea why he was dressed so formally on a hot, Arizona morning. I wondered how he knew where I lived. Why was he here?

I let him in. He took a moment to survey our hell hole of an apartment.

"Geesh, it is worse than I imagined," he said. "You better wake your friend up. Both of you need to hear this."

"Oh my God, is Sierra alright?"

Gus held up his hand. His face looked more riddled with wrinkles than before.

"Don't worry, me boy. She is fine. Just wake up your friend. Let's start with that."

I was totally freaked. I didn't ask Gus why he was at our place or why I needed to wake Thad. I did what he asked because I needed Thad's presence. As much as Thad annoyed me, I needed him to share the disturbing arrival of Gus. Thad was curled in his sleeping nest on the floor snoring quietly, his thin lips slightly parted. I nudged him with my foot.

"Thad, wake up."

He did not budge. I bent down and nudged his shoulder. He stopped snoring and opened one bloodshot eye.

"What the fuck, Cody!"

He was not happy I woke him. Up until this moment I never had a need to.

"This guy from the sanctuary wants to talk to us."

"What?" Thad slowly got up from his sleeping nest. He was barely awake having no doubt spent most of the night engaged in one of his role-playing games. His curly hair was shaped into a block shape. It would get that way whenever he washed it and went to bed while still wet. I called him mallet head whenever it was shaped that way. Now was not a time to mess around.

Thad followed me out of his room. Gus gave him a quick glance. He sighed upon seeing disheveled Thad.

"Son," said Gus, "Put some pants on. Your junk is hanging. Besides, the three of us have to go for a ride but let's chat first."

Thad turned to me and asked; "Who is this guy? What the fuck is going on?"

"His name is Gus. He works with me at the sanctuary. I don't know why he is here."

Gus held up his hands. He could tell we were rattled.

"Boys let's calm down. I just stopped by for a little chat. Put your pants on. We can talk. Cody, could you be a pal and bring me a chair from the kitchen? You two sit on the couch. I'll have the chair. My knees are barking."

Thad grumbled as he went back into his room to get a pair of shorts. I got Gus a chair from the kitchen. He motioned us to sit on the couch as he lowered himself into the chair with a contented sigh.

"Baseball ruined my knees. I loved the game, and I loved catching. I caught since I was a kid, played the position until I couldn't squat anymore. I was thirty-nine when I stopped. I played with a bunch of guys about your age, semi-pro. It sure was fun."

Gus smiled. He had a faraway gaze dreamily reflecting upon his days of glory. Thad and I looked at each other. I thought the old man had lost his mind. I gently brought him back from his reverie.

"Gus, why are you here?"

He snapped out of it. A hang dog look spread across his face. His shoulders slumped. He stared straight into my eyes.

"Cody, we gave up looking for your parents long ago. We didn't look for you too hard. It was not your fault. Then you show up at Birds of a Feather, geesh! You know, I thought I was out of the business, just like I was as a catcher, I hung up my spikes. Then you come along. I had to tell the boss. I didn't want to, but things have changed. He needs to find your parents more than ever. If his family found out I knew where you were and didn't tell them, well, they would not be happy to put it mildly. Your little friend must come for the ride because you live together.

The boss wants to have a sit-down talk, that's all. No one is going to get hurt if we all play nice."

"What are you talking about, old man?" Thad asked, clueless "Are you off your meds? Cody, what's wrong with this dude?"

Thad got up from the couch. I grabbed his arm and pulled him down. I knew who Gus was talking about. I shuddered even though the morning sun made the apartment already feel like an oven.

"You work for Sal?" I asked Gus.

"I don't anymore. I got out of the business, but since I found you by pure dumb luck, he asked me to bring you in. A standing request. Look, Sal just wants to talk. He knows you were not responsible for running off with the money. He's not even mad at your dad. Sal knows he was just a stooge, pardon the expression. He wants your mother. She handled the money. If you help him he would be forever grateful."

Thad pulled a pack of crushed cigarettes from his pants pocket and lit one up. It was bent and compacted like a tiny accordion. I could tell by his furrowed brow he was trying to assess the situation. I was confused by Sal wanting to find my mother. I assumed my parents were dead. I figured their break from Sal Martino's Peter Dinky's Fun Factory toy company was considered a betrayal even though she ran off with the advance from Melvin K. Putz's Happy Timez Toys. I assumed the disappearance of Putz, and my parents was Sal's work, a payback for disloyalty and stealing his good revenue stream.

"The last I saw my parents was the night before they vanished. I thought they were . . ., I thought Mr. Martino had them . . ."

"Killed?" Gus finished what I could not say aloud. "Nah, he wouldn't do that, at least, I don't think he would. He hasn't done stuff like that in a long time. He's been pretty legit for a long time."

"Then what happened to Putz?" Thad asked. He caught on. Thad remembered Putz disappeared at the same time my parents split. Most people knew of Martino's shady past with his family's crime syndicate in New York. Back then Martino was nicknamed "the magician" because he had the ability to make enemies disappear.

Gus frowned. For a few unnerving moments he stared down Thad who puffed nervously on his bent cigarette.

"Between you and me, Putz was the exception. He stole your family's business from Sal. You and your parents were still a big ticket even though you were getting older, Cody. It nearly brought down Peter Dinky's Fun Factory. Besides, Putz was a shiftless weasel. Sal hired a couple of young guns who "convinced" Putz to sign Happy Timez Toys over to Sal. He was roughed up but was given enough money to get out of the country, make himself scarce. One of Putz own people ratted on him, and said Putz was going to the police. That was the last I heard of him."

I was spellbound, witnessing the transformation of Gus. For weeks I thought of him as an affable, fun loving uncle type. Now he appeared as a cold, hardened thug.

"My parents are alive?"

Gus' face softened to the kindly, old man I knew at the sanctuary.

"You didn't know?" he asked, a trace of sadness in his voice.

I nodded no. I thought he was going to cry.

"Geesh, that is rotten. How could parents do that? You were just a kid. What a mess."

"So, problem solved," Thad said. "Cody doesn't know where they are."

Thad stood to leave. Gus quickly pushed himself from the chair wincing as one of his knees audibly cracked. He firmly placed his hand on Thad's shoulder.

"No, you boys still got to see Sal. He will want to hear it from the horses' mouth."

Thad already sucked his cigarette to a butt. He pushed Gus' hand off his shoulder and turned to me.

"Come on, Cody, show this old man out the door. We don't have to go anywhere."

Gus pulled out a revolver that was holstered snuggly to his side. Thad and I froze.

"Boys, I didn't want to resort to this. You gotta see Sal. Play along and nobody gets hurt."

Chapter Six

The moment Thad and I saw Gus brandishing his revolver we became programmable robots. He told us to put on shoes. We obeyed. We followed his directions like obedient, little robots while he stayed close behind. A dark limo pulled into the lot. He motioned us to get in. Dutiful, terrified robots that we were, Thad and I stepped toward the back seat passenger side door that someone behind the tinted windows opened for us. Then we heard his annoying voice. It was Lesmour. I cringed.

"Where are you guys going? Is that a limo? Can I come?"

Lesmour was carrying another six pack of cheap beer. He was on his way to our place for a round of MLB The Show with Thad. Gus leaned near us.

"Get rid of him," he said.

"Impossible," Thad said, "He follows me everywhere . . . like a dog."

Gus rolled his eyes, he motioned to Lesmour.

"Sure, sonny, come along for the ride. It will be fun."

Thad, Lesmour and I piled into the back seat. It was a large limo with two back seats that faced each other. There was a muscular man in a dark suit, bleached blond, short hair wearing sunglasses. He looked up to Gus who was standing by the door.

"Another one?" he said.

"Yeah," said Gus. "It's a regular party now."

The bleach blond goon shifted to a seat facing the rear of the limo as we slid into the backseat. I was sandwiched between Thad and Lesmour. I squeezed my butt so to avoid touching their thighs. Gus got in last sitting next to the goon. As soon as the door was closed the driver took off. From my vantage point I could not make out the driver. He had large, rounded shoulders and a thick neck with a tattoo of something partially sticking above his white collar. He also had tattoos on each of his huge, thick fingers. They looked like some ancient lettering of a long-forgotten language.

"Who wants a beer?" Lesmour offered us his latest cheap beer find, Brown River Beer brewed in Cleveland. It was so cheap it did not have any label design although I suppose no one could make the image of a brown river appealing on a can. Bleach blond turned his head toward Gus.

"Sure, why not?" said Gus.

Lesmour passed each person in the back seat a can. I popped the flip top and took a swig. It was extremely carbonated. After two gulps, I needed to burp but I suppressed it afraid to make a sound. I don't know why I drank the beer. I think at this point I was so overwhelmed I would have been open to any suggestion. If someone suggested I jump out of the limo, undress, and run naked through the streets, I would have.

"What about me?' The driver asked while keeping his eyes fixed on the road. I saw in the rearview he had small blue eyes sunken in on his heavy face.

"No. You got to drive," said Gus.

"It's great to have a designated driver," said Lesmour. "Now we can get blasted and not worry. I can buy more beer. Where are we going, anyway?"

"It's a surprise," said Gus.

I was amazed how oblivious Lesmour was to our situation. He was delighted when Gus said where we were going was a surprise. I thought he might have picked up on Thad's reticence. Thad was acting completely out of character. He sat motionless staring out the window. He usually had a sarcastic quip anytime someone opened their mouth. I also said nothing but that was not uncommon for me especially after spending time with the two of them. I wondered why I wasted my time living with Thad and putting up with Lesmour. I had a perfectly normal evening with Sierra and realized sitting in the limo, possibly facing death, all the time I wasted hiding out for years. I should have lived more.

Gus sipped his beer, winced after tasting it and then smiled, shaking his head. He transformed back into the sweet, old man I knew at Birds of a Feather.

"This beer is awful," he said. "Reminds me of the swill my brothers-in-law used to deliver. One worked for a Schlitz distribution company, the other Rheingold. They used to have arguments over which beer was better. It was a lark because they both stank. Both distributors were mob owned, that was in Connecticut. Back in the day a lot of businesses was mob owned, legit ones and ones not so legit. It was alright, nobody got hurt. Everybody got a piece of something, made some dough, no problem. I was just a kid when I got started. They would see me hanging out on the street, come over and say, "Hey kid, want to make some money? Run this envelope across the street," we had nothing to eat, so I did it. Helped my mother and sisters out.

Those guys got to trust me, and I got a regular gig running envelopes. They liked I didn't ask questions. They got chummy with me. They were great guys as long as you did as you were told."

Gus relaxed, reveling in the old days. His glassy eyed smile was derivative of a person who had his share of liquor over the years. His brow furrowed; the dreamy smile gone like when the sun is vanquished by a rogue cloud. He took a deep breath and sighed. I wondered what Sierra would think, if she could see us now, with Gus, who had a fondness for the cockatiels.

"Look, I know you boys are scared and I feel rotten I gotta take you to Sal, but as long as you tell the truth, Sal won't do nothin'. He is just as tired as me with the business. He only needs to tie up loose ends. Your mother, Cody, is a big loose end. Don't worry, you boys will be fine."

Lesmour laughed, his stupid, little puppet character laugh, a high-pitched giggling abomination.

"Oh, I get it!" he said. "This is one of those role-playing events. These guys are lame mobsters taking us to see their "boss", how rich is that?"

Gus shook his head at Lesmour while Thad and I squirmed. Our dim witted, round headed companion stopped laughing. He looked nervously at Thad and me seeking assurance, comfort. He found none. Finally he assessed the gravity of our situation. Gus never took his eyes off Lesmour.

"Yeah kid, you got it right. You are a regular Einstein."

The driver got on I-10 then took an exit near the state fairgrounds in Phoenix. It was an older part of the city cluttered with abandoned industrial buildings. One of those buildings was once the Happy Timez Toyz Company, previously owned by Melvin K. Putz, vacant now for ten years after Putz disappeared. The large, square three-story brick and mortar building with parking lot and underground parking garage was surrounded by a six-foot-high chain link fence. Our thug driver pulled into the entryway. The bleach blond sitting across from us got out, unlocked the padlock on the gate and swung it open. The driver rolled the limo past the gate and waited for his fellow goon to close it and climb back in.

Hanging above the main entrance was the Happy Timez Toy sign coated with desert dust. A chaotic mess of black widow webs and pigeon poop adorned the lettering. Below the lettering, was a cartoon character cut out of Marvin K. Putz. In life he did look like a cartoon character, bespeckled, wiry, bald, and wrinkled. The difference between himself and his cartoon likeness was the animated Putz wore a gold crown.

The life size cutout on the building, however, was missing a head. As we left the limo I noticed near the entrance the Putz head. It looked as if it was cut off by a Sawzall and was discolored by urine. Its unmistakable odor assaulted my nostrils. The reek was intensified by the rising heat.

Bleach blond unlocked the door and walked in while Gus motioned us to follow. I saw the limo guy reach in the back seat and grab the two remaining cans of Brown River beer before driving the limo to the other side of the building to a shaded parking garage. The three of us were silent, terrified. I thought I heard Lesmour whimper but could not be sure. My legs felt like jelly. My breath was short and rapid like a little dog that had too long a walk. Noticing that only increased my panting as well as my heartbeat. It reminded me of my bird, Phoenix. I once heard its wild heartbeat through a stethoscope. I wished I could fly. I had only just found Sierra, the idea that I could live a happy life.

We walked down a dirty hallway past closed office doors with nameplates of people who no longer worked there. We reached a French door at the end of the hall. Gus opened it and showed us in. The interior was impeccably decorated with brown leather furniture, a pool table near a dry bar and a massive cherrywood desk.

Behind the desk sat Sal Martino. He had changed little since I last saw him ten years ago. He was average build and weight, slightly curved back, dark eyes, dark hair. The only feature out of the ordinary was his large mouth and lips that looked as if it stretched to his ear lobes. One thing that looked different was his hair. Last I saw him, the early stages of balding began to encroach his scalp. His hair was now jet black, full, and wavy, an obvious toupee and a cheap one at that. He still had a gold ring on every finger which always unnerved me. I remember as a kid how pleasant he was to me, but I could tell by his interaction with adults he was not the lovable toy company owner he presented himself to be. The gold rings were my first indicator that he was nothing like his cartoon avatar, Peter Dinky. The two bore some resemblance, especially the big-mouthed smile, but Sal would never wear a striped, red, white, and blue suit with top hat, and I never saw him with a giant candy cane walking stick.

Now Sal motioned us to sit on the leather couch. It creaked and groaned under our weight.

Sal asked Gus, "Why three?"

"One is his roommate, the other approached us, you know, friends . . . eyewitnesses."

Lesmour bolted from the couch.

Bleach Blond grabbed Lesmour by the shoulder and shoved him back to the couch.

"I don't know these guys! I was just bringing them beer as a favor!"

"Shaddup and sit down!" he said.

Thad eyed Lesmour with contempt, mouthing "fuck you" to the little rat.

"Take it easy on him," Sal said to Bleach Blond. "No need to shit our pants. We are just having a conversation here."

Sal turned his attention to me.

"Hello Cody."

Although the room was blasting cold with some sort of polar ice cap air conditioning, I began to sweat. I managed to speak although my voice came out dry and high pitched.

"You look well, Sal," I said.

"I wish I could say the years have been kind to you, Cody but I have always made it a practice to say what I mean," he said. "You look like hell."

"He says he doesn't know where his parents are," Gus said.

He and Bleach Blond were standing on either side of the couch. I was grateful that Gus was trying to help. I believe deep down; he really was a nice guy. That guy I knew from the bird sanctuary.

Not a mobster hit man.

Sal sighed. His shoulders slumped a little more. His face softened with a genuine look of concern.

"I always liked you, Cody," he said. "You got a bum rap with your parents. Coming from my family business in New York, it was in our blood to spot a con. You were used, robbed by your own mother. Your father was a piece of shit that never stood up to her. He should have defended you, got you out of the business, let you be a kid, but money talks. Money always talks."

He stood, walked to the front of his desk then sat on its' edge. He bent forward until his face was a foot from mine. I smelled stale coffee on his hot breath.

"I know you're not responsible. Your mother did the cash upfront deal with Putz to sell a Cody Redd toy product line while your family was still under contract with me. Then she took a three-million-dollar cash advance from Peter Dinky's Fun Factory and skipped town. I don't care she swindled Putz. He deserved it. We got even with him anyways, but she made me look bad to my family. Martino's don't like to be showed up. I can't let someone besmirch my family name. I came out here with Gus because we didn't like the strong-arm stuff. I wanted to be a regular family man, got a wife and two kids, now grown. I am going to be a grandpa soon. You see, I was the black sheep of the family. I wanted to go straight, have a regular life. My family made a deal with me. They footed me money to take over, eh start a business as long as the Martino name was not disrespected. I held up my end of the deal until your mother fucked me over. They were willing to let it slide, seeing she could not be found. People in the business figured we took care of her. We always knew you stayed here but we left you alone. You were an innocent victim, but things have changed. My father recently passed, and my asshole brother is running the operation. He wants to make an impression, show who's boss. One of his lieutenants has been snooping around. If he gets wind Gus has been working with you at that bird joint and didn't turn you in . . . let's just say, they would not be pleased."

Three million dollars. I had no idea it was that much money. My mother sent me fifteen hundred a month while she was rich.

Sal sighed and turned his gaze to a picture on the wall. It was a black and white family photo hung over the dry bar draped in shadows where the floor lamp's beacon did not reach. I summoned some courage, seeing Sal had mellowed, speaking almost kindly, like a remorseful dad that was forced to waste his son.

"If I knew where they were, I would tell you. What my mother did was wrong, to you and to me. I thought they were dead."

Sal averted his stare from the family photo then leaned even closer toward us.

"Cody, tell me the truth. You really don't know where she is? If you do, we can make this all go away."

I nodded in the negative. Sal looked up at Gus, who simply muttered "geesh".

Sal was about to speak until Thad sheepishly interrupted.

"I, I can find her," Thad said.

Sal scratched his toupee which shifted slightly on his head.

"How can you find her?"

"I can hack any system and track her down. It's what I do for fun. I do it all the time."

I knew Thad was lying because he tried to find my parents before but was unsuccessful. It was the first time in ages I appreciated Thad's bullshit.

"Yeah, he can find anything on the computer! He's really smart!" shouted Lesmour.

"Shaddup!" said Bleach Blond. "No one's talking to you! Whadda you know, you can't even buy decent beer!"

"It's true," I said. "He can find anything, anyone."

Sal looked at me suspiciously.

"You're telling me he never looked for your parents? That seems like something you would have been curious about."

I almost panicked, did my best to keep a poker face.

"I wrote them off. At first I thought they left me then I believed you got them. Either way I didn't care if they were alive or dead. Why would I after they stole my childhood and pretended they loved me."

All those years of portraying the part of a happy kid playing with his dad in front of a camera, paid off. I could tell Sal bought into my lie. The old Martino ability of reading a con was apparently no match for the Redman clan for my mother duped him, and now, I. It helped when I mentioned the part about my parents stealing my childhood and pretending to love me tears welled in my eyes. I had never vocalized that truth before although I thought it many times. Hearing me speak the truth caught me off guard. The tears were no act.

"You got three days to find them," Sal said.

"Three days? I need at least a week." Thad acted indignant. It was a negotiating tactic he used on his parents in his phony greatest novel ever written scam. He always pushed for extra time to meet the minimum hoops they set before him to jump through in lieu of living expenses.

"Three days, that's all you got." Sal hardened again. He did not like being challenged, "You young men are not to breathe a word. I made Putz disappear and I can make the three of you go bye-bye, too."

He stood up quickly, moved to the pool table and grabbed a cue. Gus motioned us to stand and leave. Bleach Blond took the lead while Gus followed behind.

The limo came around to pick us up but the driver we had before was not behind the wheel. The new driver was a lot younger. He had a crew cut and was missing the pinky on his left-hand. Gus asked him where "Stubby" went. The new driver said he drank the beer and took a nap on a vacant office couch. Gus called Stubby a lazy ass and told us to climb in the limo along with Bleach Blond. We did not say much on the way back. Gus spoke one time, trying his best to put a positive spin on our situation.

"This is good. You got three days to track down the parents. Once you do that, you boys are off the hook. Everything will be squared away."

"Yeah," was all Thad could say. It was not a convincing yeah at all.

Gus wiped his long hand across his face in exasperation.

"Geesh, what a mess."

Despite what my parents did to me, neither Thad nor I wanted to turn them in. Thad's lie bought us time to figure something out.

The limo driver pulled into The Oasis parking lot. Gus told him to wait while he walked us to our apartment. He followed inside and closed the door.

"Look," he said to Thad, "I can smell a lie a mile away. Sal's talk of reading cons is bull. His family was good at it, but not him. That's why they let him do his own thing out here. He never had the Martino instincts. All I am telling you boys, if you don't come up with something in three days, Sal will be forced to do something."

He placed his hand on my shoulder.

"If your buddy can't find your mom, you boys better make yourself scarce before Sal pulls one of his magic tricks on you."

Gus ambled out of our apartment into the searing heat. The three of us were silent taking in what had just happened.

"You can find Cody's parents, can't you?" Lesmour whispered.

"Idiot, I am not even going to try. Make yourself useful and get more beer. I got work to do."

Chapter Seven

Thad sprung to action. He lit his bong and took a huge hit. I asked him if getting baked was a good idea considering our lives were in jeopardy. He said he was too nervous and needed to chill in order to think. It made a lot of sense, so I joined him. It did not help me much. I kept thinking about Sierra. I wanted to tell her but could not endanger her or her family. Thad and I brainstorming was more a drizzle of random f-bombs and mumbling "what to do". Lesmour arrived with another six pack of Brown River Beer which we guzzled. The apartment's AC was lacking more than usual. We were sweaty, high, our minds crawling toward drunkenness.

Our only option was to escape, but where? Although Thad and I suspected Sal Martino and his crew were not the most efficient mobsters, we couldn't take any chances especially since Martino's brother was out to make an impression and establish himself as the new crime boss. With limited funds, it became problematic where we could live. My stomach churned realizing I would have to leave Sierra.

Lesmour was worthless. He sucked down two beers then did a line of coke on our filthy coffee table. It was unusual. He never snorted in front of us. He knew we disapproved. After the coke kicked in, he rambled endlessly and suggested we should go off grid in some remote area like the Montana woods were we would build a cabin and live off the land. It made Thad laugh.

"Right," he said, "I can really see you roughing it. When was the last time you hunted a deer? You can barely order take out."

A little vein of Lesmour's forehead popped out while he mumbled how "cruel" Thad was. He then babbled a story in defense that he used to hunt with his uncle and shot a turkey with bow and arrow.

Thad stood.

"I have an idea. I need to work in peace and quiet."

"What am I going to do?" Lesmour asked.

"You can suck your dick for all I care," Thad said, slamming his bedroom door.

Lesmour grumbled bitterly and turned on the game system, deciding to invest his time in a role-playing game. I thought it ironic his decision to spend valuable time playing a game which had elements of life and death situations while he, Thad and I were encountering the same in real life. I was shaken. I thought of calling Grace, but realized I could not confide in her and risk her knowing. I decided to text Sierra. It was a selfish, bad idea. I wanted to see her even though I knew I could not say what happened, but I thought just being with her would calm me. I messaged asking if she could meet on Mill Ave. in Tempe by the old Harkins movie Theater. She was at ASU, but her last class ended at 6pm. I told her I needed to see her. I kept it vague.

"Can't get enough of me?" she wrote back. It brought a smile to my face.

"Busted," I tapped.

Meeting her downtown Tempe was a wise move, I thought. During the school year Mill Avenue hopped, full of students crowding sidewalks participating in bar crawls, eating out or just taking in the many musicians that crooned on street corners. I was concerned I might be followed, even though Sal had promised us three days. I was astonished not to find a limo in The Oasis parking lot. Pretty shoddy of them. Even so, I constantly checked the rearview during my drive. Considering my paranoia from the day's events and the weed I smoked, I felt confident I was not being tailed. I got there half an hour early so I could park in a crowded municipal lot and navigate the packed sidewalks in case someone was following me. I couldn't bear it if anything happened to Sierra. When I reached the old Harkins Theater, Sierra was waiting. She smiled her beautiful dimple smile. We hugged. I held on a little too long wanting to feel her against me.

"This is a nice surprise," she said. "I like spontaneous things, are we seeing a movie?"

I did not consider seeing a movie. I did not consider anything. The old theater was simply a convenient landmark.

"Ah, sure," I said.

Sierra read my uncertainty, tilting her head in that funny questioning way she had. A feeling came bubbling up from inside my poor, whittled heart, "God, I love her." Every head tilt, every expression made me love her more. It was horrible. I didn't know if I would ever see her again.

"We don't have to," she said. "I ate before class but if you are hungry I can nibble on something."

I looked up and down the street for a place to talk. The bars and restaurants were packed, many had lines of people waiting to get in. I almost gave in to the idea of the movie until I saw a place called Dusty Memories across the street at the next light. I pointed it out to Sierra.

"Let's go there."

"Sure, looks fun."

We wove our way through sidewalk traffic crossing at the intersection. Dusty Memories was a sort of antique shop minus furniture loaded with thousands of items from yesteryear. Books, records, magazines, toys, kitchen utensils, household bric-a-brac, tools, posters even old photos of people from long ago, nameless family photos that were once cherished, now lost, and forgotten were claustrophobically packed within the narrow, two story shop. So full of curiosities, I almost forgot the days' events. Sierra and I picked through all sorts of oddities. She liked the cigarette ads in magazines where sports stars and doctors expounded on the merits of smoking. She grabbed a 1965 issue of Arizona Highways that had pictures of "modern day" Phoenix. She said her father likes researching the state's history and would enjoy how sparse Phoenix looked long ago. We were separated for a few minutes. I was hung up looking at record albums from the 50's and 60's. The contrasting designs of the psychedelic rock albums of the day and the mainstream albums were interesting. Sierra wandered off to look at books but came back with something unexpected.

"Look what I found," she chirped.

Sierra giggled as she held an unopened Peter Dinky's Fun Factory firetruck with action figure firefighters and two poorly modeled figurines of my father, and I dressed as firemen. In the upper left-hand corner of the box was the cartoon figure of Peter Dinky dressed in top hat with red, white, and blue clothes and a regal robe. He looked cheerful. In the bottom right corner was a photo of my father and I in firemen outfits holding a toy fire engine. I remembered the shoot for the product. I did not want to wear a fireman outfit. I was nearly twelve. In the picture on the box I displayed my standard fake smile. I did a decent job hiding my contempt in those days but if one looked closely, on the outskirts of my smile, one could detect the beginning of a sneer. Sierra stopped giggling when she saw my sour expression to the toy I used to hack.

"Cody, you ok?"

I felt rigid. I tried to cover it up, not make a big deal of the picture of my old self and the lies I was fed in youth. I tried to recreate my old fake smile.

"No. I am not."

"Sorry. I should have known it was a bad memory."

If it were not for the day's events, I would have laughed it off. I wanted to let go of the past, especially with the good fortune of finding Sierra. The problem was these memories were no longer dusty. They were shaken and wiped clean with the looming threat of Sal Martino and his motley friends.

"It's not that. It's something else, something I can't tell you," I said. I immediately regretted admitting it. It was like cracking open Pandoras' box and peeking inside.

"Yes, you can," Sierra said. "You can tell me anything."

I stared at the worn floorboards of the shop ashamed and

afraid to involve her. I was selfish to seek comfort from her. Sierra tugged my hand, saying "come on" leading me to the second floor of the shop comprised entirely of magazines on rows of metal racks. I would have loved this place if I wasn't so upset. She practically pushed me onto a loveseat near two small tables ostensibly set up for readers to peruse before buying. No one else was on the second floor. It was as quiet and private a place one could find on Mill Avenue on a weeknight.

"What's wrong?" she asked me.

"I can't tell you."

Sierra waited for more. I had to give her something. She deserved it.

"Something came up." I took a long time before continuing. I stared at the floorboards again concentrating, trying to find the right words, choose them carefully so her safety would not be jeopardized. "I can't tell you. The less you know the better. I shouldn't even see you. It is something my mother did long ago. People are looking for her. I can't say any more."

"You are in danger?"

"Yes, so are Thad and Jeffery. Thad is trying to find a way out. That's all I can say. This was stupid of me. The last thing I want is to put you in danger."

"Wow," Sierra said. A young college student in a red miniskirt and flowered short sleeve blouse reached the top of the stairs. She saw us sitting in the back of the room then turned and retreated downstairs picking up on our vibe for privacy.

"The three of us have to leave, quick. I don't know when I will see you again," I blurted it out without thinking. I wanted to cry.

"No. There has to be a way to work it out, whatever it is."

Sierra spoke like she was trying to convince herself. I said nothing. I held her hand and then felt tears running down my cheek.

"I am sorry. I didn't want to hurt you."

It dawned on me I most likely would have to leave Sierra, similar to what my parents did to me, something I would never wish upon anyone. Tears were in her eyes. She was fighting to stay strong.

"I was afraid of someday falling for an undocumented boy and then hearing he was deported," Sierra said. "Instead, I find, a sweet, American born boy and now I don't know what will become of him."

We held each other for a long time. Then we kissed long and hard. I wished it would not end. Sierra pulled away and grabbed me tightly.

"Can you meet tomorrow, at night? I have classes during the day. " she said.

"I will try. Where?"

She thought for a moment.

"Encanto Park, Enchanted Island by the carousel. That should be safe, no?"

She must have realized why I chose a busy place to meet knowing neither of us are big on swarms of people. Encanto Park is an area inhabited by children and parents. It seemed safe to me. We hugged on the sofa until the girl with the red skirt and flowered top came back with two girlfriends. They were loud flipping through magazines laughing at old hairstyles and clothes. Sierra took my hand, and we left.

Back on the street felt foreign almost otherworldly. People everywhere getting drunk, having a good time, musical notes from various live acts spanning through the night air did not jive with the way I was feeling. Sierra was quiet. She suddenly looked older, somber. We reached the street corner.

"I better go, see if Thad came up with anything."

We stood looking at each other on the street corner. Somebody brushed against my shoulder said, "sorry, man" and moved on. Sierra stood on her toes, cradled my face in her hands.

"Now I am going to worry about you like I worry about everyone else I love."

We kissed, neither wanting to stop, until she said, "go."

Sierra walked down the block. I waited for the crossing signal to change from the red pedestrian to the little, green walking man. An automated voice told me and a handful of other human pedestrians to wait. I was tired of waiting for better days. I wanted to walk into traffic and take my chances, but the thought of Sierra stopped me. I turned to watch her walking away. It was a matter of seconds before the sea of drunken humanity swallowed her diminutive but sturdy frame.

Chapter Eight

At the apartment nothing had changed. Thad stayed sequestered in his room. Lesmour hadn't left, still high, absorbed in the insipid video game. I rummaged in the fridge finding a new six pack of beer, surprisingly a name brand I recognized, Corona. There were lime wedges in a bowl. This had to be Thad's doing. I could see him thinking he needed good beer to concentrate. I unscrewed the cap and pushed in a lime slice. It made me dream of being on a Mexican beach with Sierra. It tasted wonderful. The thought of being with her away from the madness was a beautiful fantasy. Then my heart sank, realizing we would probably never get the chance. It was more likely my two motley friends and I would be dead by the end of the week.

I took my beer to the living room and slumped in the bean bag chair. On the coffee table among uncollected food wrappers were three empty cans of shitty beer.

"Did Thad buy the Corona?"

"No, I did," said Lesmour, still playing his game, "It's sort of an apology. I felt bad pretending I didn't know you guys. I was scared."

I was wrong, again.

"We all are," I said." There is a bright side to this."

"What's that?" he asked. He stopped playing the game. His ancient warrior character stood still while a dragon roasted him to kingdom come.

"The bright side is we are finally drinking good beer."

Lesmour laughed.

I raised my bottle. Lesmour grabbed an empty can and tapped mine to complete the toast. He stopped smiling.

"I lie all the time," he said.

"I know."

"I hate the world," Lesmour said. "I hate myself, and my parents. Both were mean drunks. They were decent sober, but that was rare. When my father got really drunk he did weird things. One time he burned me with his cigarette when I was not looking. He thought it was a joke. I make up shit because it's better than the truth but some of the things I tell you guys are true! I really work on Saguaro Lake. I am a pontoon boat tour guide!"

"That sucks about your parents," I said. It was amazing he was not a total lunatic.

"You guys are my best friends, my only friends. You both treat me like shit."

"I know. I'm sorry. Tell the truth more often, we will get off your back. It comes off like you are trying to impress people. Besides, you don't have to impress losers like Thad and me. All three of us suck."

"Thanks, Cody."

"Want a Corona?"

He smiled and nodded. I tapped on Thad's door, asked if he wanted a good beer. The furious tapping on his keyboard ceased.

He replied "indeed" then resumed his work to save our lives. None of us slept. Thad hunkered in his room. Lesmour and I alternated between playing some medieval role play game and talking. We finished the six pack of Corona. I volunteered to get another and some Taco Bell. On the way out to my car I recognized Bleach Blond slumped in an older model Buick in The Oasis parking lot. We were now being watched.

I was sorry Thad and Lesmour were involved because of my mother's thievery. Talking about my dysfunctional mother with Lesmour lead to an interesting conversation, comparing each of our parents. We concluded out of the three of us Thad had the most damaging parents. The abuse Lesmour and I experienced from our parents was blatant and we no longer interacted with them; Lesmour cut them off, mine ran away. Thad's parental abuse continued. Although well-meaning they were textbook helicopter, delusional parents. It was a much more subtle, insidious abuse. They appeared to be wonderful, supporting parents in his feigned pursuit of creative freedom. It was plain their overzealous care demoralized him. They slowly suffocated their only son's life.

Thad came out to grab a beer and bean burrito not saying a word. He was deep into internet wizardry in the attempt to save our asses. Occasionally we heard him behind his closed door emitting a guffaw of triumph followed moments later with a high pitched "fuck, fuck, fuck." It went on for hours and was unsettling. In the wee hours of the morning he burst from his room, bleary eyed, obviously drunk, and elated.

"Mission accomplished!"

Thad staggered to the fridge, grabbed the last beer, and dropped into the beanbag chair. It made a pop sound when he landed. Styrofoam stuffing flew out looking like a brief snow flurry. He took a swig. Jostled by his crash to the beanbag, suds bubbled down the side of the bottle onto his shirt. He forced a burp then smiled.

"Well?" I said.

"We are escaping to Lemuria Down," he stated.

Lesmour and I exchanged baffled glances.

"Where's that?" Lesmour asked.

Thad chortled, "Where's that? Do you live under a rock? It is paradise on Earth! A new utopian society that is highly guarded to keep riff raff and criminal elements out. Only the most qualified, worthy people are invited to join this society until now, thanks to your buddy, Thad."

Lesmour was agitated by Thad's gloating superiority over his ignorance. I quickly told our round headed friend about the experimental burgeoning society off the outer reaches of the Hawaiian Islands: how the wealthy, mysterious investor Darby Summers created a place where everyone had a purpose, everyone invited was carefully selected to join after passing rigorous psychological and sociological tests to be sure they would be happy and productive citizens. Thad nodded and smirked as I related all this to Lesmour. He was very pleased with himself.

For once, Lesmour remained silent, the rusty wheels in his head working overtime trying to comprehend Thad's masterplan. Then his face clouded over.

"I will lose my job. I loved being a pontoon captain," Lesmour said, crestfallen.

Thad chortled.

"Better than losing your life!" he said. "Besides, I hacked into their data bank and gave each of us sweet jobs and new identities. Pumpkin Head, you can work at their marina taking people on tours, fishing, sightseeing, whatever recreational crap they dream up. I am working in the research and development lab for this brainy scientist named Robinette. Cody, you will be the resident ornithologist slash naturalist cataloging and researching wildlife."

Unbelievable. All those years of Thad being a dick head on the internet paid off. The merry prankster hacked into Lemuria Down but not without two major flaws: him and I. The thought of Thad helping a scientist was a stretch but me being an expert on the natural world was ridiculous.

"How are we going to pull that off?"

"Easy," he said, "I hacked their system. They had an assistant to Robinette lined up, but I replaced her with me. I introduced myself via e-mail then recommended you because you are a respected ornithologist and would be invaluable in preserving the natural habitat."

"Thad, I helped nurse a fledging. I don't know shit about birds or habitats."

"Well, neither do they, you just fake it. Spend your days combing the island photographing birds, and other critters. Identify what they are with online pics. Then you write some believable bullshit about how they are affecting the island. My job as an assistant largely consists of popping research stuff into his database . . . easy. We can pull this off. We are great fakers. I faked it with my parents for years and you played the part of a happy kid for half your life. Lesmour actually does know something about boats. I looked it up. He really is a pontoon tour guide."

My heart sank. Even if we were able to pull it off I would be far from Sierra with no chance of seeing her. Disheartened I realized it was safest for her to be as far away from me as possible. Our flowering relationship was over.

"There is one catch," Thad said. "We must sneak onto the island. There is an official receiving area at the main port where new residents have to scan their Lemuria Down ID cards. I can make convincing fake IDs but have to fudge the barcodes. They won't get past their scanners. The western side of the island is undeveloped. We can dock there undetected then trek into the main village bypassing the scanners. We fly to Kauai, buy new clothes, get grown up haircuts to look professional, print out fake, official Lemuria Down ID's and charter a boat to the island. I saw our new digs on Google Earth, all we gotta do is get there and set up shop. No one will know we snuck in. They will assume we were screened at the port."

"Why new identities?" asked Lesmour. "Is it so the mob guys can't find us?"

"No dummy," said Thad. "They aren't that smart. I had to create our new selves and phony history in order to get onto the island in case they tried to cross check us. They might have been able to link us with our old selves if we kept our real names."

"What about your parents? Won't they miss you?" I asked.

"I'll tell them I am going to do research for my novel in Oregon. They will believe anything and give me some extra cash for my travels."

Lesmour stared blankly at Thad as if he was in a dream state.

"I can captain boats off Hawaii?"

"That's right, my round headed friend."

Lesmour was elated. I was skeptical but realized as chancy as Thad's scheme seemed, hiding in a society of highly skilled people was our best option. Being losers, no one would think to find us there.

"That bleach blond dude is parked outside. He will see us leave for the airport."

"I know. Lesmour told me after he got the Corona. I have an idea for a diversion."

"When do we leave, Thad?" Lesmour asked eagerly.

"We board a red eye tomorrow morning to LA.; we hang there then catch an afternoon flight to Kauai."

"Hawaii," said Lesmour, "It seems like a dream."

Or a nightmare, I thought.

Chapter Nine

We avoided the Oasis parking lot where Bleach Blond was perched in the limo and walked to a nearby ATM withdrawing all cash from our paltry accounts. By the time we got home the night sky was washed grey by the rising sun. Lesmour curled on the couch while Thad and I crashed in our bedrooms hoping to rest for the big day ahead.

I slept little. Thoughts about my parents, leaving Sierra, Sal's rank coffee breath, even Phoenix, my rescue bird ran rampant. I was planning on adopting him. He would have been my first pet. I ruminated about my wasted life for hours. I woke twice with the inhale of a snore, unaware I had fallen asleep. The swamp cooler was down once again. I got out of bed damp with perspiration. It was past 9am.

Lesmour was asleep on the couch dreaming happy, little dreams about his new life as a sea captain. I felt sorry for him. In the past twenty-four hours his world was turned upside down and his life threatened. And he was happy. To him this was a cheerful event. I let him dream. Maybe if I hadn't found Sierra, I would have been happy too.

Thad was awake tapping away on his keyboard. He rarely woke early. His huge tower PC was humming.

"Just putting some finishing touches to our getaway," he said.

"I want to meet Sierra before we leave."

"That's doable. Our flight out of this hell hole isn't until 11pm. Just be back by nine."

"Oh shit."

"What?"

"I forgot about Bleach Blond."

"Ask your geezer co-worker for help. He's on our side. He doesn't want anyone hurt."

I called the Birds of a Feather landline, their only number. Gus answered.

"I want to see Sierra tonight after she gets out of classes. I don't want to be followed. Can you help me?"

"Geesh, you are putting me in an awful spot, kid."

"Please. That bleach blond guy has been camped out in our parking lot all night."

"I know, I know. Ok, here's what I can do. Another goon is going to take his place in about an hour. The new goon is grousing about watching you guys because he has softball playoffs tonight. I'll act like I'm doing him a favor and take his shift. That will give you a couple of hours, no more."

"Thanks, Gus."

"I feel responsible for this. You're a good kid, but I wish I never met you. Be sure to get back no later than eight. If he comes back and you are gone then my ass will be on the line."

I got off the phone and messaged Sierra to meet at Encanto Park. There was a knock on the door. Thad sprung from his swivel chair tripping over loose garbage as he swung open the door. A FedEx carrier handed Thad a package. He signed for it.

"Thank you, my good man," before the carrier could reply he slammed the door on his face.

Thad tore open the package pulling out a small circular electronic device and a tiny remote with a singular button.

"This ought to do," he said proudly, holding it up. "All we need now is the accelerant. While you are out get a Styrofoam cup from Circle K and squirt some gas into it."

I was stunned, "huh?"

"We need a diversion for our getaway. While you are out, tape this box to a cup of gas and attach it inside the engine compartment. When you get home I'll press this little button, and your crappy car goes out in a blaze of glory. We call the fire department, and police then have an Uber lined up a block away to take us to the airport."

"You're going to torch my car?"

"Yes. It will be perfect. In the smoke and confusion we make our escape. I always hated that car. It'll be fun."

If someone told me a scant two weeks before I would willingly allow my beloved beaten down Honda to be torched I would have thought them mad. Now it seemed like a practical thing to do like having a checking account. I certainly wasn't going to need it anymore. I only needed the car for one last drive to meet Sierra at Encanto Park.

Thad scurried to his room to work on printing fake ID's for Lemuria Down. He said that once we landed in Kauai, he and Lesmour would get professional haircuts then we all have photos taken for our new ID. Lesmour was still sleeping even though when I checked on him there were rivulets of sweat on his brow. In the privacy of my room I sent Grace a text saying I had to leave the country, I would be alright, but it is best we do not talk until I get back, if I ever get back. I thanked her for listening and being a friend. The less she knew, the better. I doubted Martino's goons would be able to track her down, but I didn't want to take any chances.

Lesmour finally woke so we all walked across Van Buren to get breakfast. Thad wanted to go as a group as an experiment. He was curious to see if Bleach Blond would follow. We purposely walked through the parking lot past the limo. Thad now feeling confident about our impending safe escape brazenly marched up to the limo and tapped on the driver side window. The window rolled down. Bleach Blond was gone. A new goon was in his place. He was weasel faced; a scalp cut hairdo with ears that stuck out almost perpendicular to his head.

"Where's the other guy?" Thad asked.

"I'm watching you assholes, now. Where you going?"

"To Circle K, want a beer?" Lesmour chipped in. Even he seemed confident, not I.

The tense squint of Weasel Face relaxed.

"It's a little bit early, but why not? I got to follow you guys though."

"It would be better if you drove us," Thad said. "You can't lose us that way."

Weasel Face' eyes narrowed as if he was contemplating the vastness of the cosmos. Then the limo's door locks popped up.

"Get in back."

I nostalgically got two hot dogs and a blue slushie thinking it might be the last time I get to eat a vile breakfast. Thad bought his usual churros and coffee. Lesmour got an egg, bacon, cheese burrito thing and Arizona Iced Tea that was ironically produced in New Jersey. Thad told Lesmour to pick out cheap beer for the goon. He came back with one from Nogales, Mexico called Heavenly Parrot Hero. It had a cartoon of a buffed parrot wearing a sombrero with a halo encircling the hat. Thad was very pleased. He also bought a bag of pork rinds for Weasel Face saying he wanted to give him both the six pack and the rinds hoping it would make him "shit his pants."

Getting in the limo Weasel Face was very pleased with our offering. He popped the top of a beer taking a big gulp then belched, ripped open the bag of pork rinds and shoved a few in his mouth. Thad grinned imagining the havoc it would wreak upon the goon's digestive system.

"I got softball playoffs tonight," he said while pulling out of Circle K. "We are going to get the championship."

"Yeah?" said Lesmour. "What do you win?"

"We get a trophy and a championship t-shirt."

"How grand!" said Thad.

Weasel Face snarled at Thad's sarcasm but brushed it off choosing instead to take a swallow from his beer. He parked in the same space at The Oasis as before. Lesmour wished Weasel Face good luck as we got out taking our breakfast booty to the apartment.

We spent the rest of the day packing, (it took ten minutes considering we owned next to nothing), and getting stoned, because we could not take our stash with us. Thad emailed a

PDF of his manuscript to his parents with a missive telling them he had to travel to Oregon for "research" and would not be in touch for some time. He had already received his "living expense" allowance with added money for travel expense via Venmo from his parents which he drained from his account seconds after receiving.

I cut off my intake of cannabis edibles around noon so I would not be baked when I met Sierra. I was stuffed because we were munching everything that was left in our crummy kitchenette cabinets, crackers, cookies and whatever else not far past the expiration date. Thad told us in Lemuria Down we would be eating fresh food made by first rate chefs designed to make our mouths water while being beneficial to our health. I wondered if our bodies could withstand it.

When it was time for me to leave I felt drowsy, so I made a cup of coffee to be alert on my drive to Encanto Park. We had instant coffee in the house Thad drank late at night when he was engrossed in devious internet pranks and didn't want to make a Circle K run. The coffee was stale and bitter, but it helped. I grabbed my keys and stuffed the igniter box in my cargo shorts pocket then stepped out the door. There was a little cloud cover. It was not scalding hot but still oppressive. The limo was there. I could not see who was sitting inside because sunlight reflected off the tinted glass. I was nervous until the driver's window rolled down and I saw Gus. His face was particularly drawn, and sad, much more than usual. He nodded and called out.

"Remember kid, be back by eight."

"Thanks, Gus," I said as I got in my car.

"Hey kid," he said. I stood up from my crouch on the way to wedging myself in the Honda, "You didn't tell her about me, did you?"

I emphatically nodded no.

"Smart, kid," he flashed a sad smile. "Keep it that way."

Encanto Park was not far from The Oasis. I met Sierra at the entrance of the Enchanted Island Amusement Park which is a part of Encanto. I remembered I did a shoot for The Cody Redd show in what felt like a million years before. It was a promotional shoot for the park in which my father and I went on a bunch of kiddy rides. He got motion sickness on the carousal and immediately threw up once the record light on the camera went off. My mother was pissed off at him in her cool, controlled way.

Sierra's eyes were red. She ran to me. We hugged then she took my hand and dragged me to the pedal boat entrance. The place was crowded but we managed to secure a pedal boat and paddled through the waterway mingling among other pedal powered boaters, geese, and ducks. I didn't know what to tell her. She didn't know what to say. We got to a point where only a few around. A mallard was following us hoping for bread crumb handouts. I surveyed the surroundings. No goons as far as I could tell. For the moment, we were safe. Sierra reached into her tight pink jeans, briefly struggled, then pulled out a cell phone. She handed it to me.

"Ever see one of these?" she asked.

I hesitated.

"It's, it's a cell phone, right?"

"It's a burner phone. It's disposable. You can buy them, use up the minutes, recharge them or get another. They are hard to trace especially if you keep buying new ones. Here."

She reached into her pocket again pulling out a piece of paper. Tears started to run down her cheek. I missed her smile. I did my best to suppress my tears as I glanced at the paper with a phone number written in red ink.

"This is my burner phone number. We can text and speak as long as we keep switching phones. We must tell each other the new replacement number every time our old burner phone time runs out."

"Sierra where I am going, I don't know . . ." she finished my thought . . .

"It must work, Cody! I must know you are ok! God, I don't even know if you are ever coming back but I must know you are safe! You don't understand. I lost too many people who tried to cross the border never to hear from them again. Not you. Not this time. I must know you are safe! If I never see you again..."

I held her as tight as one could in a pedal boat on an Enchanted Island waterway. I stroked her long, dark hair. We stared into each other's eyes with disbelief, sadness, and love. Then we kissed long and deep in the middle of ducks, geese, pedal boats, carousal music and screaming, joyful children. It was surreal. It made my phony childhood seem quite normal compared to all that transpired in only a few days.

"I will try like hell to talk to you," I told her. "If there is any way I can get back here and be with you I will. You know that, right?"

Sierra nodded and forced a weak smile. I cupped her face in my hands. We kissed once more. We pedaled to the dock then walked the park holding hands, past children at play to a little bridge that crossed the waterway. It looked like a tropical paradise. I thought soon I would be living in a tropical, utopian society but knew I would gladly stay with her in this false enchanted island.

"I will keep Phoenix at my parents' house until you get back," she said. "I officially adopted him."

I smiled, wrapped my arm around her, drew her close. Sundown was near. A spectacular pink, orange, and purple sunset developed. I had to leave. My smile faded. I needed to say something I wished I didn't have to say.

"You are so wonderful," I told her. "You give the gift of flight to everything you touch. If it gets too hard for you I want to give you that same gift. Fly if this gets too hard. I want you to be happy."

"There's the man I knew was inside," she said, "Caring, thoughtful man, soulful man. I will wait but thank you."

We walked to the parking lot. Our cars were in opposite directions. I studied her sweet face wanting to remember every detail right down to the faded scar above her eyebrow. She put on her best smile, turned, and said, "See ya around," then walked away.

Once again I watched her disappear in a sea of humanity. I got in my crummy car and sat numbly for a short while. This was happening, I told myself. I looked at the burner phone and the paper with her burner number. I thought I would try it out. I messaged: "I love you."

I put the key in the ignition and blasted the AC fan. A bunch of hot air blew out. I heard a notification ring.

"Love you too," was her reply.

Driving back panicked me because traffic bottle nosed on I-10 due to an accident. I had to stop at Circle K and buy a Styrofoam cup of gas then attach it and the device under the hood of my poor beleaguered Honda. A roll of duct tape I used once to tape a split radiator hose would come in handy. Since I had to swipe a cup from Circle K, I also bought a decent six pack of beer for our last night in Phoenix. It felt awkward paying for the beer and giving an extra dollar for gas. The cashier was bony with sleeve tattoos, gage earrings and rotted teeth. I figured he was a reformed meth addict. It is unnerving when a dude like that looks at you like you have two heads.

"A DOLLAR FOR GAS?" He stared with bloodshot dark, piercing eyes.

"I'm selling it. Just need enough to get me to the guys' house," I lied.

I couldn't tell him I needed it to torch my own car.

"Ok, big spender," he said, "You got a dollar on pump four."

I put the beer in my car and pulled out the cup then pretended to put a dollar of gas into the Honda. I held the cup close to the filler hole trying to gently squeeze the pump handle so the gas would pour out slow. I failed miserably. The gas gushed out, slopped out of the cup, and sprayed my hands and forearms. On a second try I successfully filled the cup and put on the plastic lid but reeked of gas. I got out of there fast. The cashier saw what I had done. He stood by the Circle K door shaking his head. He yelled something but I did not catch it with the AC blowing full blast.

I pulled over in a neighborhood side street to tape the cup with the remote electrical igniter under the hood of the car.

It is not easy trying to duct tape a cup of gas and igniter onto a filthy, grease and dirt encrusted air filter cover. Terrified I might combust myself considering I had a rich cologne of Unleaded 87, I sweated profusely and cussed until I managed to tape it in place, for how long, I did not know.

Every pothole and speed bump on the way back to The Oasis caused me to clench the steering wheel believing it would ignite a blazing inferno. I cursed Thad and his dumbass plan. It was ten minutes before eight when I parked in the lot. The limo was there. I began to hyperventilate fearing Weasel Face had already relieved Gus. When the tinted window of the limo rolled down and revealed Gus I sighed with relief.

"You cut it close, kid," he said shaking his head.

"Sorry. Please keep an eye on her, ok?"

He smiled his sweet, grandfatherly smile.

"You can bet on that, kid. Take care of yourself and good luck."

I nodded, keeping my distance because I didn't want him to pick up the scent of my gasoline cologne. I strode to our apartment with decent beer.

As I stepped in I nearly tripped over two bags Lesmour and Thad had readied by the door. Lesmour's face was lit up like a Christmas tree. I never saw him so happy, excited to be starting a brand new, shiny life in Lemuria Down. His tiny-toothed smile grew ever wider when he noticed I brought more Corona. We each popped open the sweaty bottles and split the last of the food in the apartment, a stale bag of potato chips.

"Let's toast our new lives in paradise!" he said.

We raised our bottles in toast and took a slug. Within our

hovel, our roach and ant haven, bat, and mosquito refuge beyond our newspaper blind windows, we heard a firetruck in full alarm approaching, getting louder. It was not an uncommon sound. A part of me was glad to be leaving Phoenix.

Thad bragged he erased the hard drive and decided as an extra precaution, to toss his Tower PC in the far lot dumpster for garbage pick-up early next morning. It would be buried in the landfill, "Let them look for it," he said. He packed his spare laptop in his carry-on bag saying he would need it to work on our new identities. I was about to ask Thad what my new name was, but the fire engine siren was startlingly near and joined by several police car sirens.

"What the fuck?" Thad said.

I opened our door. The choking stench of burning rubber and black billows of smoke rising above the buildings emanated from the parking lot. We ran to the lot and peeked around the apartment building so as not to be seen. There was my poor Honda engulphed in flames. Two fire engines and three police cars had already arrived. The cops shouted to bystander residents to get back as firefighters donned oxygen masks and frantically unspooled hoses. Weasel Face was there with the limo, but a cop was gesturing for him to move the car.

"Did the cup melt and catch fire?" I asked.

"No way," said Thad. "The dark site I got the device from said it won't ignite without the remote."

Thad gasped. His eyes rolled back in his head as he slowly reached into his back pocket. Lesmour and I gawked as he pulled from his pocket the remote. Its green light was blinking.

"I put it in my pocket just for a second . . ."

"You ignited it with your butt!" Lesmour blurted.

Thad's mouth drooped open in a weird oval shape, his lips curled outward, quivering.

"We gotta get out of here . . ." he whispered. "We gotta get out of here . . ."

We ran back to the apartment, grabbed our bags and were about to slam the door behind us when Thad stopped in his tracks.

"My PC! We got to dump it! They could trace us with that!"

Thad shoved his two bags in my arms and dashed into his room. I heard him grunting and cursing as he staggered out with the bulky PC in his arms.

"Go to the east lot!" he grimaced in pain.

Thad didn't get far before dropping the PC. The smoke from the fire plus its bulk and weight made it impossible for him to carry it alone to the dumpster at the far end of the parking lot. I took Lesmour's bag so he could help Thad lift the PC. With bags piled high I looked like a bell boy from some old movie I saw long ago barely able to see where I was going. Together Lesmour and Thad carried the PC only a few yards before it started slipping out of their sweaty hands.

"We got to leave," I said, "The cops will want to talk to us. Weasel Face has to be close by!"

"We can't leave it here!" Thad panted.

He and Lesmour were bent over gasping for air. None of us were in peak physical shape. Lesmour pointed into the murky night of The Oasis brown zone.

"Dump it there."

In the flickering fluorescent gloom of The Oasis was the green slime of the community pool.

"Won't they find it?" I asked.

"Cody, when was the last time that pool was drained and cleaned?" Thad sputtered between gasps.

"Like never," I said.

I dropped the bags on the sidewalk. Together we hauled the PC to the pool. Thankfully but not surprisingly, the pool gate lock was missing. We lowered the PC as quietly as possible into the deep, green abyss. It bubbled and burped as it went down making a final thud on the bottom, wherever that was. It would be impossible to find unless the pool was drained. We grabbed our bags and ran to the back lot. Thad slowed, sticking his head around the corner of the east building to see if Weasel Face was there.

"Shit! He's coming!" Thad whispered.

We freaked. Lesmour hopped like a cat in those videos when a cucumber is placed nearby while it is not looking. The only place to hide was behind a poorly lit stairwell leading to the second floor, but with our bags and three bulky bodies, it was a tight squeeze. Thad smelled like onions and smoke. Lesmour just had this kind of sweet, rank scent. I reeked of gas. Weasel Face rounded the corner with a cellphone pressed to his ear. I held my breath because I was panting loudly. My head was pounding. It was agony.

"Yeah, almost there. Where are the other guys? OK, OK! I'm hurrying!"

He broke into a trot. It would not take long for him to get to our place and find us gone. We made our escape to the back lot. Thad spoke in full sprint.

"We can't wait for an Uber! They will get us!"

Then we saw it, the limo idling under a street lamp. We froze in disbelief.

"Did he really leave it running?" said Thad.

"It's like a mirage," said Lesmour. "Anyone in it?"

With its tinted windows under the bleak light of the parking lot, it was impossible to tell. In the distance we heard the fire roaring and the fire marshal commanding something over a loud-speaker. We realized then that we were standing in the middle of the lot. If anyone was in the limo they would have come out by now.

"Come on," Thad waved, we followed.

I glanced at Lesmour. He was equally hesitant. He smiled weakly, shrugged his shoulders then ran after Thad. I was not far behind. Thad grabbed the driver door handle and swung it open like one would rip an adhesive bandaged off a hairy leg. A waft of cool air rushed from the limo. No one inside.

"The idiot let it run to keep it cool, hop in."

Thad took the wheel and floored it, screeching tires, careening off the curb on the way out of the lot. He immediately jammed on the breaks when a black SUV speeding into the lot almost hitting us blocked our exit. We were trapped. Lesmour whimpered in the back seat. The driver window to the SUV rolled down. It was Gus. Thad rolled down his window.

"Jesus, Mary and Joseph!" he yelled. "Get the hell out of here. I didn't see you. Go east. Everyone else is coming from the west side."

Gus threw the SUV in reverse. Thad took his advice slamming the gas pedal to the floor to gain speed and distance. We raced to Mill Avenue in Tempe and managed to wedge the limo on the top floor of a full parking garage. There wasn't an available space so he parked it at the end of a row making sure drivers could get around. He quipped he hoped it would get towed as he tossed the keys in a bottom floor trash can by the elevator. We darted past college students to the light rail station at University Drive and Rural Road. The train arrived. Grabbing the nearest available seats we caught our breath absorbing the narrow escape. Thad and Lesmour were crimson. Thad wheezed and coughed. Out of the three of us, he was the biggest sloth.

"We lost them, right?" Lesmour's eyes darted about, his nostrils flared. I thought he resembled a sexually aroused swine.

I tried to calm him and to be honest, reassure myself too.

"It will be a while before they get a call about their limo being towed. They might figure we took the light rail to hop a flight but then would have to guess which terminal and what time we were leaving. We should be long gone by then."

"Damn! What a rush!" Thad shouted. "If I wasn't afraid of dying I would have tried something like this years ago."

A primly dressed Hispanic couple sitting nearby stared at Thad, spoke in Spanish under their breath then got up and moved to the other end of the light rail car.

Reaching terminal four an hour before our red eye, we hurried through security. Thad booked the tickets using our real names. Thad said he would rebirth us in Kauai to be respectable members of the fledgling utopia Lemuria Down. Our primary objective once past security was to hit the first open bar we could find, each ordering tequila shots to sooth our nerves. It helped.

It was late, not many people in the bar. The quiet was surreal after the tumult of escaping. The atmosphere was reminiscent of a time Thad, and I broke into a church the first week his parents took me in. It was Thad's idea. He thought it a good diversion to break me out of the shock of suddenly being orphaned. The church was two blocks from his house. We waited until his parents went to bed. It was easy to break in. There was a partially open window near a side door. All we had to do was go back to Thad's and get his father's crowbar for leverage. We climbed in and fumbled in the dark until our eyes adjusted. After examining the altar we sat on a pew in the back, not speaking for a long time. Thad heard the place was haunted. He wanted to see for himself if it was true. We sat in the stillness waiting for something to happen.

There is a strangeness in places designed to house many people and left vacant after hours. I thought of all those church goers believing in God or at least wanting to believe. I wondered if God was there. At that most vulnerable time in my life I wished God was. Maybe they were right to congregate and pray. It sure felt like something was there besides Thad and me, something besides ghosts.

"Do you think there is a God?" I asked Thad.

He studied the church, squinted eyes, took in the pulpit, the stained glass, the cross, the quiet that filled the vast space.

"Doubt it," he said. "Probably not even ghosts."

The airport bar held the same eerie quiet. It was oddly

comforting. The bartender was sullen like he didn't want to be there which was fine because neither of us felt like talking. Time was needed to process our escape and future. Thad felt confident his scheme would work. I trusted him like an infant trusts a parent because there are no other options. I thought about his big idea to set my car on fire as a distraction and how it prematurely went up in smoke. I squirmed and asked for another tequila shot trying to drown the doubt swimming in my mind.

"Time to board," Thad said. "Drink up."

Thad treated us to first class. He was able to splurge because he made an investment that paid off. He and Lesmour sat together while I had a window seat across the aisle. Even in my heyday as a YouTube child star I never flew first class. Once we went as a "family" to shoot a Disneyland episode. My mother took a first-class seat while my father and I rode coach. She justified it by saying she needed quiet to plan the next several Cody Redd episodes but when I left my seat to check on her after my father had fallen asleep, I saw her drinking champagne and flirting with a male airline attendant. She had a funny little laugh which I never heard before or since. See was happy.

First class was great. The seats were wider, comfortable and clean. The attendant asked if we wanted a drink, but we had enough already. An old gentleman sat next to me. He had angular features with dark bruises on his long, withered hands. His hair was so thin you could see his scalp. He sat next to me, smiled briefly then began to hack a watery, phlegm filled vile cough that almost made me throw up. The attendant asked my travel mate if he was alright. He managed to wheeze out, "yes, just water please". He caught his breath then apologized. I glanced over at Thad and Lesmour. They found my predicament amusing.

Once he got his glass of water his coughing subsided. We had a conversation, him doing most of the talking, saying he was a retired professional piano tuner for classical musicians worldwide. He traveled to great concert halls hired to do his magic for some of the world's greatest virtuosos. The previous year he retired. His arthritic fingers could no longer coax the wires into sweet notes. He raised his hands to make his point. They were long and lean with swollen knuckles. He was flying to LA to visit his grandchildren.

"I loved my work, all the brilliant people I met, the travel, but it's over," he said, "Life is a series of adjustments, like a piano, you have to tinker with the strings to get the best sound possible."

I almost told him I was flying to Lemuria Down to join the newfound society supporting the lie I was an ornithologist given the job to preserve the delicate balance of avian life. I resisted scratching the old itch of trying to be something I was not because being who I am was humiliating. Instead I nodded politely and said things like, "awesome, great, cool" until he settled in for a nap. Thad and Lesmour reclined in their comfy seats already asleep. The cabin lights were low. I pulled out the burner phone Sierra had given me. I messaged her, said I was no longer in Arizona and was safe. I told her I missed her before falling asleep.

After a long layover in LAX, the flight to Kauai was uneventful. I sat with Lesmour this time while Thad sat next to a regular human. I did get Lesmour to calm down after he and Thad sniped away before boarding to Kaui. Sierra sent a text saying she was glad I was safe.

We landed in Lihue, Kauai's tiny airport, deboarding on a truck with pull up stairs to the tarmac to an outdoor covered baggage claim. The first thing that caught my attention was the soft, moist breeze. It felt like my dry, Arizonian skin was greedily absorbing this pure comfort. A fragrance of flowers permeated rather than choking jet fuel. It gave me a sense of calm and renewed energy. Even Thad was impressed. He kept repeating "everything is so green," as if he were in a meditative trance.

We took a shuttle to the Tip Top Motel Café and Bakery. Thad already reserved two rooms where we could stage our transformation to be responsible citizens of Lemuria Down. Lihue was the main commercial hub on Kauai even though it only had a max population of seven thousand. It also had a Walmart where we could shop for clothes cheap and a nearby barbershop to help clean up our act. I could use a trim even though I had my mop cut before my first date with Sierra. Thad and Lesmour both needed grown up haircuts. The motel was a short drive from the airport. Our shuttle driver gave us a condensed overview of Lihue's main attractions stressing we must go to the local beach and eat at a bar where the best poke' on the island is served. None of us knew what poke' was so we took him at his word.

The Tip Top Motel's Café and Bakery was a small two-story motel and restaurant. It looked old and simple in design, two stories high, no-frills block construction architecture but well kept. We intended to get our room and go immediately to sleep, but our olfactory receptors were greeted with mouthwatering enticements as we stepped out of the shuttle. Bacon, eggs, strong coffee, cinnamon, fresh baked bread, sirens of the culinary world bade us to enter the heavenly restaurant. Wordlessly we stepped inside the café, inhaling the rich, warm aroma. A friendly waiter said aloha and seated us. His forearm was tattooed with a bearded and dreadlocked troll-like figure brandishing a spear. Thad told the waiter he liked his tattoo. The waiter beamed.

"It is a menehune, a creature that roams the forest at night. It is like a leprechaun."

Thad said it was cool. I was surprised how pleasant Thad was acting, not his usual sarcastic self. It was as if he was put under a spell after stepping off the plane. We each ordered the Tip Top Grand Slam, a massive serving of two soft, buttery pancakes, two eggs, rice, hash browns and Portuguese sausage, tearing into the meal while downing several cups of the best coffee I ever had. The waiter was amused by our zeal. He said, "I see you are enjoying your breakfast." I gave a thumbs up, Thad nodded affirmatively. Lesmour tried to say something with his mouth full but was unintelligible. While I was eating, I almost forgot everything. It was as if we were on vacation.

We ate until we could eat no more. Finally Thad spoke after taking a last gulp of coffee.

"I feel gross, I ate so much but God it was good! Today we rest up, hang low, but much to do tomorrow. We get haircuts, buy new clothes, and get photos for our ID cards. We got to charter a boat, too."

I was about to ask Thad what my new name was, but Lesmour swallowed his last mouthful and asked Thad, "Where do we get the boat?"

"There's a harbor close by. I found a boat owner that will drop us at the uninhabited part of Lemuria Down. We meet him tomorrow afternoon."

We took our meager belongings to our rooms. Thad got a room with a king-size bed. He reserved a room for Lesmour and I with twin beds. I was too full and exhausted to protest having to share a room with Lesmour. Our room was sparse but clean, a framed picture of a beach, another of a fishing boat, twin beds, with one nightstand between, and a tiny dresser with a small TV propped on it. We dropped our bags, drew the thick curtains, and slept off the trip and food stupor. Lesmour snored like a drunken sailor. The times he slept over on our apartments' sticky couch he kept me awake most of the night. In the dark room once I put my head on the pillow not even his snoring disturbed me. I did not wake until Lesmour nudged me. I opened my eyes to see he and Thad looking down. The drapes were pulled back. The room was dark because the sun was almost down. We slept the whole day.

"Let's check out the beach," Lesmour said.

We took an uber to Nawiliwili Park. The driver dropped us by the beach where the magenta sun was touching the horizon as we walked past several shops to a restaurant called Duke's Kauai. Near the shops was a beach cove bordered by green, tough grass with benches, and picnic tables backdropped by the shadowy shape of a low mountain range jutting to the ocean. An ocean liner was docked further down, luminously lit in fading daylight. We took off our shoes and dug our feet into the cool, damp sand. It was marvelous. A gentle wind made the palms breathe a sleepy, continual whisper. If only Sierra were here.

Thad and Lesmour laid in the sand. I got up, walked to the

water's edge, sticking my feet in. It felt good to be out of the desert. I pulled out the burner phone and messaged Sierra.

"My feet are in ocean water. I wish you were here." A few minutes passed. She replied. "I am jealous. It is very hot again. Someday we will be together on a beach."

Chapter Ten

The next day was hectic. After another overindulgent breakfast at Tip Top Café, we took an Uber to Walmart. It was hard figuring out what educated, successful people wear, seeing we didn't know any. Lesmour needed deck shoes for his seafaring captain gig, and I had to get hiking boots, thick socks and khakis for bird watching along with binoculars and a digital camera, field notebooks, all the stuff a birdwatcher would use. Thad's attire was easier. He had to dress geeky like an Office Max employee. Our biggest transformation were our haircuts. An old-time style barbershop near Tip Top called Sonny's Clips and Shave was the next stop.

Sonny's was a little off the beaten path, a narrow, winding street with large, leafed trees that covered it like a canopy creating perpetual shade. We witnessed several chickens, a rooster with black body feathers, black tail with red hackles. Several hens with brown feathers and yellow-orange hackles, one with black hackles laced in gold, a salmon breast, and black tail wandered around clucking dully while pecking. The two ancient island barbers who could have passed for twins said domestic chickens gone wild were a common site on the Hawaiian Islands. I thought, "at least I know one invasive species to control in Lemuria Down."

I was first in the chair. The barber asked me what I wanted.

I told him a trim that would make me look professional which made him grin. He thought I was joking. I further clarified I was hired to do important work and needed to look the part. He nodded gravely then proceeded to give me the kind of low maintenance cut I had when I was a kid. I contemplated my new identity and realized another reason I was so attracted to Sierra. She was without pretense. She is a what you see is what you get person. Once again I was playing a role rather than being myself, whatever that was.

But my haircut was refreshing. I felt lighter in spirit. While Lesmour's cut was an improvement, it made his head appear as a neatly trimmed basketball. Thad's was the most startling. Gone were the tangled web of curls. I saw his ears for the first time since I have known him. His hair was so short I could see his pale scalp except for some locks on the top combed to the side. The new look accentuated his straight nose making it appear larger than before.

Finding the business that was going to take our photos for our fake IDS was challenging. It was a little camera shop inland which our young, hippie Uber driver never heard of. How Thad found this business online I don't know.

A small, stocky man with copper-toned skin and black framed, thick lensed glasses had us take turns standing on a red line to properly frame us for our ID pic. After we were snapped he ushered us past a black felt curtain to the back of the shop where a young girl in her teens hunched over a laptop in a corner. Thad gave her each of our new Lemuria Down identity cards. She said the cards were not the right paper stock. She would print new ones then transfer our photos to them. She had several other fake ID's to do ahead of us. We could pick ours up at the end of the day.

Lesmour and I got to see our new names. Mine was Kody Hillman. Jeffery Lesmour became Jefferson Brown. Thad said he wanted our new first names to resemble our originals to prevent confusion. My last name was a nod to my origin of Fountain Hills. Lesmour's new last name, Brown, was paying homage to Charlie Brown, the original pumpkin head. Of course Jeffery went off the rails.

"That's really cruel! You change it!"

"Sorry, Charlie, the die is cast, no turning back."

"What's your new name?" I asked.

"Thaddeus Story, I thought since in my past life I was a phony writer, Story was appropriate."

The hippie Uber driver was sitting on the hood of his car playing with his cellphone when we came out. Thad had asked him to wait. On the way to the marina, he lit up a joint and passed it saying he was originally from San Francisco and came to Kauai five years ago to work and party for the summer. He never left. He worked as a waiter, an Uber driver and bus boy at a second restaurant to pay his share of rent for a cramped cottage he shared with three others his age. He said it is not easy, but he loved the island lifestyle.

Our charter boat was at a marina that lay in the shadows and wake of the giant cruise ships docked in Nawiliwili Harbor. Thad said the captain he hired to take us to the far end of Lemuria Down would meet us in a boat named Ursula, after the evil underwater Disney character. We clomped along the dock, unsteady by the lazy, rolling waves passing several trim vessels until finding what could best be described in nautical terms as a garbage scow with the name Ursula haphazardly painted on the prow. The cabin cruiser was weathered with chipped, dull paint and rust from the railings streaking to the waterline. The cabin windows were clouded by saltwater residual. When we walked across the plank, the worn wood of the deck groaned with each step. There was a figure laid out below deck in the cabin sleeping quarters. Thad called hello. The burly figure sat up and stretched. I was shocked to see it was a woman. So was Thad.

She was solidly built, big forearms and calves, broad shouldered with straight, blond hair tied in a ponytail. Her freckled face was flaking, and dark red, from sun damage.

She climbed out of the cabin and offered her hand. Thad didn't shake it.

"Where's the captain? I spoke to someone named Chris."

"You must be Thad, I am Chris. People on the phone mistake me for a guy, especially when I give my name. It's short for Christine."

Somewhat reluctantly Thad shook her hand as he peered at the boat.

"It don't look like much, but it will get you to your paradise," she said.

"I hope so," he said, "We are lousy swimmers."

"I'm a good swimmer!" said Lesmour, "I am a boat captain too." Chris beamed at Lesmour.

"You can be my first mate! So you know, you guys aren't the first to get there through the back door."

Lesmour was elated by Chris's offer to be her first mate. She twirled her hair, staring longingly at him. He returned the gaze with a dopey smile.

"We are sneaking onto the island to hide from mobsters that threatened Cody!" he blurted.

Thad punched him in the arm. In high school, Thad and I used to have punching contests; taking turns hitting each other's arm until someone conceded defeat but that was just in sport.

"Asshole," he muttered.

"Don't worry," Chris said. "I can be discreet. This is not my first rodeo doing a covert operation." She winked at Lesmour who was rubbing his arm. His grimace reverted to his dopey grin.

"We want to get there before sunrise tomorrow," said Thad. "Is that doable?"

"Sure. I'll sleep onboard tonight. I'll be ready when you are. Do you have the cash?"

Thad reached for his wallet, hesitated, then looked at Chris.

"Listen," she said, her smile vanished. "You can pay me now or tomorrow. I ain't going nowhere."

"If it's all the same, I'll pay tomorrow."

Chris stared a second longer. Her gritted toothed jaw relaxed, waved her hands dismissively.

"Sure, whatever dude. I'm easy." She looked over at Lesmour, winking once again.

Lesmour emitted a high-pitched schoolgirl laugh. Thad glared at him.

The hippie Uber driver took us back to the motel, passing us a new joint on the way. Thad asked the driver if he could return at three in the morning. He wanted to make sure there was ample time to reach Lemuria Down before sunrise. The driver was not too interested waking that early until Thad offered to pay double the fare. He was rapidly blowing through the extra cash his parents gave him.

"That would awesome," said the driver, "I can make rent early this month!"

Before he dropped us off, the driver recommended Lihue Joe's Bar and Grill on the beach for lunch or an early dinner.

"The weed got me hungry," he said. "It's awesome food at a cheap price."

His suggestion of food suddenly made us hungry; the weed was strong. We hurriedly packed the clothes we bought, making sure our new IDs were in the suitcases then dressed in swimsuits, old t-shirts and did something we never do, walk. The restaurant was a little over a mile but mostly downhill, our version of exercise. Thad said the new society we were about to infiltrate encouraged all residents to walk as much as possible. There were community electric vehicles people could reserve but none privately owned. I especially had to get used to walking if I was going to be cataloguing birds on the island.

On the way I messaged Sierra, asking if she was free to talk later. I wanted to tell her about Kauai, how soft the breeze is, the scented landscape, the warm water lapping gently against the white sand shore. I knew it was dangerous, but I wanted to share this enchanted place with her. She replied quickly. "Sure. I miss your voice, and the rest of you." She concluded it with a heart emoji.

On the way, we spied a beautifully plumed rooster in a tangled thicket underneath a large palm tree. It was regal and seemed proud to be wild unlike its domestic cousins. I smiled, thinking we also flew the coup of our Phoenix apartment. Besides missing Sierra it felt good to be out of that self-imposed hen house. I glanced at Thad who was grinning.

"Thanks for getting us here," I said.

"It was scary as hell," he said, "But I am almost glad our lives were threatened. We would not be here if that old guy didn't recognize you."

"And I would not have met, Christine," Lesmour said. "We made a connection!"

Thad's old sarcastic scowl reappeared.

"Great, Pumpkin Head is in love. Don't get used to it. Once she drops us off, it's over."

"You're not my father!"

"Thank God for that!"

Thad and Lesmour pecked at each other. The rooster having more sense than my two chums, scattered into the protection of the underbrush upon hearing the raucous squawking. Fortunately the bitter exchange of words was short. Hunger generated by the weed propelled us to Lihue Joe's Bar and Grill which was steps from the beach. The establishment was low key and casual, high tops by the bar and wooden booths near a deck with several sliding glass doors pulled open to access the umbrellaed metal tables that overlooked the beach and harbor further on. We took a booth closest to the sliders with beach view ordering two Poke' Bowls for Thad and I. Lesmour had a Maui Burger which was basic except for aioli sauce.

I never had Poke' before but felt adventurous. I was not disappointed. The ahi tuna was soft and fresh, marinated in sesame oil and soy sauce with crushed red pepper, chopped macadamia nuts and slivers of green onion on a bed of rice. We split a pitcher of a microbrew called Kauai Sunset to wash it down. Thad and I ordered another bowl to split.

Afterward we took a dip in the ocean, bringing a local brew six-pack named Lihue Gold purchased at a minimart adjacent to Lihue Joe's. I couldn't imagine a better place to be or better way to live. I wondered if Lemuria Down, the new utopia, could be any better than Lihue, Kauai.

Thad and Lesmour, being true Arizonans, soaked up as much ocean water as possible. I got out eventually toting my burner phone and beer to a palm grove. I sat on a bench and called Sierra.

"I miss you," I said.

"Are you safe?"

I spouted like a volcanic eruption telling her almost everything since we left Phoenix minus the location, substituting Kauai with "a tropical island". I doubted it was wise. Sharing any information at all was a risk.

"I am glad you are safe. Phoenix likes his new home," she tried to be cheery, "Gus asked about you."

"Don't tell him anything!" I practically shouted in the earpiece. She was alarmed.

"Relax, Cody. You know I won't. I told him we broke up. That way I can be upset and not have to hide it."

"I don't want anything to happen to you."

"I'm good. I'm fine."

I did relax, realizing Gus surely thought it a natural thing to ask seeing that I was no longer there. He knew it might be perceived as suspicious if he did not inquire. I took a swig of beer trying to get some liquid courage for what I had to say.

"Where I am going, I don't know how well this phone will work. I did buy a bunch of burner phones in case they do."

"If not send me a quick e-mail from a business, not your current e-mail address. Better yet make a new email address and send it to me. Make it like you are looking to volunteer at Birds of a Feather. Say you are Mary Torrens."

"You are so clever."

"I am adaptable. So are you."

We spoke until Thad and Lesmour dried themselves from their dip in the ocean. Thad waved to me and shouted: "Come on, time to get our IDs." It was hard to end our call.

Thad hailed another Uber. Minutes later, a beat-up subcompact driven by a heavy Hawaiian with a long ponytail pulled up. We crammed in, creating a sauna effect with body heat, wetsuits, and towels. He knew exactly where the camera shop was, saying the owner was his cousin.

"You men picking up pictures?" he asked flashing a big, toothed grin, one of which was gold.

When we answered in the affirmative, he laughed.

"Yeah, my cousin does a good business these days. You would think with digital photography people don't want physical photos but that's what he sells the most. Kiana is my niece. She works in the back. She is a nice girl."

We looked at each other hesitant to speak.

"No worries, men. It is the best-known secret in town. My cousin is very discreet."

Arriving at the camera shop, the Uber driver said he would keep the car running because we wouldn't be long. He was right. The IDs were ready. After Thad paid for them he passed the cards to Lesmour and me keeping his. I was surprised. I held a rainbow colored ID with my new, fake name, Cody Hillman and Lemuria Down spelled across its top.

"Looks official to me," I said.

"They do," said Thad, " but the bar codes I added won't get past the scanners at the processing center. We still have to bypass them."

We wedged into the Uber taking the uncomfortable ride back to the Tip Top Café and hotel. A late afternoon rain began to fall. Outside the café, we paused to feel gentle gusts of wind that made the palms sing. The coffee and fresh bakery aroma drew me inside the café. Thad and Lesmour followed to order coffee and a variety box of cookies to munch while we finalized packing.

I cut a slit in the lining of my suitcase with fingernail scissors I bought and slipped our former identities inside. Thad wanted to toss them, but I suggested it would be a good idea to keep in case something went wrong and needed to get back to the mainland. I was more interested in keeping mine in hopes of finding a way back to Arizona to be with Sierra.

Outside on a narrow balcony to our room, Lesmour and I draped our wetsuits over the rail as the tropical storm passed. Suitcases packed; clothes we would wear for our early departure were set out. We were ready. The three of us sat on the balcony, overlooking the bay. Night had come. We said little between munching cookies and coffee sips. Lihue was tranquil. The lights of the cruise ship in the harbor glittered. The rising moon illuminated slow, undulating waters of the Pacific as white foam stroked the beachhead. I relished this one moment of peace.

"I wish it could always be this way," Lesmour said, finishing the last cookie.

Thad could have said something sarcastic but simply nodded. Away from the squalor of our apartment life he was behaving in a manner I had not seen before as if he was a different person. Maybe it was just the change of scenery or the peace at the end of day. Tomorrow we would steal our way to the shiny, new, fabricated paradise. I relaxed on the lounge chair, exhaled contentedly, focused on the gentle coo of an unknown bird in a nearby palm. Could Lemuria Down be any better than this?

Book Two:
Lemuria Down

Chapter Eleven

The coffee late in the day kept me up until midnight. The alarm was an auditory bolt of lightning striking my brain. Lesmour somehow slept through it. I jostled him. He groaned a little. I gave him a good shove then said, "Come on, your girlfriend is waiting."

That did the trick. He pushed himself out of bed and quickly dressed. There was a knock on the door. It was Thad.

"Come on ladies, time to go."

In a dream state, we plodded down the hotel steps to the parking lot. The hippy Uber driver arrived on schedule. He had a Grateful Dead tune on his phone which added to the early morning waking weirdness. Getting in the car, I realized we left our swim suits on the deck railing.

"Screw it," said Thad, "They are probably still wet. We each have another suit anyway."

The driver wanted the fare up front in cash. He was happy when Thad handed it over mentioning again he could now pay his rent early. There were no other cars on the winding backroads that lead to the marina where Chris kept her boat. Wordless and numb from lack of sleep I listened to the only Grateful Dead song I knew as we drove to the marina.

"Ripple in still water
When there is no pebble tossed
Nor wind to blow"

I thought to myself rather dramatically "fare thee well old life, welcome new life" feeling oddly nostalgic and excited. Deep down I thought I would never see Sierra again. That part of my life was over. The prospect of better days was intriguing although it was hard to imagine them being better without her. I hadn't a clue about the impending tempest that would befall us. Not the greatest mentalist in the world could see what was coming.

Reaching the marina, the headlights of the Uber shone upon Chris's shoddy boat, Ursula. The stocky captain clambered from below deck holding a large cup of coffee. The cabin lights gave a subdued, hazy glow.

The hippy driver wished us a "bon voyage" as we took our luggage out of the car. He said when we got back to look him up, he would be glad to show us around Kauai. I felt sad to leave him. He was cool, he had looked after us. Lesmour sprang back to life seeing his heart throb Christine. He was the first on the deck acting like a puppy that hadn't seen his master all day.

"Ahoy, captain!" he called out.

"Jesus," said Thad.

I followed Thad on board. He reached into his pocket and pulled out a wad of cash, handing it to Christine. She smiled as she counted the money carefully.

"Everything looks good to me," she said. "You guys ready?"

"What can I do to help?" Lesmour asked. He was so excited I thought he was going to hump her leg.

"I'll fire up the motor, you unlash and push her from the dock. Help yourselves to coffee below deck."

Thad grabbed Lesmour by the arm before he set off to do his chores.

"Keep your mouth shut on why we are here," Thad said. "You spouted off too much already."

Lesmour gave a fat lipped scowl and shook loose from Thad's hold. Thad went below deck to the galley and retrieved two cups of coffee spilling some passing one to me. I was sitting on a bench that faced the stern. Christine hunched over the motor and mightily yanked the starter cord three times causing the boat to rock. On the third try, it coughed black billows of exhaust until she adjusted the trim. It chugged grudgingly to life.

Lesmour nimbly freed the mooring lines from the deck rings then pushed Ursula from the dock. He joined Christine at the helm after getting coffee, chattering like a male parakeet witnessing sunrise. Thad and I took sips of the black, hair-raising coffee. The dark silhouette of Kauai's shoreline grew small then vanished entirely in the night. I imagined this was what death was like. It certainly felt like death, gently rolling away from what you knew, the good and bad of living without an explanation or definition of what it was about, all fading to nothingness slicing through endless waves to a place you had never been, a rumored paradise.

"You're goanna miss her," Thad said, breaking the silence.

"Yep, already do. You think this will work?"

"I think so," he said, "regardless, it was our best option."

"I have my doubts," I said. "I don't know if I can fake being an ornithologist, but then again it can't be such a perfectly run society if we are able to sneak through the back door, right?"

Thad grinned, taking a large slurp of coffee with satisfaction. It had cooled to a non-scalding temperature.

"You underestimate me, my friend. I am an expert worm. I found their soft underbelly and I exploited it, but you are right. If they were perfect I would not have been able to sneak in. The truth is of course nothing conceived by humans is perfect. There is always a crack in the armor. I found the crack. I exploited it well."

The coffee was strong but not bitter. I was surprised Christine could brew a good cup on her garbage scow. I surmised it might be a state law that all coffee in Hawaii must be awesome. Christine and Lesmour laughed uproariously. Thad took a quick glance back at them, gritting his teeth.

"That bothers me," he said. "Pumpkin Head got the hots for her. He can blow our cover. I wish we could have dumped him."

"Cut him some slack. He sort of means well. He had a harder life than us."

Thad gruffly agreed. I changed the subject trying to avoid unpleasantries.

"Lemuria Down, how'd they come up with that?"

Thad tittered.

"I looked into it," he said. "Lemuria is a legendary sunken continent in the Indian Ocean where humans supposedly began and were all knowing, mystical bullshit creatures. The word "down" of Lemuria Down means rolling hills. It represents the land this place was built on, volcanic rock core filled with the fertile ground of their new civilization. It is the kind of cockeyed type of name I would dream up."

The stealth cruise reached the far shore of Lemuria Down before dawn. Christine found a secluded white sandbar with her fog light where she could safely beach. She cut the engine letting Ursula drift harmlessly until the bow sunk into the embankment, tossing an anchor overboard so waves would not dislodge the craft. In the dark, beyond the sand strip there was dense foliage and what appeared to be a steep rock face that towered to the stars. Christine managed to lean the gang plank to the shoreline so we could haul our luggage without getting them, or ourselves wet.

After everything was on shore, Lesmour walked back up the gangplank and hugged Christine. They spoke briefly murmuring something we could not hear. Thad shouted, "Come on!"

Aggravated, Lesmour walked across the plank calling back to Christine, "talk to you soon!" He and Thad helped feed the gangplank to Christine. She grabbed a power pole using it to shove off then motored slowly from the shore. We picked up our luggage. Looking at the climb ahead I could see why Thad advised us to wear hiking boots.

"It's not so bad, there is an access road about a quarter mile up. It leads to where we need to officially register."

We were at the eastern base of the dead volcano, the foundational building block of Lemuria Down. We had to climb a steep grade a quarter mile long through thick vegetation and loose volcanic rock. It was torture. The first rays of sunrise did not penetrate as we hiked through rainforest tangle, cold and damp. I suggested compact camp flashlights I bought but they did little to light the way. The leaves on low hanging branches were bigger than our heads proving difficult to push aside as we stumbled several times over ground vines, panting and groaning after only a few minutes of exertion. It took nearly an hour until we found the unpaved access road, collapsing in a heap.

I made the mistake wearing shorts, while my companions wore long cargo pants. My unprotected legs were scraped and bleeding. A light tropical rain began to fall. Our clothes became soaked in sweat and rainwater. Thad said we had to follow the road north around the dead volcano to the main port where the receiving office for new residents was located.

"The receiving office is a block from the port. We can act like we just got past the ID scanners on the morning boat and funnel in with the latest batch of new Lemurians."

We walked for another hour. Ahead in the access road, vibrant shafts of rainbow ribbons looked as if they touched the road. Thad sang "Somewhere Over the Rainbow" very poorly. I told him to shut up although, I thought it was funny. Lesmour blabbed about how great Christine was and he couldn't wait to see her again.

Of course upon hiking to the end of the rainbow spot, it ceased to exist. The access road dipped to the fresh paved road to civilization. Further down, a small harbor sparkled in early morning sunlight. A smattering of one-story homes and other small buildings all topped with solar panels nestled into lush landscape. Thad had read the architecture was inspired by Frank Llyod Wright blending in with nature incorporating material from the land itself. What stood out most was the white roads of Lemuria Down. Thad explained they were painted a very resilient white coating that would not absorb heat and lesson the effects of climate change. It was not a yellow brick road, but it gave a magical, fairy tale appearance.

"Hello!"

I practically jumped. So intent on studying our new life ahead, we did not notice a paved side road cutting into the access road where an elderly lady with curly shoulder length hair was seated in an electric car with a canvas top. She wore a big tropical floral pattern dress. Her bright smile bared dazzling white teeth and her skin had a bronze, healthy tone. The only wrinkles were crows' feet and smile lines. She was probably three times our age but looked much healthier than any of us.

"Need a ride?"

She noticed our bags and then saw my legs cut up from the fall.

"Oh my, you are hurt, come on. I'll take you to the clinic."

I looked at Thad and he motioned to get into the lady's vehicle. We placed our luggage in a large, wire basket in the back. The car had two bench seats. Lesmour and I got into the back seat with some difficulty while Thad sat in front.

"Actually, can you take us to the receiving office?"

She looked at Thad with a trace of suspicion.

"You just got here? Why didn't you go right to the welcome center?"

I squirmed in my seat. Thad was caught off guard momentarily. He leaned toward her and whispered as if he was in a confessional booth doling out a dreadful sin.

"You see, my colleague is an ornithologist. He is here to study and help maintain the natural beauty of the island. He is a bit of a loon himself, if you get my drift. He saw some rare bird and went chasing after it right off the boat. We lost track of him until now. He had a tumble while he was traversing the wilds."

I wanted to slap him across the back of his head, but the lie worked. She nodded knowingly.

"My uncle was a botanist. He would disappear for days in the woods . . . strange man."

She looked back at me and smiled. I felt the heat of my blush but said nothing.

"I am Lois, you folks will love it here. People are so friendly. There are plenty of birds to admire!"

Lois insisted taking me to the clinic first to get my legs treated. We rolled down the white roadway toward the center of town. Lois waved at every electric car motorist and pedestrian she passed. She told us she and her husband Nigel were resident artists. The artist commune, a series of small buildings in town center was a special enclave where artists displayed their work and offered lessons to any resident. She encouraged us to participate. I found myself starting to get excited. This place was real. We were here.

The town center was slightly elevated from the bay and harbor near a white sand beach and seafood restaurant at the end of a pier about the length of a football field. People were lounging and playing on the beach, strolling the pier, dining in bright, open-air restaurants and slowly debarking the cruise ship to become new citizens.

Through a quiet residential area, we rolled past manicured yards of homes with lots of glass to afford a view of the Pacific

Ocean. The town center was like no other I had ever experienced. One cannot describe the serenity of a place devoid of combustion engines. The air was clear, clean. Snippets of conversation could be heard as we rolled by residents. On several street corners, musicians and singers serenaded passersby.

The town had an open-air market with a huge array of fruit, vegetables, and seafood as well as locally produced crafts. Scents of fresh, roasted coffee and a fruity ambrosia permeated. Lois identified the sweet scent as Buddleia Asiatica, also known as a butterfly bush, a roadside long thin leaf plant with small white flowers shaped like dog tails. I eagerly made note of various restaurants we passed that specialized in every conceivable cuisine worldwide. I officially pronounced myself as a foodie.

"The center of town is designed for the mind and soul," Lois said. "Music, art, food, and drink abounds giving us a special glow amid great meeting places to build community. You must go there after you settle. First let's take care of those lacerations."

She drove a few minutes more to "the clinic," several buildings spaced out on lush grounds with a tall fountain statue of Poseidon at the entrance. Lois parked her car, plugging it into one of several charging stations in the lot. She proudly told us the water in every town fountain was perfectly safe to drink. Each building housed a separate practice of medicine. The one we went to was for general practice, but she told us there was a building for surgery, one for dentistry, psychology, yoga, exercise, and massage.

Lois strode into the general practice with me as if I were a child and needed to be escorted or a mad bird lover who might wander off upon hearing an exotic bird song. She lead me to the front desk, explaining to the receptionist I just arrived and injured my legs in a fall. The man at the desk had an accent, possibly from the Caribbean. He knew Lois by name and stood from the desk to hug her. I was immediately taken to an examination room, no paperwork, no ID, or insurance asked. I had not even a chance to examine the room when a member of the medical staff came in and cleaned my wounds, applied gauze around a gash in my calf and handed me an antibiotic sending me out the door.

Thad and Lesmour sat on a park bench by the Poseidon fountain arguing but quieted when we approached, trying their best to behave. Like chicks following a mother quail, we followed her to the vehicle. Lois drove through a residential area to the harbor receiving office. It was another cluster of buildings that housed different elements of town functions such as public services, road maintenance, housing, sanitation, post office, and shipping.

"Here is your stop," she said. "Welcome to Lemuria Down! Don't be a stranger!"

We thanked her, then carried our luggage to the receiving office. A sign by the front door read Aloha in script encircled by a lei. It had a rustic feel. The interior was open and airy with wicker chairs in the lobby illuminated entirely by skylights.

The front desk had a bowl of tropical fruit. On a separate table were two coolers, one with water, the other fresh squeezed lemonade. A stout woman who I surmised was of Hawaiian descent was finishing up with two women ahead of us.

The woman behind the desk declared they were now official residents of Lemuria Down. The couple embraced. We watched them gleefully roll their baggage to an open glass door on the south side of the building where a teenaged boy greeted them then loaded their belongings into an electric car. The couple hopped in with the teenager and were driven away. Now it was our turn.

"Mahalo friends!"

We shuffled to the desk, Lesmour aka, Jefferson Brown filled a glass with lemonade, drinking it down in three gulps as she inspected our fake IDs. Lesmour encouraged us to have the lemonade. He was on his second glass, whispering "so good" with alternate gulps. As I reached for a glass, the desk lady said, "Kody Hillman, do I know you?"

I was afraid my haircut might have reclaimed my former boyish appearance. A chill came over me.

"I, I have never been to Hawaii. I doubt it."

She crinkled her brow, stared directly at me for what seemed like a week. I glanced at Thad and Lesmour, both steadying themselves for the worst.

"I know who you remind me of! My nephew in San Jose! You look just like him!"

The three of us made feeble attempts at laughter.

"Your new homes are ready. They are in the north end of town by the research and development consort, up the hill from the marina. Since you are acquaintances we made sure you will be neighbors and close to your areas of interest. Tomorrow at 9am come back here for orientation. Afterward you will be taken to your places of core interest. For now feel free to rest, relax and wander. Your homes have already been stocked with some of the island's culinary delights."

She glanced to the side door where a new driver was waiting.

"Ah, Albert is here! He will take you to your new homes. Welcome to Lemuria Down!"

Albert was an African American, nearly bald. He grinned and gestured for us to join him. We climbed in and made the slight, winding ascent to our new homes on the north side of town. Albert pointed to his left down a road that led to the marina where Lesmour was to play as a sea captain, his dream come true. The marina could be seen from the top of the road. It had a dozen boats for various pastimes, whale watching, fishing, pleasure cruising. At a right fork further up, Albert pointed to where Thad and I would find our "place of interest," the research and development quad. Thad was assigned to assist a man named Robinette, a brilliant inventor and innovator. I had my own, separate pod devoted to the study of Lemuria Down's natural world, focusing on our feathered friends but I was to report to Robinette since he was the head of research and development. Cynically I wondered if the island was a true natural environment considering the town proper was built upon an extinct volcano with countless tons of landfill in which vegetation was planted later. I might as well have been a resident naturalist in Disney Land.

"I am surprised the vehicles need drivers," Thad said aloud. "I thought they would all be autonomous."

"Oh, they are self-driving cars," Albert said, "But some people rather have a driver like me or drive it themselves. I was a cabbie in Chicago. I loved the work, but the city brought me down. This is like I died and went to heaven."

He chuckled, then took a sharp turn into a cul-de-sac with six small houses, three symmetrically set on each side. He pulled off to the right and stopped.

"Here are your new homes!"

Albert offered to help with our bags, but we declined. He drove away with a wave and a chuckle. Thad told us all the homes and buildings were carbon zero. Everything was built with recycled material and what little waste was produced in Lemuria Down was reused for fertilizer, fuel, or new structures. Our homes were about the same square footage as the apartment Thad and I lived in but the use of glass, and open floor plans made them seem much larger.

We each had our own personal decorative theme. Lesmour's was nautical, much to his delight with ships at sea paintings, a sculpture of an old sea salt among other things. This is so cool," he said. "Christine is going to love it." My place was a bird and nature motif, more paintings, sculptures and even some ambient, programmable bird calls in nature I could control by voice command or a remote. Thad's was all tech, clean, modernistic, too sparse for my taste, but he seemed pleased. Basically, anything was amazing compared to our shithole apartment. All of this felt too good to be true and I wondered again how Thad was able to get us here. I stepped into my new digs to unpack, the three of us agreeing we meet at my back patio after settling in. It was private and beautiful, a perfect place to get stoned.

As I put my clothes and field equipment away I realized I would finally be living on my own. I lived with my parents until they flew the coop then was taken in by Thad's parents until a year after we graduated from high school. We moved to the fungoid Oasis apartment complex and lived there ever since. That was when Thad changed my name to evade media vultures and old fans and make it more difficult for Sal's mob buddies to find me. No one ever did until I decided to save the bird Phoenix and met Sierra.

I sat in a recliner listening to a native Hawaiian bird, 'Akepa through my bird call sound system. It made a shrill, loud burst followed by a two-note repetitive, lower tone. I was almost touched thinking back on the years after my parents abandoned me how Sal chose to let me live. He spared me from my mother's indiscretions. Of course when I was discovered by Gus, Sal had to act. I was no longer a boy, and the Martino family wanted retribution to preserve their family pride.

I was about to check out the contents of my refrigerator when I noticed Thad on my back patio, swinging in a hammock smoking a joint. I wanted a snack and then nap but instead rolled back the sliding door and joined him. The sweet fragrance of a white flowered shrub was overwhelming. I later learned it was named a mock orange shrub. It almost over-powered the skunk scented weed Thad was smoking.

"I could get used to this," he said. "They set me up with locally grown, kick ass weed. Want a hit?"

I took a toke kept it in my lungs too long coughing most of it out.

"Won't that effect your work?" I asked.

"It never did, why should it now?"

"For one thing, you never had a real job, maybe they will expect you to be professional."

"What they want me to do is easy, just entering a shit load of data and making sure no one else gets to it. The hardest stuff will be troubleshooting crap, but I don't mind. It is child's play."

"I wish I was self-assured as you."

"Cody, that's your problem, always looking on the downside."

I laughed, "You're one to talk!"

He laughed, the effects of the weed, kicking in. "I suppose you're right. Yeah, but look at this place. What could go wrong?"

Lesmour joined us. He grinned like a fool.

"I forgot," Thad said, gesturing toward Lesmour, "That could go wrong."

Lesmour became defensive, of course.

"What's that supposed to mean?"

"Even in paradise, you are such a bummer." Thad replied, "What took you so long, having phone sex with your girlfriend?"

"No! We were just talking, you pervert!"

They launched into a barrage of heated words. Thad told Lesmour to dump Christine, she was shady. Lesmour countered yelling that she was "really cool," saying Thad was jealous because he hadn't had a girl in years. I was horrified that I would be sandwiched between lunatic neighbors. So much for paradise.

Chapter Twelve

Lesmour and Thad took an autonomous car to the welcome center. I decided to wear my ornithologist outfit, taking the mostly downhill walk. My cuts and bandaging stung and pulled but I didn't mind. I thought it a good idea to build up my legs and play the part of a naturalist. Below, the community, nestled in the bay with its brightly colored buildings and swaying palms, did look like paradise. Fit and trim passersby waved or called "good morning." It was plain to see my two companions and I stood out because of our paunches. Lesmour was tanned as much as anyone we saw. I had a little color from volunteering at Birds of a Feather, but Thad was a ghost. Right before the welcome center, they passed me in the autonomous car shouting out to purposely startle me. A couple of people near the center looked up, puzzled at the sudden ruckus. I felt like a fool in my naturalist costume with my very unnatural friends.

The welcome center had a back garden area with tables and chairs and a small podium. I met Thad and Lesmour by a sign that said, "Welcome new neighbors!" near an open gate joining ten other people of mixed ethnicities already seated. Lois, the woman that gave us a lift the previous day, breezed through the open slider door.

She wore an ankle length flowing white dress and was bare-foot. With hands clasped she surveyed the new recruits in a state of rapture. Lois recognized us and trotted over to where we sat, her curly white mane bouncing. She smelled of patchouli.

"And how was your first night in Lemuria Down?"

"Good," said Thad. "You have kick-ass weed here."

Lois laughed, nearing a fit of hysteria. I smiled sheepishly fearing at any minute we would be discovered to be the phonies we really were. Lesmour began bitching to Lois about Thad being cruel like he was snitching to a teacher about a bully. I discreetly balled my fist and rapped him in his thigh which shut him up temporarily.

"Yes! We do have excellent "weed"," she used her middle and index fingers to simulate quotes saying the word weed. She was a little too cheerful for my liking. "If you excuse me I will now perform my interest as orientation comforter."

She swooshed away as if she were a dandelion seed taken by the wind to the front podium where she greeted and kissed a thin elderly man. He sat at a front table with two other men. The animated talk of the new residents was quashed when Lois picked up a brass bell and hit it with a striker three times gaining everyone's attention.

"Welcome all! Welcome to Lemuria Down! I am Lois, your orientation comforter. It is my interest to provide you with an introduction to our beautiful island like a mother would greet a long-lost child with arms open and a heart that is full!"

Lois gushed at length on the merits of Lemuria Down, mentioning the introductory correspondence that we, the new residents, were briefed on before our arrival. I looked at Thad with raised eyebrows seeing that we were officially in the dark. He shrugged his shoulders and whispered: "I didn't have time to dig that up."

Without the introductory correspondence, I was able through her speech to learn fragments of info such as Lemuria Down had no monetary system, not even a barter system. Everyone was recruited to work a specific function that they were skilled at and enjoyed. The skill was called an "interest." In turn, each resident would be provided with a beautiful home, abundant food and creature comforts, sports, educational, art and music programs in a pristine town in a temperate climate. Healthcare was free and exceptional. Communications free, utilities free, transportation free, everything free provided you did your job "interest" and contribute to the greater good. One could even change occupations if they desired in which case another person who is qualified, and a psychological fit, would be recruited to fill your previous job from the outside world. Much of the revenue to support the island would be through the tourist trade focused on wealthy visitors and also through scientific discoveries sold by the Research and Development department.

I stopped listening. My sad, feeble mind entertained whether it was possible a group of people could get along and be happy having all that they could possibly want. It seemed logical to me but what did I know? I wanted to talk to Sierra, hear what she had to say about this radical concept. She was the most practical person I knew. Thinking of her being far away while I was banished to paradise made me sick. I felt trapped in Lemuria

Down rather than freed from repression. I tried to snap out of my funky thoughts by listening to Lois.

"None of this would be possible without the visionary work of our benefactor Darby Summers! By the end of this week all our new neighbors will have arrived. We estimate in one month our paradise will be full throttle. It is then Darby Summers will arrive at our graceful shores to see the living embodiment of her vision. As you know it is her mission and ours to show the rest of the world how to live in peace and harmony!"

All stood cheering and applauding including us. Thad and I put on an enthusiastic act to blend in, but Lesmour was sincere.

"Dear new neighbors, it is time for you to meet your destiny. Each of you will be escorted to your interests where you will meet fellows in the field of your passion!"

With clockwork like precision, small driverless electric cars arrived. From the welcome center came four smiling people. Each person broke off to a table of new residents. A young woman from the line greeted us. The nametag on her purple dress read Nandi. She knew who we were and where we needed to go and led us to an electric car. She pressed a green button on the car dashboard and told the car the destination. She had a British accent. I asked her is that where she came from. She said yes but she was born in South Africa, her parents moved to London when she was two. Her parents were world class chefs and applied for residency to Lemuria Down. They were excited to be part of the grand plan. She wasn't. Nandi said she missed her home and friends even though she thinks the island is charming.

The car first took us to the marina. Nandi playfully asked

if we noticed anything unusual when we pulled up. The docks held many boats of various sizes and purposes. Most were for recreational use except for one fishing boat that was leaving the harbor. That's when I figured it out.

"It's quiet, no outboard motors, no diesel fuel."

Nandi laughed, "Good for you! Not a spot of fossil fuel on this island! All is either electric, powered by wind, ocean current, waterfalls, or sun."

Lesmour excitedly said "awesome" under his breath and got out of the car. "Where do I go?"

Nandi pointed to the only building nearby, a light blue split-level construction with big decks and sliding glass doors opened to the ocean view. "Henri should be in his office. He is expecting you."

Lesmour trotted to his destiny, waving his left hand without bothering to look back. Nandi told the car to "commence." As it turned around I saw on the horizon a cruise ship arriving. Nandi said it was carrying the last shipment of residents. She said next week the cruise ship will bring the first tourists to the island. On the southern shore a resort was built for a limited number of tourists. Only the wealthiest people on the planet could afford the accommodations. Nandi said the resort was already booked a year out. Apparently the super-rich wanted to see utopia in action. The revenue generated from the tourism industry would go to purchase items beyond Lemuria Down's shores, products that cannot be produced on the island.

The car took us to Thad and my "interests." It climbed the hilly road where Lois found us the day before, making a right-hand turn past the access road to the back of the island. It cut through a rainforest with many streams and giant, large, leafed plants. I felt out of scale like I was in that old movie Honey I Shrunk the Kids, an ant of a human. We arrived at our future place of "interest," the Lemuria Down Research and Development Consort. It consisted of several types of pod-like structures tucked into the base of the volcanic rock mountain. One of the pods was much larger than the others. Nandi told us it was "the brains" of the island. There we would meet Dr. Robinette, the head of all scientific study. He would be our supervisor and chief liaison.

We took the walkway lined with colorful stones and solar ground lights to the front of the central research and development building. The entryway was a large common area. In the center was a green framed glass cubicle with a man sitting at a bamboo desk. He was feverishly tapping on a keyboard oblivious to our entry.

The man was dressed in tan, khaki shorts, and a tight-fitting, white t-shirt. Dark skinned, muscular with strong features, he was bald on top with greying, close cropped hair on the sides. Perfect posture, he sat in a brown leather swivel chair. Thad approached the man.

"Dr. Robinette?" he asked.

The man held up a thick finger then went back to his hectic typing. We waited. With a bit of a flourish he finished, stood and held out his hand.

"I am not Dr. Robinette," he said as he shook our hands. He grabbed mine tightly. I missed the full palm shake as he gripped my fingers so tight my knuckles hurt. "I am his husband, William. He is poking around in his lab. Follow me."

I noticed William was barefoot. He caught my gaze and smiled.

"I was in the military and construction in my early years. My feet are better off without shoes."

We followed William to a room marked simply "lab" on a small bronze plaque near the door handle. There was a flashing red light above the door. William pointed to it.

"Don't ever go in unannounced when it's flashing," he said. "That's when he doesn't want to be disturbed." William lightly tapped on the door and called out. "Your new co-workers are here..."

There was silence for a moment. Faintly a voice mumbled, "just a minute."

William sighed, turned his head and smiled, "He is so dramatic."

The shared confidentiality of his husband made me grin. I liked William.

"Is it hard working with a spouse?" I asked. I was thinking of Sierra and how we worked well together.

"Oh lord, no. I don't work with him. That wouldn't do. I sometimes help at the front desk when new arrivals or visitors are scheduled. Besides, that cubicle is a fine spot to write. In my later years on the mainland I was a journalist, that's how Jayson and I met. I did a free-lance article on him for Scientific America. I am now working on my memoir which will culminate with us moving here."

"Come in."

Dr. Jayson Robinette perched awkwardly on a chair by a desk with stacks of paper. He examined a slide held toward the sunroof. Tall, with salt and pepper hair, pale as Thad, lean with rounded shoulders from what I assumed was the result of years hunched over microscopes, test-tubes, lab tables he casually put down the slide and peered at us with an uncomfortable intensity. I wondered how long it would take for him to realize we were frauds.

"Welcome gentlemen. Pull up a chair. Sit down."

He fixed his eyes on William with the same intense stare then smiled broadly.

"Thank you so much, William. How is your memoir proceeding?"

"I am on a roll!" William said, then addressed Thad and I. "Jayson can be unnerving at first but once you get to know him, he has a heart of gold. Enjoy, men."

Dr. Robinette watched his partner exit then returned his focus to Thad and me. He was a low talker; the kind of person you had to lean slightly forward to hear. In time I learned even the most mundane things he spoke carried a weight and confidentiality because of his whispered speech.

"I read your profiles, very impressive. You will be extremely pleased to be a part of the grand experiment. I know I am, and I am hard to satisfy. My career has been hampered by the constraints of university and government funding. They always had a protocol which I found restricting. Here I am free as a bird. Darby Summers chose me personally and encouraged me to work on anything I wish. She knows the creative mind is best at play. Before coming here, I was forced to put several projects on the back burner. No one would fund my research. Not anymore. She sees the potential economic opportunities for Lemuria Down in my work. Many of my projects once perfected could be sold beyond our shores and bring revenue to our community. Thaddeus, tell me why you chose to come here?"

Thad had to think for a minute. He tried to act intelligent by placing his forefinger to his chin like he was deep in thought. He needed to concoct a good lie. No way could he tell Robinette he came here to avoid the mob.

"For the same reasons, Dr. Robinette. I found the constraints of a monetary society oppressive."

Dr. Robinette beamed.

"I know we will make a great team. All I ask is you gather and assimilate my various projects, safely store the data, and help me find resources to further my studies. I am sure someone of your ability will find it child's play. You will have ample free time to pursue your own interests. Now Cody, I imagine it must be fascinating for you to be here. Tell me, how will you determine what is natural on an island that was essentially created from scratch?"

I expected a similar softball question that "Thaddeus" got and was caught off guard because there was not a simple answer. I looked up through the skylight, blue, blue, not a cloud in sight or a decent answer to satisfy an intellect like Dr. Robinette. His constant, smiling stare was unsettling. I had a pang of paranoia wondering if he already saw through my foolish disguise. I stared at my clean, barely used hiking shoes, was conscious of the lame bird watching outfit I choose. I felt like a total fake. I was a total fake! Aware of the silence I blurted out the only thing that came to mind.

"No chickens!"

The good doctors' smile vanished. For a seeming eternity, he stared blankly at me. I wanted to run away. Then he threw his head back and bellowed with laughter. Tears ran down his cheeks.

"Yes! Of course no chickens! The Hawaiian Islands are fraught with them! Oh my, I do enjoy humor," He wiped the tears with his lab coat sleeve, "You dear Cody will be the freest of all. For now you are the only naturalist on the island so you will have your own pod and full reign of the animal kingdom. Ms. Summers did have a naturalist consultant. The consultant stocked the island with what she deemed were non-invasive animals. This consultant was to oversee assembling a staff in her residency but inexplicitly backed out days before her scheduled arrival. For now you are on your own."

"I will do my best, Dr. Robinette," I said like a loyal boy scout.

"Thaddeus, Cody, please, call me Jayson. We are equals here. Now Thaddeus, I will take you to your adjoining pod and show you the ropes, so to speak. Cody, William will escort you to your pod. You will find him in the lobby tapping away. You might have to wait for him to finish a thought, though. He is very dramatic. So nice to meet you both."

I exited to the main entrance and found William typing just as Jayson said. He averted his eyes momentarily from his keyboard and said, "let me finish this thought." It took several minutes before he finished with the same flourish as earlier. He sprung from his seat and asked me to follow. My pod had a rustic look inside, a lot of wood paneling and soft lighting, a live edge office desk and a floor to ceiling bookcase. William noticed my fixed gaze on the bookcase.

"The field biologist that never showed preordered all these books. Most are about native wildlife and vegetation of Hawaii. Your office laptop also has hundreds of files you can reference. Any questions?"

I had a knot in my stomach. I knew nothing about nature. I carried a defenseless fledgling in a contaminated rice box and now I am supposed to be nature boy in charge of keeping the ecological balance of a fledgling society. Sierra can help, I thought. I did have a question for William.

"Do you like it here?"

William gave a nervous laugh, embarrassed.

"I don't hide it very well, do I? Let me just say, I like it wherever Jayson is. I could be wrong, but I sense you have an ambivalence being here too. Don't worry. You will get used to it. Are you and Thaddeus…?"

"No, old friends from grade school."

"So good to have old friends. Jayson and I don't. That's why we are so close." He put his hand on my shoulder, "I'm going back to writing. Settle in, get comfortable. We will talk later."

After William left I wandered around what was to be my refuge from Thad and Lesmour. I would use this as a sanctuary to get away from their bickering and the ensuing troubles in paradise. What was to become a comfort zone initially was overwhelming. I had to step up, do nature. There were hundreds of books each displaying in words and pictures everything I did not know about the natural world. I hated science in school, and I never ventured from our cruddy apartment. Besides Phoenix, my rescue starling, the only other animals I was familiar with were the mosquitos from the green pool water of The Oasis and the fat cockroaches that scurried from cabinets in our apartment, parasites and bottom feeders, like me.

I sat in the slim leather swivel chair at my desk and was about to lift the laptop screen but stopped. I couldn't begin to fathom the immensity of knowledge in the book collection. I shuddered to think what else was stored in hundreds of additional files of information. I spun around in the chair and spied a patio with a hammock, round table, and chairs. It looked like a good escape route from responsibility.

Stepping out I intended to lay in the hammock and not open my eyes until dusk, but a light rain began to fall. I noticed a tree with leaves the size of my torso. One branch jutted out toward the flagstone patio. I put my palm under one of the leaves to catch the trickle of rainwater. Then I saw the path. The path was narrow with low clearance for a human, overhanging branches making it difficult to pass. I wondered if it was created by human or beast. I found later there were no large native animals in Hawaii. This path was formed by humans before Darby Summers bought the volcanic rock island and filled it in for her own purposes. Adventurous native people used to dock at the volcano base under its great peak. The path I discovered was originally the volcano's shoreline.

Curiosity got the best of me. I had my hiking shoes, my Dora the Explorer outfit, so I explored. The rain was so light to not be an issue as I squeezed through the opening into the thick foliage.

The path was overgrown, roots protruded from slick, muddied turf. A bird nearby made a loud chu-weet call but was silenced after I snapped a twig underfoot. I learned the bird was a Hawaiian 'Amakihi, a small honey creeper with a tubular tongue that fed from flower nectar and ate small invertebrates.

Eventually the path became easier to walk without crouching. Long tendrils of a parasitic plant wrapped around the base of large trees dangling from many branches. I figured Tarzan would enjoy this place. An Arizona desert rat, such as I found the humidity stifling. The rain stopped but I was still pelted lightly by runoff from tall trees. A moss covered boulder ahead became a comfortable place to rest. The rich, earthy smell I inhaled with relish, taking in a sweet aroma I later discovered were plumeria flowers creating an interesting olfactory blend of fresh rainwater, musky rot of fallen trees with rampant moss and mud. I closed my eyes inhaling deep while I became aware of a muffled rumble. Standing, I continued on the path toward the sound.

With each step the rumble grew louder. Getting closer I discerned the sound of rushing water. My heart raced in anticipation. Through an entanglement of branches and vines I saw the source. From the upper regions of the volcano an avalanche of water cascaded into a riverbed frothing and churning to a grand whirlpool. Tears pooled in my eyes; it was so beautiful. I went off the path to get as near as possible having to stop briefly to dislodge a thorn that pierced my shoe jabbing the ball of my foot.

On a tree trunk I admired the awesome sight. Halfway to the peak of the volcano sprung a waterfall. The tumbling water emanated from a cavernous hole. I heard a thousand bird calls deep in the rainforest, none I could recognize. A hawk swooped out of nowhere to the water below, dove into the shallow withdrawing a panicked, flapping fish. I wept and could not stop.

A waterfall of emotion poured out, regret about all the things I missed in life, missed adventures and opportunities lost, used, and discarded by loveless parents, cowardly choosing a life of mediocrity with Thad. Self-pity, self-loathing, I found someone real, someone I could love only to lose her. I found this rainforest, something natural and eternal alone and perfect. I could not share it with her.

Afternoon faded to dusk. I hurried back before nightfall, not wanting to get lost on the path. Even though the trek was mostly downhill, my legs cramped, and I was forced to stop in order to rub out the pain. It was dark when I made it home. On my back patio, Thad and Lesmour were waiting. The weed they were smoking had a strong, acrid scent. I reached for the joint.

"Where the hell were you? I had to talk to Pumpkin Head by myself!"

Lesmour said something nasty, but I chose not to listen. Several empty beer cans from a Maui microbrew sat on my oval patio table. One was laying on its side by a table leg. I picked it up, sighed and placed it back on the table. Living in paradise and they were still slobs. I told them I found a waterfall then asked Thad if he liked working with Jayson.

"It was sucky. He expects me to work. I had to store and secure a ton of files, but he does have some weird ass projects going on."

He offered me a beer. I slumped in a patio chair. It felt better than sitting on a damp log. I guzzled the beer, realizing how thirsty I was, so I had another. Thad lit a new joint and passed it around.

"Nobody asked how my day was!" Lesmour grabbed the joint after me and toked.

"Captain Jeffery Brown how was YOUR day?" Thad used his most sarcastic tone. It did not stop Lesmour.

"Guess what, guys? The chief said he will train me for the whale watching cruise! I never saw a whale before. I am so pumped! Then and then..." he hesitated for dramatic build up. Thad rubbed his face and muttered, 'kill me now, please', Lesmour ignored him and continued, "Christine called and asked if I wanted to hang out with her. She is coming over tomorrow for dinner."

"Cretin, she is full of shit. She is using you to worm her way into this place."

Lesmour stood up clumsily. He tried to look menacing but lost his balance and knocked empty cans off the patio table including the one I just picked up.

"No! You're full of shit!"

Lesmour stumbled back to his house.

"Why don't you cut him some slack?" I was getting tired of the constant bickering, "Maybe she does like him."

"Look at you," he said. "You're a regular Romeo now. Did you hear from her yet?"

"No. I will call her in a few."

"Pumpkin Heads' girl is no good," Thad said. "She has a shady transport business. I checked her out. She had a couple of busts, went to trial for taking people on an illegal shark hunting charter but got off on a technicality. Very sketchy bitch."

"I guess you would know a sketchy person if you saw one."

I stared at Thad with raised eyebrows. I thought he was going to slap me at first. Instead he laughed and nodded.

"Touché"

I was hungry. Even though our refrigerators were pre-stocked, we went online and ordered a Hawaiian pizza from a place by the harbor called the Lemur Café. Between the weed and the beer I had a good buzz going by the time the pizza arrived. It was delivered by a spirited girl named Colleen. She was short and full figured, her face covered with freckles. Cute. Thad invited her for a slice and a beer. She accepted because she didn't have any other deliveries. Colleen refused the weed; said it made her feel weird the only time she tried it. This temporarily put off Thad, but I could tell by the way he was acting he liked her. He wasn't his usual obnoxious self.

"I'm going to hit her up," he said after she left.

We spoke a little more until he declared he had urgent business to take care of and left. I was tired but wanted to speak to Sierra. First I sent a text to Grace to let her know I was safe.

"Glad to hear it. Stay that way, don't let your meat loaf! LOL!" I figured maybe that was it, my friendship with Grace. I wondered how long we would stay in touch. Then, I messaged Sierra to see if she was available. She called right back.

"Are you alright?" she asked.

"I am safe, but I miss you."

We spoke every night the first week. The conversation at times became tricky. I did my best to edit the details of where I was so she would not have knowledge of my exact location which caused a few awkward moments. Her side of the communication was normal, anecdotes about school, classes, her family, and the day to day events at Birds of a Feather. Twice I asked about Gus. In retrospect, it was an asinine thing to do. The second time Sierra questioned why I was so interested in Gus. I couldn't tell her the truth that I was concerned his ties with Martino might jeopardize her safety.

On the seventh night we spoke I could tell something was wrong. Sierra seemed nervous and distracted.

"Are you ok?"

"Not really, my family had a sad event. My tía in Sonora passed. She was struck by a car. My father left to make arrangements for the funeral. My mother and I are leaving this weekend for the service."

I had to ask what the word tía meant. It was Spanish for aunt, her dad's eldest sister. Sierra said she met her once when she was very young. She also said she was worried about her father going to Mexico. Her family immigrated to the United States because he was forced into a gang as a teen. The gang was still active. They do not forget those that leave.

"Do you have to go? It sounds dangerous."

"It's family, Cody. We must be there for each other."

I decided to tell her without going into detail I oversaw a natural habitat. Despite her worries she found it amusing and baffling. I told her it was one of Thad's ideas to set me up in a field I knew nothing about. Sierra joked that Phoenix; my adopted starling missed me. I suggested someday she could escort Phoenix to where I am and be my assistant bird watcher. My silliness cheered her.

"When I get my degree I will be qualified to assist the great Cody, bird whisperer in his secret location," she teased. "In the meantime I will leave Phoenix at the sanctuary. Gus and the staff will take good care of him."

I could barely keep my eyes open after spending all day in the rainforest, filing a lengthy report in my pod afterward, then smoking the weed with my friends. As we were saying goodbye Sierra insisted we switch to new burner phones even though we had plenty of minutes left on the current ones. I asked her why and she simply said, "just to be safe." We exchanged the new numbers and said goodnight. I showered and laid in bed exhausted. Before drifting off I wondered if it was possible to get Sierra to Lemuria Down. It was a good bedtime thought even though she would not leave her parents. Her request to use new burner phones was disturbing. Even though she seemed more herself by the end of our conversation I could tell something was wrong. She joked and teased as always but it was mechanical, her voice flat at times with little emotion. I assured myself it was because her aunt passed and was worried about her father returning to Mexico but felt there was more she was keeping from me. I tossed and turned the entire night.

Chapter Thirteen

The weeks that followed were an odyssey of uncertainty and worry. Lemuria Down proved to be as close to paradise as anyone could imagine, but I was torn apart by Sierra's absence. The ocean breeze calmed the initial anguish of her not returning calls. I listened to the waves at night trying to convince myself she was too busy to talk, she was in a location without cell phone towers. I was lying to myself. She did not text or call. It was as if she disappeared. I tried not let myself think about Martino's nickname, the magician. Sorrow grew with each passing day.

I was miserable in paradise. A day of intemperate weather came with gusting winds and periods of rain from morning to night. Normally it was fair, breezy with late afternoon tropical showers that would dissipate to a gleaming night sky crowded with stars. Lesmour was in heaven, excited to be the captain of whale watch excursions and equally elated to have a half-assed girlfriend. Since she was not an official resident, Christine was only allowed to have limited overnight visits as Lesmour's guest. Thad's misgivings about her seemed unfounded. Even Thad let his guard down and treated her decently whenever she came by. It could be because my old friend was getting a life for himself. He warmed up to working for Jayson Robinette even to the point of admiring his intelligence and pure creative genius. Thad kept a tight lip about what Jayson was researching and developing. One thing he did mention was that Jayson and island engineers were attempting to drill into the volcanos' deep ocean base. They believed the long-capped lava field fathoms below could be a permanent source of thermal energy for the residents.

He also "hooked up" with Colleen the delivery girl. It was very casual, which according to Thad, mostly amounted to exuberant sex and then eating cold pizza. I must admit he was the happiest I had ever seen.

On a regular basis William joined us for late afternoon drinks. Thad boasted to William one day at the Research and Development Consort that he too was working on a book. He invited William over to talk writing, which was a load of crap because Thad was more a clever plagiarist than writer. In his spare time, he worked on his great American novel, continuing the ruse with his parents speaking with them every other week and jettisoning via email his latest chapters. They still believed he moved to Oregon. His parents remained confused about the content and non-existent storyline but assumed it was simply beyond their artistic acumen.

The initial pretense discussing the craft of writing with William quickly devolved into an observational criticism of the experimental society we lived in. After too many margaritas, Thad confessed one night to William that "The Three Amigos" as William termed, Lesmour, Thad, and I came to Lemuria Down to escape a perilous situation. Like William who was a resident solely because Jayson was recruited to be part of the attempted utopia, we were all here by need, not choice.

Thad, Lesmour, and I needed to preserve our lives. William needed to preserve the love of his life. We formed our own private social group with William dubbing it Parasites in Paradise.

Occasionally we met at William and Jayson's home situated near a gorgeous manmade pond designed for swimming, complete with lily pads and tropical fish. Its natural replication required zero maintenance. We often took dips then retired to their front porch for ahi-ahi poke' appetizers and white wine. Other get togethers were mostly at my cozy back patio where sometimes Lesmour and Christine would stop by, or Colleen would swing by between food deliveries and laugh at us. She could not understand why we made fun of Lemuria Down.

The more I sunk into despair with the disappearance of Sierra, the more I obsessed about my naturalist "interest." It helped keep my mind off her. I spent hours in my pod reading books, filing reports with an occasional teary eyed meltdown. Daily excursions in the rainforest was the most effective way to get out of my head. It became my fertile playground. I roamed and took notes, snapped pictures, recording audio on several trails that wound around the islands' original base even venturing to the west side access road where we first set foot on Lemuria Down. After a while, I felt myself to be what I said I was, a naturalist. My legs and lungs became strong. I carried a backpack with recording instruments, a camera, field glasses, field guides and got into the habit of eating the pre-made healthy, plant-based snacks and meals delivered to our homes weekly. My paunch melted away. For the first time in my life I liked the way I looked.

Still, I tried texting Sierra pictures of my latest finds, a Rose-

Winged Parakeet, a Java Sparrow, the Hawaiian Hawk by the waterfall that I grew to love. I grew reckless, told her she should come, live with me. I called her in the evenings leaving messages with pleas to call back. One day her mailbox was full. I attempted our failsafe plan. I sent her an e-mail from my office account stating I was Mary Torrens enquiring about a volunteer position at Birds of a Feather. There was no reply. I feared the worst. The last I last spoke to her; she was going to Mexico to join her father and the troubled past he left behind. Did something happen to her in Mexico? Did Sal get to her?

I asked Thad if he could trace Sierra's whereabouts. All he found was Sierra and her mother entered Mexico through Lukeville, Arizona the border town into Sonora. I wanted to leave the island and try to find her, but Thad convinced me week after week to stay. He said it would be a veritable needle in the haystack. He promised to continue searching via internet. If he found anything concrete then it would make sense for me to leave. In the subsequent weeks he only confirmed where they were not. Sonora was their original destination, but he saw no evidence they arrived, no credit card receipts at gas stations or restaurants or lodging. He did not even find any local information on funerals that matched her surname of Gonzalez.

Some days I stayed blessedly lost in the natural wonder, traversing the increasingly familiar paths. I delved into learning the islands' wildlife. On dark days I would give in to the despair of losing Sierra. Those days were spent mourning at the waterfall. At times I entertained thoughts of climbing to the mouth of the waterfall then leaping to its rocky bottom. I was saved this dramatic ending to my life by observing the Hawaiian hawk. Initially he was hard to pick out. My first siting of the hawk diving to the waterfall base was pure luck. It was the only time I saw it plummet to pluck a fish. In a field guide I read they mostly fed on smaller birds and non-indigenous mice or lizards. Lemuria Down, although it did not have chickens, had plenty of non-native plants and animals. It was a fool's folly to attempt to create a purely natural environment where humans trespassed. Even the hawk was procured from the Big Island, its only true remaining natural habitat.

The hawks' grey and white plumage made it hard to spot in the rainforest but once I heard his distinctive eee-oooh screech I was able spy him using field glasses by a nest on the other side of the waterfall. His mate was settled in the nest guarding her chicks. One morning I saw a hatchling stick its head out when the mother shifted. The male only came to the clutch when he had food. After dropping off a meal he took off to roost beyond my view at the top of the falls.

A month passed. The highly anticipated arrival of our utopian visionary Darby Summers did not happen. At every weekly town gathering came a new announcement of her delays. The first reason told was we were not quite up to speed as a society. Construction and the general functional flow had not reached the optimal peak. We wanted, or should I say, our spokespeople wanted Lemuria Down to be humming perfectly before her arrival. As each week passed another visit was postponed. Often it was announced she had pressing engagements on the other side of the world that needed immediate attention. A pattern set in. Every expected arrival date was followed by a cancellation and a new excuse. At first people were disappointed but then it became an island joke with amusing guesses at what the next excuse would be. It could have developed into an issue had it not been for the fact that almost everyone was totally pleased with life on their oasis of humanity.

My small circle of friends attended one town center gathering, not because we became model citizens and loved our fellow Lemurian Downers. We went for the food, music, drinks, and weed that was abundant at every event. The island had a dozen musicians who could play anything. Sometimes they played as a mini orchestra but this time they broke into three or four smaller bands and played at different locals. It was great to stroll and stop at splendid vendors on every street then relax with a stiff drink in hand while live music played within earshot. Thad's girl, Colleen loved it and cajoled him to dance after he had a couple of drinks. It made me laugh because I never imagined Thad dancing, or being among a crowd of people, or laughing without a sarcastic edge. It was obvious they were no longer just hooking up.

I watched them having fun. A pang of loneliness crashed upon me like in the old roadrunner cartoons when an Acme anvil dropped on the coyote. I felt nauseous. I had to leave and find a quiet spot by the ocean, close my eyes, and listen to the steady lapping waves. In desperation I called Birds of a Feather thinking insanely Sierra might have come home and gone back to the sanctuary. My call was answered on the second ring. My heart sank when Gus answered. I said nothing.

"Hello?" he said, he was silent for some time waiting for a response then spoke, "Kid, is that you?"

I was shocked. It loosened my tongue.

"How did you know?"

"Just a hunch. I figured you would call someday. Just tell me this, but don't give specifics, is Sierra with you?"

I was a cement mixer of sadness and relief. Gus asking about Sierra's whereabouts was devastating but he being as clueless as I was also a relief. I was terrified Sal Martino might have made Sierra, and her family "disappear". I thought if she was taken out by Martino, Gus would know.

"No. Sal, didn't, did he?" I needed confirmation.

"I doubt it. I rarely see Sal and his bums since you left. He never asked about her. I doubt he knew you two were dating. Look don't come here looking for her. He is mad as hell you boys skipped town. Last I heard his family is pissed off."

"Did she say anything before she left?"

"She asked if I could take care of your bird, and she mentioned she was going to look for your father. She didn't say why, and I didn't ask. The less I know the better, for all of us."

I couldn't believe what I was hearing. I said "What?"

"Kid, you didn't tell her what you got wrapped up in, did you?"

"No! I would never do that! I just told her how messed up my parents were, that's all. I don't know why she lied to me. She said she and her mom were going to Sonora, Mexico to be with her father because a relative died."

"That's not what she told me. Hey, don't get bent out of shape. People lie all the time. You should know that by know. It was probably for a good reason. She doesn't have a mean bone in her body. She is trying to help you I bet."

"Something happened to her. She doesn't return my calls or texts. It's driving me crazy. How would she know where my dad is?"

"I don't know. Look, I will do some snooping, see if her parents are still around."

I told Gus how Thad traced gas receipts of Sierra and her mother crossing the border at Lukeville.

"All that means is her car crossed the border, and her credit card was used. Maybe she went there with her mother, or maybe she didn't. Maybe someone stole her car and credit cards..."

It sent chills down my spine thinking how someone else could have her car and credit card.

"Give me a week to sniff around. I will check their rental and neighborhood out. Call me back here same time next week. I'll see what I can find."

I thanked him and hung up then rejoined the merry throng to drink myself to oblivion. Thad genuinely seemed concerned about my behavior. He called for a driver to take me home. It was Nandi, the girl that escorted us after our orientation a month earlier. She and Thad helped me as I staggered to the vehicle. She buckled me in saying, "You are pissed! Don't throw up!" I slumped in the seat as she drove while singing an old Brit pub song.

The rest of the evening was a foggy blur. I do remember a staggered mad dash to the bathroom in the middle of the night making the toilet in time to throw up. I remember drinking a gallon of water afterward. Then there were flashes of Nandi helping me into my house taking me to bed and taking off my sandals. She was the same height as me and muscular, said she played football for her school team in the U.K. Her perfume was strong and made my mouth water close to the precipice of vomiting. She laid my head on the pillow and looked me over.

"You trimmed down," she said. "Quite handsome I would say. Sweet dreams, luv."

She patted my head then left. I had a brief bout of the whirlies before passing out.

I attempted to sleep in although to describe my burrowing under the sheets with a splitting headache as sleep would be an exaggeration. It was more a hiding from the world. Eventually I gave up the idea of sleep and got out of bed, took a shower, and tried to scrub the foul taste of puke from my mouth with a toothbrush. I made a pot of coffee and looked in the fridge to see if there was something my stomach could keep down. Some artisan baked rolls from yesterdays' food delivery seemed reasonable. I thought one might absorb the remaining alcohol inside me. When Thad and I first moved to The Oasis my morning after recovery method was coffee and a buttered roll from the deli down the street. Having the artisan bread and coffee with my first Lemuria Down hangover was meager comfort.

Thad rapped on the back patio slider. He walked into the kitchen and helped himself to coffee from the pot. He took a large bite out of one of three rolls I had set aside on a plate.

"Dude you got ripped last night," he said, mouth full.

I told him about my conversation with Gus the previous night.

"I want out. I want to find my father."

"No fucking way," he said, "There is no way you can find him. It's a waste of time, Cody.

"If I can find him, maybe I will find Sierra. I got to . . ."

"You can't. You can't just leave this place. If someone decides to leave, they have to go through an outgoing process. They want to know why someone would leave a perfect society to see if any improvements can be made. There is an interview, a psychological exam, and then, then they recheck your background to see if they missed anything in their invitation. If it comes to that, they will find you are a phony and since I recommended you they will kick me off the island too. We might even be prosecuted!"

"I'm stuck here?"

"Poor baby," he muttered bitterly. "Stuck in a tropical paradise."

I sank in a kitchen chair.

"I got to find her. I got to know she is alright. I can't live like this."

He sighed, topped off my coffee, and shoved the plate of remaining buttered rolls under my nose.

"First things first. Get rid of your hangover, go look at birds. I'll see if I can trace her or your dad. Be patient. It won't be easy. Besides maybe your old man bird buddy can find something by then. Maybe between the two of us we can get answers."

I nodded and was about to grab a roll when I saw Thad's hand swoop into my line of vision and take one more roll before leaving.

I did not "go look at birds" as Thad suggested. I stayed in my gilded cage, spending the day wallowing in self-pity. I entertained the idea of drinking again to see how sick I could get but resorted to smoking an excessive amount of weed, watching very old movies on an island channel. It was an all-day marathon, movies starring Humphrey Bogart. I had a memory of watching

Casablanca with my father, telling me how romantic it was. I closed the blinds in my cage and huddled on the couch with a blanket and pillow bingeing black and white movies while high. I cried during the last scene of Casablanca when Bogart let his old flame get on the plane with her husband. It ended when he walked off into the fog with his newfound friend beginning a beautiful friendship.

I imagined there were some twisted parallels between the movie and my life. I said goodbye to Sierra trying to protect her and save my ass while flying away with Thad and Lesmour, not so newfound friends. The weed made it seem spookily similar. Accompanied with the weed and movie fest I also ate most of the day picking out the least healthy food in my pantry. When I ran out of low sodium chips, gluten-free pretzels, and trail mix with yogurt raisins, I ordered from The Pig and Poi Grill near the port built for tourists. My fellow islanders were too health conscience to admit they order take-out from there although Thad's girl, Colleen told us many residents get it delivered after sundown so no one else can detect their guilty pleasure.

Colleen delivered the bar-b-que pork, took one look at me, saying Thad was worried about me and she could see why. I assured her I was fine, closed the door and gluttonously consumed. I must have passed out on the couch because I awoke after sundown to the sound of Thad's voice. He was on his back patio engaged in an argument. Since I heard no other voice I assumed he was on his phone. It was peculiar because he rarely spoke on phones, using them only for texting. I went to my kitchen to get a glass of water thinking maybe he was arguing with Colleen. Curiosity set in. I leaned against the slider pressing my ear to the glass to hear better.

"I don't want to do this anymore! It's not right! He's my friend but what would you know about friendship . . ."

Thad's doorbell chimed. He swore then said to whoever he was speaking to he had to go. I opened my slider and sat outside with my water. I could hear Lesmour's annoying voice but could not make out what he was saying. Thad shouted, "if you are so concerned why don't you ring his doorbell instead of bothering me?"

I let them argue for a few moments giving myself some time to process who Thad was speaking to on the phone. I figured the only way to find out was to ask him.

"I'm awake!" I shouted from my patio.

Thad and Lesmour pushed through the brush that separated our backyards. Thad's eyes were bugged out.

"How long have you been out here?" he asked.

"Who were you talking to on the phone?"

"What did you hear?"

"You said something about someone being your friend, you not wanting to do it anymore. Were you talking about me?"

Thad averted my stare. I have known him long enough to know when he was at a loss for words, he was hiding the truth. He finally turned to Lesmour and said, "Why don't you make yourself useful and get some beer."

Lesmour who was fidgeting nervously left to get beer without complaint. The stall gave Thad a chance to come up with a lie. He drew close and whispered he was on the phone with Christine,

Lesmour's girl. Thad said she had been harassing him to convince Lesmour to move in with her on Kauai. It was a pretty good lie to make up under pressure. I knew he was really talking about me to someone, but who? Frankly, I was afraid to find out what Thad was keeping from me, and I felt heartbroken to know that I could no longer trust him. How long had Thad been lying and about what? I decided to play along. For now.

"You were right," I said. "She can't be trusted."

I stared until he looked away. Lesmour pushed through the brush with a six pack. I left them on my patio to drink. After last night's binge, I couldn't look at a beer. In my bedroom, I heard them argue a few minutes before retreating to Thad's place. I showered. All was quiet next door as I went to bed but could not sleep wondering if Lesmour was part of whatever Thad was keeping from me. I considered approaching Lesmour to see if he would take me to Kauai. From there I could book a flight to Mexico. I still had access to my bank account and figured I could subsist in Mexico with the monthly check my mother had set up for me so long ago.

After a couple of hours tossing and turning my brain was fried. I resolved to stick out the week until I could talk to Gus again. It would also give me time to determine if Lesmour was a willing partner to Thad's secret. I opened the bedroom window and listened to palms stir in the breeze. It was cool and soothing, scented with flowering plants. Chilled, I curled to fetal position. Finally, gratefully, sleep came.

Chapter Fourteen

I woke before sunrise. There was some bird chittering outside, but I did not record it like I had been doing since I came to Lemuria Down. It was my routine to record what I could, take a picture if possible and then attempt to identify it with what resources I had in my office and field guide. I had already identified and entered in my field notes several bird and lizard species. It seemed all in vain now even though I was beginning to enjoy it, especially the part of hiking through the rainforest and spending time at the waterfall. Still, I wanted to leave — even if I could not find Sierra. My best friend was keeping something from me, and it was big. I resolved to act as if nothing was wrong, pretend I was into my work until I could figure a way to leave without anyone knowing. I even ruminated over reaching out to Christine since she was not adverse to stealth and shady doings.

Coffee and the remaining rolls stabilized my fragile state of mind. I was hungry and the coffee was strong, earthy, life affirming. It helped while I put finishing touches on a report to Jayson Robinette that was overdue. I had to file a weekly summary of my findings for him since he was the overseer of research and development. It seemed like a formality in which he often responded with a simple thank you within minutes of sending the emailed report. However when I sent it this time, he did not reply with his usual thank you. He asked me to meet him at his office. I agreed, replying I would be there within the hour.

After getting dressed and gathering my gear for a day in the rainforest, I walked to the Lemuria Down Research and Development Consort. Entering the foyer I saw William settling into the reception desk. He looked up and smiled saying Jayson was waiting in his office.

"He has a surprise for you," he said.

I thanked him but thought that the last thing I needed was another surprise. Dr. Robinette's door was partially open. His tall frame was bent talking to someone in a chair, but I could not make out who it was because the partially open door blocked my view. When I got close I recognized the British accent. It was Nandi.

Stepping into the room, I saw her dressed in clothes suitable for hiking. There was a backpack on the floor with a pair of binoculars strung to it. Jayson greeted me.

"Cody, here is your new assistant!"

Nandi shot up from the chair, grinning broadly introducing herself in a formal manner.

"So good to see you again, Mr. Hillman."

I shook her outstretched hand as Jayson explained.

"Nandi is very interested in the wildlife of Lemuria Down. She volunteered to be your assistant to pursue her new interest. Isn't that wonderful?"

In my current state of misery, a tagalong was the last thing I wanted. Her handshake was firm. She held on a little too long. It didn't feel right. It was the same feeling I had when I was a boy and first realized that the playdates my father and I had with toys were being watched by a million kids. There was a week of nervousness every time my mother said the camera was rolling. I eventually got used to it.

"Show her the proverbial ropes today," Jayson said." You can discuss how you conduct your research while Nandi gets the lay of the land."

I fully envisioned my week of waiting until I could call Gus to be spent moping in the rainforest by the waterfall continuing the ornithologist ruse so not to draw attention while I figured a way off the island. Nandi's perky demeanor was forced. She had an agenda. What it was, I did not know. I dusted off my old acting chops and pretended to be pleased to have her on my team.

"Great," I said, "Let's not waste any time."

As we hiked to the waterfall, I told her about my plan to petition the natural wonder to be named Sierra Falls. She countered that it already was named after a popular fisherman/loner from Kauai who long ago spent nights at the original formation. I stopped abruptly and turned. She read the anger on my face and said little after as I pointed out flora and fauna, bird sounds, identified certain insects and toads all the time taking notes in a small, leather-bound book as she walked. I was smugly self-aware how much I had learned in the short time on Lemuria Down.

The air was unusually still, encouraging mosquitos to mill about our heads. We worked up a good sweat. At the falls we rested on the fallen log that had become my favorite observation point, taking drinks from our water bottles. The hawk called above the din of the thunderous water. I pointed to the nest, and she took out her binoculars briefly adjusting the focus until she spied the mother in the nest. She was delighted.

"Brilliant," she said. "I am impressed you are able to identify that bird, considering you misidentified half of the natural world on our hike."

Nandi smiled. There was a predatory fierceness in her eyes that scared me.

"How would you know?" I asked feebly.

"As the good Doctor Robinette said, I have acquired a taste for our natural surroundings. I am a quick study. I already know more than you. The question I have for you, Cody, is who are you really and why are you on this island stocked with well-trained, world class experts?"

I knew she had me and her cheerful attitude annoyed. I decided to be flippant.

"If you're so smart why don't you tell me? I am at the point where I am not so sure myself."

Nandi took a swig from her water bottle laughing lightly, before redirecting her gaze to me. She seemed to be relishing the moment.

"When you first came here, you had me fooled. You were stodgy and out of shape, looked much older than you truly are. That night you got wasted, that was when it hit me. You looked more like you when you were on the Telly. I used to watch you for hours while nanna sat for me. My parents were always working. It was just me; the Cody Redd Show and nanna in our London flat."

I was shocked. I did not realize The Cody Redd Show was viewed across the pond.

"I liked watching you play with all the toys," she continued, "Most of all I liked that you had the opportunity to play with your father. My parents were rarely around. I had an enormous crush on you but was also envious."

The hawk called out again. We watched him leave the nest. He began a large ascending circular flight. It struck me that Nandi was like the hawk, a predatory animal. She was circling in.

"'io," she said, I looked at her blanky. "'io, is the name of that bird. You called it a Hawaiian hawk, which it is but not truly its name."

"What do you want from me?"

"I fancy you."

I was dumbstruck. I thought Nandi wanted to expose me, take my job.

"You were adorable when I first saw you in an unkempt, ramshackle way, but last night I saw how handsome you have become. I am bored. I want you to keep me company like you used to when I was a tot."

Nandi placed her hand on the back of my neck and tried to pull me toward her. I stood up. I shook with anger.

"What the fuck? You think you can use me like that? I'm your fucking little, toy now? I play with you, or you will tell everyone I am an imposter. Well here's news for you, I hate this fucking place. I have a girlfriend, and I want to be off the island so go ahead do me a favor, tell everyone. I really don't give a shit."

Nandi stood abruptly and shoved me with such force that I

fell backwards and sprawled on the muddy turf. She stood over me pointing her finger.

"Fool! Did I threaten to turn you in? Did I? I was just saying I fancy you; I know who you are, and I wouldn't mind getting on with you. Since you have a girlfriend I won't. I'm not a whore!"

I got to my feet slowly. I noticed how well toned her legs and arms were. I noticed for the first time that she was pretty. The back of my shorts and shirt were soaked and muddy.

"OK," I said.

"OK, what?" she demanded.

"If you want, we can hang out, look at birds and shit."

I was too embarrassed to look her in the eyes opting to wring the dripping mud from my shirt. Nandi shoved my shoulder to get my attention. When I looked up, she was smiling. We laughed until tears rolled down our cheeks.

On our way back, I told her about my sorry predicament. Although she was four years my junior, Nandi was a good listener. I liked that she did not take pity on me or try to provide solutions. She listened and asked questions so she could understand. I realized, unlike me, she would be an excellent naturalist because she focused on gathering information before drawing conclusions. We reached the consort. I needed a shower.

"What are you going to do?" she asked.

"Wait a week and see what Gus and Thad come up with."

"No, you twit," Nandi said. "I mean after your shower."

"Probably stay in, eat and drink, do nothing."

"Wrong. You are going to shower and meet me at the beach.

I'll bring a picnic basket. Bring a blanket. I had to hear your sob story now you must hear mine."

Nandi's sob story was not as dramatic as mine. She tried to get into the University of Liverpool because of its excellent football program. She did not make the cut and got into some "bad company" her parents did not approve. They threatened to cut her off if she did not come with them to Lemuria Down. Like Thad, Lesmour and me, Nandi considered Lemuria Down a default destination not a dream choice.

For the rest of the week, Nandi and I were inseparable. Being with her was also a convenient way of avoiding Thad. He asked after a couple of days of me missing our patio soirees if I was dating her. I told him we were just friends. I made it clear to him not to give up looking for Sierra. He said he wouldn't, but I knew I couldn't trust anything he said. Nandi and I spent the days exploring the rainforest, recording whatever wildlife we could find ending each day in my office cataloguing our discoveries. She kept my mind focused on tasks rather than dwell on Sierra's disappearance.

After work our favorite way to kick back was to meet at The Pig and Poi Grill to watch tourists dine to cap off their day of frolic. Some locals who knew us stared at our brazen ways, eating unhealthy food in public in broad daylight. Lois, the elder Lemurian Downer caught sight of us as she passed on a tandem bicycle. She was riding with a silver haired, thin man who Nandi told me was her husband, Nigel. Lois playfully wagged her finger at us in admonishment.

One day we returned to the beachfront with another picnic

basket of good eats supplied by Nandi's parents. She brought a soccer ball and teased me to play until I finally relented. It was a game of keep away using only our feet which ended up being comical. She took the ball from me within seconds. It was impossible to get near her to even attempt to kick the ball. This, of course, made her laugh uproariously until I quit. Saturday night, we were invited to Jayson and William's for dinner. Jayson got in his head Nandi, and I were an item. He said he was pleased to be partially responsible for us being together. I didn't let on that Nandi, and I were platonic. It was a good cover until I could leave the island. She played along a little aggressively holding my hand during cocktails then leaning in to kiss me on the cheek when William said we were a cute couple. When William and Jayson went to the kitchen to serve tuna and salmon poke', I told her: "You are playing the part of girlfriend a little too much." She laughed saying she was just having a bit of fun.

I was glad to have her around. I would have been a wreck trying to pass the time until I could call Gus. Even though Nandi was engaging and upbeat, I still could not keep my mind from wondering if Sierra was alright. Trying to sleep was the worst. I purposely stayed up late because I knew once I put my head on the pillow a storm of thoughts and worries would precipitate and rain the entire night. One day after I mentioned to Nandi I couldn't sleep she proposed an all-night movie fest. We had kettle corn and drank beer watching old black and white movies on the little island station until falling asleep on the couch. I woke in the morning with an erection. I had fallen asleep sitting up. Arising and arousing from dreamland I noticed why I had such a hard on.

Nandi was asleep curled on the couch with her head on my lap. My hand rested on her bare shoulder; her wavy rivulets of shining black hair brushed against my fingers. I moved my hand to touch her hair, felt my heart pound then resisted standing abruptly waking her in the process.

She dreamily gazed at me from the couch. I had sweatpants on. My member was pushing against the fabric. I fumbled to straighten it out feeling my blush.

"Want to do something about that?" she smiled; her eyes flashed toward my crotch.

"I can't."

Nandi sat up rubbing sleep from her eyes.

"Correction," she said, "You can do something about it, but you won't. No worries, luv. I understand."

There was a knock on the patio slider. It swung open and Thad rushed in. I made a mental note to start locking the doors.

"I got to talk to you in private," he said, nodding toward Nandi.

Nandi stood from the couch, pecked me on the cheek, saying she had a lovely time, and she would pop by later. After she left, Thad paced a little then plopped on the couch.

"Is this about Sierra?" I asked. "Did you find her?"

"No. I think I did something stupid."

I was going to make a sarcastic comment, but I could see he was distraught. I sat in my recliner and asked what happened.

"Nothing yet, at least I don't think so. Pumkin Head and Christine were over last night. I got so wasted. I was upset you and I are not talking. I've been going at it heavy lately. I passed out before they left and when I got up this morning, I went to log in my work account. My laptop battery was drained. I thought it weird because I always leave it plugged in, and it wasn't. I started checking my desk and stuff was moved inside, somebody went through it. I have a small notebook of passwords buried under shit in my bottom drawer. I could tell the stuff was moved and the notebook was open at the page with my work password. Also two USB drives are missing. I think that fucking Christine hacked me."

"Did you tell Lesmour?"

"No, I don't trust him. I was just over there. He said Christine spent the night but had a job to do in Kauai in the morning. I acted like nothing was wrong to see if he would slip up."

"I doubt he would be involved with anything she would do. He is a tool, but he wouldn't want to get you in trouble."

"Trouble? That's putting it lightly! I would be so screwed if they found out I allowed anyone access into what Jayson is doing on the island. If this gets out, they might think I was a part of some espionage act especially if they learn that we are all fakes. Cody, you have no idea what Robinette is working on!"

"Did you say anything that might have made her want to hack you?"

He rubbed his face then intertwined his fingers resting his forearms on his knees. He stared at his hands.

"I might have . . . I was really drunk. Lesmour was being an asshole bragging about his job and his girl. Colleen and I got into a fight over me drinking too much so of course, I drank more. I remember saying something about his job was only to entertain tourists and mine actually meant something. I can't remember much else."

"You should tell Jayson. Maybe he can do something."

"No way! That would put an end to us. He is a nice guy, but he is dead serious about how things should be done. He would turn me in and that would be it."

"How about William? Maybe he can help. He knows we are fakes, and he kept that to himself."

"Yeah, maybe. I doubt he can do anything; it is worth a try."

Thad sent William a text asking if he could come over, it was urgent. He replied saying he was near the end of writing a chapter and would be there shortly. I made coffee and brought out a stack of cinnamon sugar malasadas, a yeasty, chewy doughnut that is popular in Hawaii. The coffee and two doughnuts helped clear my head. Thad drank coffee but refused a doughnut saying he was too stressed to eat.

William knocked, then let himself in via the front door. He was in good spirits saying he had a good writing session. His spirits were dashed after Thad spilled the events of the night before. He helped himself to coffee and sat at my dinette table.

"This is not good," he shook his head. "We must tell Jayson."

"Don't!" Thad pleaded. "Maybe nothing will come of it. Maybe she couldn't find anything useful!"

"Anything Jayson does could be useful especially in the wrong hands. His research on tapping into the thermal energy from the submerged volcano alone is invaluable. If someone sells that research it would be a fortune and lost revenue for Lemuria Down. Darby Summers would not be pleased."

I heard my patio slider roll open. Lesmour walked in, grabbed a cup of coffee and doughnut. He slumped into a dinette chair. His beady eyes were red.

"Christine broke up with me."

"What a surprise," Thad said dripping with sarcasm. "She got what she wanted and flew the coop."

"What are you talking about? She told me she had business on the big island and thought it better we split."

Thad told Lesmour about the break-in of his pod the previous night. He asked Lesmour point blank if he was involved.

"That's really cruel to say! I love it here why would I mess it up?"

Even Thad, in his troubled state, could see Lesmour was telling the truth. He was just an innocent, moronic victim.

"Didn't I tell you she was no good?"

Lesmour nodded, embarrassed. Thad's bitterness subsided. He saw the remorse on Lesmour's round face. "Did she let on anything last night, say anything weird or telling in retrospect?"

Lesmour thought a moment.

"Before bed, she wondered about the important stuff Jayson was doing. Then she asked if I knew what was going on. You will hate me for this . . . I said I didn't, but you knew everything."

William groaned running his hand over his balding head.

"This is bad. This is very bad. Come, we must tell Jayson."

Thad protested. William stared him down until Thad ran out of words then evenly stated,

"There is no other way to handle this."

We found Jayson in his office panic-stricken hunched over his computer. He looked up.

"Files are missing. Thad, are you responsible for this?"

William told his husband the whole story, how we were

imposters and stealing our way onto the island with the help of Christine and how she hacked into Thad's laptop for the purpose of gaining what she could to sell to unscrupulous parties. Jayson slammed his fist on the desk.

"Years of work stolen! Were you a party to this?" he shot William an icy glare. William kept calm.

"I did not know their friend Christine was a thief. You know how I feel about them, the club we formed. What I did not tell you is our name for the club, Parasites in Paradise. It was not their choice being here nor was it mine. I only agreed to come here because I thought you would have the freedom to follow your dreams."

Jayson's anger deflated. His tall frame slunk into a leather chair.

"Did she take everything?" Thad asked.

"No but whoever gets hold of what she stole will be very rich and very dangerous. William, she stole Heavenly Vacation."

William gasped. I was about to ask what Heavenly Vacation was, but William spoke.

"Seven years ago I lost my parents. They were driving home from a party when a deer crossed the road. My father avoided hitting the deer but lost control of the car and hit a tree. Both died in the Emergency Room. I stopped working, stayed home, and did nothing but sleep. I am an atheist, so I believed I lost them for good. Jayson, beautiful fool that he is, wanted to prove me wrong. He read a book written by a doctor who researched afterlife experiences from those who were legally dead but came back to tell. Over time he developed an injection that could stop the heart and brain function for fifteen minutes. Another injection would shock a heart back to its beating state. It gave people the ability to experience the afterlife temporarily. He wanted to do trial runs on terminally ill people, but I begged him to not. If it went wrong I did not want him to be responsible. Instead I dug into therapy to work on the trauma of their passing."

Jayson hugged William.

"Wow," said Lesmour. "I would pay big bucks to try that!"

Thad mumbled something threatening to Lesmour under his breath.

"Exactly," said Jayson. "In the wrong hands and not properly administrated, it could be disastrous."

"What can we do?" I asked.

"First thing we must contact Darby Summers. She must be told. I daresay this will finally bring her to Lemuria Down in the flesh."

Thad blanched. He began to protest but Jayson held up his hand stopping him cold.

"Thaddeus, I will take some of the blame for this. I was careless to keep that research. I will also urge Darby Summers not to press charges although I will suggest your immediate removal from Lemuria Down, including your two friends."

"You don't understand," Thad weakly replied, then left.

Thad was not seen for two days. He avoided work. Nandi heard from Colleen that he was staying with her. Lesmour and I stopped by to attempt a conversation with Thad, but Colleen met us at the door. She said he refused to talk to anyone. He didn't even tell her what had happened. The days that followed after the data theft was fraught with anxiety and anticipation. Jayson said Darby Summers was due to arrive by week's end. She hired investigators to see if they could track down who Christine sold Heavenly Vacation to.

There was so much drama among our small circle of friends that I almost forgot calling Gus. I woke Thursday morning realizing while brushing teeth it had been a week since Gus told me he needed time to find what happened to Sierra. He told me to call back a week later to catch him on his Birds of a Feather shift. We spoke in the late afternoon a week ago, so I had to occupy myself the entire day. Nandi joined me to hike a strenuous path to the top of the dormant volcano. We hoped to find a plethora of nesting birds. We marveled spotting at the top of the falls: White-tailed Tropicbirds, long tail feathers and dragon-like wings gracefully gliding. Nandi, knowing far more than me, said its binomial nomenclature was Phaethon Lepturus. It was also my first sighting of a male Great Frigatebird or as Nandi correctly observed, a Fregata Minor, with its bright red markings on neck and chest that inflate for upwards of twenty minutes during mating season. The one we saw was massive having a nearly seven-foot wingspan.

On our trek up the volcanic mountain, Nandi wanted to know about what happened at the consort. Darby Summers asked all the parties involved in the Heavenly Vacation theft to keep it secret until her arrival. I was tight lipped with Nandi, but upon our descent she started punching me in the arm every time I refused to speak about it. I finally relented. We stopped for a water break on a little ridge that afforded a panoramic view of Lemuria Down's pristine bay. She could not understand the danger in a formula that would give someone the ability to experience the afterlife without permanently dying. For age twenty-one, she was worldly but in this instance her innocence showed.

"It could be a freeing thing," she said. "You could live without worry knowing you will have a brilliant afterlife."

"Maybe so, but what if your life stinks? There have been a few times I wanted to die, and I didn't even believe in heaven."

We watched a tourist boat leave the harbor. I wondered if Lesmour was captaining the vessel. Nandi broke the silence.

"If you cannot find Sierra, will you . . ."

"No. Besides she would not want me to."

"Neither do I. You are my source of amusement in this paradise. I can't even play football. I attended a pick-up game once but left before it was done. The players were shite."

It was past noon when we reached the Research and Development Consort. Nandi encouraged me to go home, take a shower and call Gus. She volunteered to draft a report of our findings on the trek, joking I was too distracted to file a coherent account. I jogged back to my place, showered, dressed, and drank two glasses of water before picking up the phone. My hand trembled as I tapped the number to Birds of a Feather. Gus answered on the first ring.

"Bad news, kid. I looked up her address in a Birds of a Feather file. When I got there the place was empty with a for rent sign on it. Her whole family is gone. I called up the bleach-blond goon that works for Sal on the guise of let's get a drink somewhere. After a couple he started blabbing and told me something you won't want to hear."

He paused a moment. I almost ended the call, so afraid of what Gus might say.

"Tell me."

"Somehow she became suspicious of me, women's intuition, I don't know. She must have done a work history search and saw I worked for Peter Dinky's. She went to the warehouse.

Bleach-blond "helped" her by introducing her to Sal. This was a day before she left saying she was going to find your father. I spent time in their neighborhood asking people, but they are tight lipped there; Mexican community, thought I was ICE."

My mind went wild trying to comprehend all the possibilities. After a week of waiting Gus found nothing definitive about her whereabouts. If anything there was more confusion.

"Kid, you still there?"

I was lost in thought numbly holding the phone to my ear.

"That all you got?"

"Sorry kid, that's it, that and my gut feeling."

I already surmised his gut feeling, but I asked anyway. I forced myself to hear it because deep down I felt the same. I wanted confirmation.

"Maybe Sal pressured her, like he pressured you. That lieutenant came back to check their books. Sal is feeling the pressure. He might have told Sierra to find you, or he would make her, and her family disappear. That is why she told me she was going to find your father, to try and get help. The fact she has not communicated to you can mean only one thing. Somebody got to her and her family. Maybe it was Sal, maybe something happened once they crossed the border. It hardly matters. If she were alive,

Cody, both you and I know she would have at least let you know she was ok."

I took a deep breath trying to hold back from sobbing. I managed to gather myself and spit out; "Thanks for looking."

"I wish it were better news," Gus said. "Sorry, kid."

The phone fell from my hand and bounced off the couch to the floor. I wanted to break something. I grabbed the water glass and threw it into the kitchen area. It smashed against the fridge shards flying everywhere. I kicked over the coffee table howling with pain because I struck it full force with my shin. I fell to the floor and rolled on my back grasping my shin bawling like a newborn.

The phone rang near my head. I saw by the caller ID it was Nandi. It felt like I was losing my mind. It was terrifying. I answered the phone out of sheer desperation.

"What happened?"

I couldn't respond. I couldn't catch a breath between sobs.

"On my way."

Chapter Fifteen

Nandi became my babysitter. She collected me from the floor, got me in bed and swept up shards of glass. Later she took me to the health center, where a nurse x-rayed my shin. I had a hairline fracture and was told to elevate and stay off my feet. The nurse also gave me a sedative to dull the pain.

Nandi, much to her parents disapproval, stayed with me. She attempted to feed me even though I did not have an appetite. Her parents culinary skills did not transfer well. Breakfast eggs were either rubbery or so runny it could have passed for soup. She ended up relying mostly on take out. Jayson told her to stay with me rather than do any field work making us both on hiatus.

I had no will to do anything. The sedatives only made me sleep. We watched old Gary Cooper westerns in bed although I could not focus on any story line. I thanked her for being there.

"No worries, luv. You've had a rough go of it. Glad to help."

By the second day I stopped taking the sedative. It was more depressing taking a pill and sleeping half the time than not taking a pill. My shin was black and blue, but the swelling had gone down. I could hobble around a bit. Late in the afternoon we moved to the couch to watch Man of the West. I remembered watching it with my father. I adopted from that film the habit of saying yep and nope like a cowboy might say. Nandi wasn't really watching. She was staring at her nails which she just painted with pink polish. The fumes of the polish gave me a headache. I sighed.

"Let's go to the beach," I said.

She did not look up from admiring her nails, trying to be nonchalant about my decision but I could tell she was surprised. Her eyebrows raised slightly.

"Ok. Get in your trunks. We are going for a dip."

"I don't really want to swim," I said.

Nandi grabbed me by the shoulders and shook me.

"I spent days watching old movies with you. No. We are going for a dip in the ocean. I will go home and get my swimsuit. Meet you at the usual spot."

Nandi hurried out the front door like she was making a prison break, not even bothering to close it. I got up from the couch to close the door but took a few moments to look outside.

Another beautiful day in Lemuria Down. Lois and her husband were on a walk. She saw me and waved cheerfully. I made a poor attempt to smile.

"It looks like you need some sun," she called out.

"I'm going for a swim," I replied.

She gave me a thumbs up then took her husbands' hand and continued down the road.

It took some time to find my bathing suit. I had not worn it since we first arrived. It was buried in the bottom draw of my dresser. It made me aware I wore pretty much a combination of three sets of shorts and shirts since I came here, the same rut, an unthinking self-imposed dress code I enacted in Arizona. I miserably pondered, have I changed at all? After everything that happened I was still a bird in a cage with a broken wing, same feathers, same outlook. The only difference being Lemuria Down was a pretty cage, and I fractured my shin.

Nandi waited at our spot on the beach within walking distance to the Pig and Poi. She had a two-piece orchid patterned suit. Her body was incredible, perfectly toned and her dark skin shone under the sun. She spread a blanket on the sand. It was windy so she used a small cooler, her sandals, and a smooth stone to anchor each corner.

She saw me plodding toward her with my gimpy, fractured gait.

"Hop to it, mate!"

"Gee, thanks."

She reached into the cooler and brought out two beers, passing one to me. I hesitated because of the meds I was taking but figured enough was out of my system to not be a factor. It almost made me laugh because the last two days I couldn't have cared if I lived or died. It felt good to be outdoors. About halfway through the beer, the aromas from Pig and Poi made me salivate. We bought some ribs. I gnawed every bit of meat I could find off the bone. We were sticky with the tangy sauce. Nandi yanked my hand.

"Time for a dip, must wash off the sauce!"

I am usually a wimp getting into water. It always seems too cold to me, but the ocean was a perfect temperature, cool and refreshing. The buoyancy took away the ache of my fracture as we waded until the water was chest high. I could not help but to stare at the buoyancy of Nandi's breasts. She caught me staring and slapped my shoulder.

"See. You still have life in you."

She fell backwards and did an underwater flip. I squatted and submerged keeping my eyes open even though the salt stung. I watched her kick and turn like a dolphin. I like the muffled sound while being underwater. When I was a kid I used to be terrified of water until my mother made me take swim lessons. I overcame the fear of drowning and would swim underwater with a snorkel, pretending I was a fish. I came up for air and floated on my back keeping my ears underwater. Nandi grabbed my hand again. I stood letting a larger than normal wave smack my back.

"It's either sink or swim, Cody."

Nandi had my other hand now and pulled me toward her. I was lighter in water, and she was strong. I was like a big game fish that had lost the strength and will to fight after being hooked for too long. She reeled me in.

"What will it be? Sink or swim?"

I grabbed her tight. We bashed teeth at first, so eager to have our mouths meet, but quickly adapted to tongues and lips working furiously with desire. I held her so hard. I had the brief thought of wanting to crawl inside her, live there, become a part of her. She was beautiful, intelligent, and witty but her assertiveness was irresistible. She was the only clarity I found on Lemuria Down.

She pulled away from my lips and whispered in my ear.

"Let's take this to your bed."

"With my leg fracture and this hard-on I don't think I could make it," I joked.

She smiled slyly. Her eyes fixed upon mine.

"I can remedy that."

She let go and dipped under water. She came up holding her bikini bottom.

"We can't let go of our suits, or we will have a revealing walk back to your place," she said working her free hand under my suit in an attempt to pull it down.

I looked around nervously. Three people were relaxing under the palms near the beach. It looked like they were having a picnic, too far away to tell. The Pig and Poi had a couple of customers, but their backs were to us. Nandi read concern on my face. She stopped tugging at my suit.

"They won't notice. It will look like two people hugging and kissing. We just can't thrash about much or scream. It will be thrilling trying to control ourselves and dangerous if we forget to hold onto our suits."

Caught in indecision, I did not say no. I thought of the old Clash song Should I Stay or Should I Go. She smiled, bit her lip then submerged pulling my suit past my rock boner down to my ankles. I tread water as I raised my feet. Nandi came up and placed my suit on my head laughing. I grabbed it as she climbed on me wrapping her right arm around my neck while keeping her left hand below the waterline holding her bikini bottom. I followed her lead submerging my suit with my left hand while embracing her waist with my right. At first it was awkward until Nandi slowly began to grind her hips the same rhythm as the waves careening off us.

"I never done this," I confessed.

"I never have, either" she gasped. "I always wanted a shag in the sea."

"You don't understand. I have never done THIS."

Nandi stopped for a moment and gave me a peck on the cheek and whispered again in my ear.

"Oh luv, you will never forget me."

She licked my ear and then began grinding again this time stronger. I felt lightheaded. My feet tingled. I wanted to make it last until eternity, but it was only a few seconds. I came inside her and could not help but groan. Nandi covered my mouth so as not to attract attention. She giggled. I could feel her laughter from within her.

"I am so glad; I am your first. I thought . . ."

She stopped herself. I felt sick. I had not thought of Sierra. I was an unthinking animal.

"No, we never had a chance to. We never had a chance."

Nandi got off and held my face in her hands.

"I am sorry. Don't feel bad. You said yourself she would want you to be happy."

"I am not happy, just desperate."

I instantly regretted what I said. She took her hands from my face while her own turned to stone. She turned her back to me, dipped under water and put on her bottom.

"And I am on the pill. Thanks for asking," she said as she waded back to the beach.

She was moving fast. I followed her until I reached the shallow water with swimsuit still in hand. My now flaccid pecker dangled in the breeze. I hurriedly put on my suit, losing balance because of my fracture, and fell to my side as a wave rolled me. I reached her just as she was rolling up the blanket.

"I didn't mean it like that."

Nandi ignored me. She tucked the blanket under her arm, slipped on her sandals and picked up the cooler. She started walking. I limped behind.

"I mean what guy would not want you. You're amazing. I don't want to hurt you. I am so fucked up inside and you have been so kind, of course I feel close to you. You tell me to sink or swim. I can only tread water now. I'm sorry!"

Nandi had gained several feet on me because of my limp. It hurt like hell trying to hurry through sand. She spun around taking three steps toward me.

"Go away, Cody! You frame the whole world through your own pathetic eyes! I am sorry you lost the love of your life, but that doesn't mean you can use me!"

A firepit of anger burned inside. The truth hurt.

"You were using me!" I yelled. "You wanted me! You hung out with me knowing I was vulnerable!"

That's when she started to cry. I was about to blurt an apology, but she kicked my fractured shin like she was trying to score a goal from midfield. I fell to the sand clutching my shin screaming.

"Fuck you Cody! Fuck you!"

Chapter Sixteen

It took two days for the kick on the shin pain to subside. It was a good excuse to hide out. I called Nandi, but she didn't answer. Apologizing again seemed like the right thing to do, but deep down I was emotionally spent. I was tired of people. Lesmour interrupted my solitude to see how I was doing. It was a well-intended gesture until he got on his own pity trip moaning over how Christine used him. I asked him to leave. Before leaving he said he saw Thad. He took up residency with Colleen since the discovery of his laptop hack. Thad asked Lesmour to say to me he was sorry. Neither of us could figure out what he was apologizing for.

William stopped by. He was saddened about all the discord. He missed our afterhours get togethers. The Parasites in Paradise group was something he looked forward to after a day of writing. Jayson was distant. He was bothered that his hard work leaked out. To remedy his worries, he interacted little with William burrowing deep into his work.

William asked if I saw yesterdays' local news broadcast. When I responded negatively he shared more troubling events.

"Lois and her husband are missing. They vanished without a trace. Worse yet, Darby Summers is arriving this weekend. Lois was Ms. Summers' main liaison. Their disappearance and the hacking of Jayson's files are not the best circumstances for her first visit."

It was disconcerting Lois, and her husband were missing. William went on.

"The town security searched their premises and found nothing suspicious. The community is organizing search parties. They want us to help. Jayson asked us to meet this afternoon in order to devise a plan."

"All of us like you, me, Thad and Nandi?"

"Yes. You and Thad have to bury the hatchet in a situation like this. Two people's lives are at stake."

"It's not only Thad and me. Nandi and I had a falling out."

William rubbed the back of his neck. A couple of veins on his forehead bulged.

"It is time to act like adults and think of others that need our help! I am off to speak to Thad and Nandi and twist their arms if necessary. Make sure to be at Jayson's office by four."

William cursed in exasperation as he let himself out.

I ordered an autonomous vehicle to take me to the medical clinic to get pain killers for my shin. Several people in hiking gear were on the white roads coming down from the rainforest. I surmised they were looking for the lost couple. I told the vehicle to take me to The Pig and Poi instead where I ordered kalua pork and a beer. I was not hungry. I thought being at a tourist hangout might take my mind off the meeting.

The place was busy. I found a seat at the bar, ordered a beer, and washed the meds down with my first gulp, not the brightest idea but I didn't give a crap. There were loud people at a table behind me. I turned and took a quick glance to see a pitcher of beer and empty bottles on their table. Tourists.

"Pity about that couple missing. That shouldn't happen in a utopia like this."

"Maybe it was a boating accident."

I shifted my weight on the bar stool facing their table and leaned into their conversation.

"I live here. I can tell you this is not utopia, and it wasn't a boating accident." They stared at me like I had three heads. I continued. "You see that big volcanic rock halfway up the mountain?"

I gave them time to find it.

"The missing couple liked hiking in that area. I told them not to go but they wouldn't listen."

I got their attention. A woman in a one-piece suit with gaudy rings asked; "What happened to them?"

"Dirty little secret," I paused for dramatic effect, "Nobody knew about them until after people started moving in."

"Who?" said the same woman.

"Ancestors that ate Captain Cook. I saw them myself. I am a naturalist. They almost got me."

The woman gasped but a man with a diamond stud earring laughed.

"You're full of it," he said, "That whole thing about Cook being eaten by cannibals is bullshit. I saw it in a documentary."

My pork came. I took the plate and put it on their table. I got up to leave.

"Hawaiian Tourism Bureau wants you to believe that. I can't eat. Thinking about them turns my stomach. Enjoy your stay."

I hobbled away as the tourists engaged in a lively exchange. The earring man blurted out, "I'll eat it if no one else will!" I would have to tell Thad about my mind fuck on the tourists. It is something he would have done. It might be a good ice breaker.

I went home showered and shaved. The beer with the meds gave me a fuzzy glow. Lesmour called, asking if I heard about Lois and her husband. He said all available boats were searching the shoreline. He docked briefly to refuel a fishing boat he often used. He chose the small craft that could take him close to the shoreline. I was impressed by the seriousness Lesmour took to the task of finding the couple. There I was, drinking beer and taking pain pills. He said he would search until sundown.

I was shocked to get a text from Nandi offering to pick me up. I agreed, encouraged that the dynamics of the meeting might not be so awkward. I waited at the end of my pathway by the road. When she pulled up she did not look at me. She hit the accelerator before I could settle into my seat, nearly falling out, saved by a last second grab of the safety bar.

"Don't think all is forgiven," she said when we parked at the science consort. "Finding them takes precedence."

"I am sorry. I am an asshole."

"I agree. You are a sorry arsehole." She smiled somewhat cruelly, nodding at my bruised shin. "How was my kick?"

"You scored."

She tried to suppress her laughter but couldn't.

"Sorry, luv, you deserved it."

At the reception desk a hastily scrawled sign was taped to the green glass stating the meeting was being held in Jayson's office.

William and Jayson were seated by a live edge coffee table. No Thad. Nandi and I sat in a loveseat by the table. Jayson looked at his watch.

"Thad is late," he said.

I was about to say I didn't think he would show when he stepped in. He was in rough shape. His clothes were wrinkled, giving the appearance he slept in them. He smelled sour and breathed heavily, wreaking of beer. Jayson gave him a disdainful glance but said nothing. William spoke.

"In the event that this get together may get heated, I volunteered to be the intermediary. It is understood there are personal differences here, but we have to unite as a group to find Lois and Nigel."

"Who's Nigel?" Thad slurred.

"Lois's husband, you nob," Nandi shot back.

Jayson closed his eyes and held up his hand saying, "please people." Thad emitted a loud belch.

"I think we should move this along as quickly as possible," William said. "Our search and rescue team has been dispatched as well as our security team, but we need all hands on deck to find the elderly couple."

"Thad," said Jayson. "I have six residents each with a drone stationed at strategic parts on the island. The cameras are linked to monitors William set up in your pod. Are you capable, given the condition you are in, of overseeing and directing the drone operators in the hope we can get a visual of Lois and Nigel? Perhaps Colleen can be an extra set of eyes for the monitors."

Thad saluted with his left hand as he stood.

"Aye, aye, Captain!"

He tried to make a precise turn to the door, emulating a serviceman. Instead he lost his balance and fell to his knees, got up and staggered out the door. Jayson shouted to him to call Colleen for help. Thad waved his hand above his head without turning. Jayson turned his attention to Nandi and me.

"William tells me you two haven't been getting along. Whatever it is, you must put that aside for now. Nobody knows the nature preserve better. We need you to work as a team, scouring the rainforest. Get your gear, get some sustenance, and leave immediately. There are a few hours of daylight left. If they are still missing, resume your search in the morning. Darcy Summers just arrived by helicopter. She has been briefed. Regardless of what we find, she wants us here tomorrow evening. No other Lemuria Down resident knows she arrived. Keep it that way. Could you tell Thad his presence is required tomorrow evening?"

Nandi and I left. We saw Colleen just arriving. We stepped into Thad's office where he was clumsily adjusting monitors so he could view them while reclining on a sofa. I passed on Jayson's message for us to be there tomorrow for a meeting with Darby Summers.

"Fan fucking tastic," he slurred.

Colleen came close and whispered.

"I'll get him sober, drag him by his ears if I need to."

I thanked Colleen. Nandi and I made it to the door. Thad called out my name.

"I'm sorry," he said.

"About what?"

"You'll find out soon enough."

My jaw tightened. I wanted to hurl insults and demand he be specific. Nandi grabbed my arm.

"Ignore him, he's pissed."

She dropped me off at my place so I could gather gear while she went home to change. We agreed to meet in our office pod. I had the clever idea to check footage of cameras set on the main trails weeks before to monitor ground wildlife. If Lois and her husband hiked the monitored trails, the cameras would have recorded it. The monitors also recorded sound for the purpose of identifying and observing wildlife. If they passed a monitor there was a chance their conversation might reveal their whereabouts.

When Nandi arrived I told her my idea of utilizing the trail monitors. Although she was still angry with me, she said it was brilliant, but it would take many hours to review all the footage. She suggested we hit the main trail first while there was daylight then spend the night scouring the footage.

"We might get lucky and run across them on the trail. They will probably need medical attention. The sooner we get to them the better chance we have saving them."

We took the trail less traveled that led to my favorite spot, the log with the view of the hawk nest and the waterfall. The other trails were more accessible and therefore more popular for residents. No doubt residents searching for the couple scoured those trails. I had to stop several times. I tried not to put too much weight on my shin which caused my good leg to cramp from the compensation. Nandi took pity on me, apologizing again for her game winning kick, then massaged the cramp. Her strong, warm hands working the calf caused arousal. I hoped she would not notice. She did.

"You should try walking on that leg."

She patted my thigh, stood, and headed up the trail.

It was odd looking for humans rather than island creatures on the hike. The turf was wet, few footprints to see. We hoped to find something they dropped which could provide a clue, or like one sees in cheap movies, a conveniently torn fabric from clothing caught on a branch, but no luck. The dread of perhaps finding two prone bodies gave the trek a sinister vibe. The rainforest sounds seemed especially muted and distant. I was glad to reach the log. The waterfall volume was thunderous as ever. No sign of Lois and Nigel.

Nandi squinted toward the 'io nest.

"I wonder where Egbert is?" she said.

We named the male Egbert one afternoon while acting silly much of the day. I took out my binoculars and got a close look of the nest. I saw the head of the mother but no Egbert.

"Maybe he's on vacation."

"Right. Maybe he flew off with a younger bird."

We made eye contact and laughed despite the situation. Despite everything. Nandi studied the sky, raised her arms above her head and shouted to the heavens.

"It is all so fucking mad! Why? Cody, why can't it be like this always?"

She stood spun slowly around in a grand sweep extending arms and hands to the thick, primordial vegetation, the towering volcanic rock face with the cascading falls, the sun, perfect blue sky gleaming above.

"Maybe God likes to torture us," I said. "Put us here and let us fuck it all up."

She grinned and closed her eyes lifting her face to the light, taking in the warmth, the musk, the falls. Nandi's smile faded like the sun shielded by a rogue cloud.

"There are times I am glad my parents moved here."

"Why did you join them? Why didn't you choose another university."

"I could have," she said, her eyes still shut. "They have money. I could have gone anywhere. I had my heart set on University of Liverpool. I obsessed about making the football team but couldn't get by the tryouts. I was stubborn, pig headed and hurt. I thought I was good enough. I am a brat. If I don't get my way I get mad."

I told Nandi I was sorry she was disappointed. I told her I was sorry for being a dick after we had sex. She opened her eyes and nudged my shoulder.

"No worries, luv. Best we get back before sundown. We have a long night ahead."

Chapter Seventeen

Limping down the trail was worse than limping up. I had to stop twice to drink water and let the throbbing in my shin quiet. With each step, I felt where the hairline fracture was. The sun went down. We used our phone flashlights to illuminate the path to avoid tripping over roots. We went back to our respective homes to shower and change out of our sweaty clothes. Nandi brought a six pack along with Pig and Poi take out and met me at the pod. What followed were hours of scrolling through trail footage. Our beginning point of the search was set from when they were last seen. Hours passed. We huddled over our laptops while sipping beer and devouring bar-b-que. It was hard on the eyes because we tried to fast forward as much as possible while still being able to detect any movement on the monitor cameras. We also turned the volume high thinking it might catch their voices out of camera range.

It was midnight. My eyes were burning and losing focus. It made me think of Thad's bloodshot eyes from perpetually staring at his screen. Nandi stood rubbing her back.

"Where can they be?" she said.

"Think it was foul play?" I asked.

"No. Everyone loves them."

I closed my eyes. We kept the monitor footage at half speed scroll with the volume up just to whittle down our viewing time. There were hours more to go. I heard the night sounds of the rainforest from the monitor. Thousands of peepers calling for mates in slow motion speed sounded as if they were drugged. I felt Nandi lean against me. Her dark, curly locks tickled my shoulder. My heart raced. Without opening my eyes, I eased my arm from behind her, hugging her close to me. She brushed her free hand against my cheek, tilted my face close to hers. I could smell beer and barbeque sauce on her breath.

"Keep your eyes closed," she said. "We have seen too much."

We kissed so hard it hurt. My ears rang. Eyes closed, I searched blindly for her body, her buttons, her skin. She pulled off my t-shirt, fumbled excitedly with my belt buckle. The couch was too small. We fell to the carpet. I heard her moan. She whispered my name like it was a mantra to a lost religion. She got on top. I tried to last as long as possible. I forced myself to think of something to counterbalance my lust. Lesmour complaining came to mind. It worked momentarily until Nandi increased her rhythm, her cries rising in volume and pitch. I thrust hard against her, slapping sounds each time we collided. I came first. She a close second, collapsing on me, shaking, our lips finding each other's, insatiable kissing.

I opened my eyes. She looked down on me, panting.

"Wanker. Kept your eyes closed the whole time."

We heard voices muffled, slowed on the footage.

"Oh my God, it's them!" Nandi said pushing herself up scrambling to the laptops.

I sprang up, grabbing my underwear. Nandi rewound the footage adjusting it to normal playback speed. The time stamp read 4pm, the afternoon before their disappearance. Lois and Nigel were walking hand in hand along the trail. Lois carried a picnic basket. They came to a stop.

"This is it?" Nigel asked.

The couple faced a small path that led off the main trail.

"Yes darling. It's not as scary as it looks. Don't worry, I will help you."

Lois pushed a large fern leaf aside letting Nigel take the first steps on the path. She followed, eased past the leaf, and let it swing behind her. Then they were gone.

"Do you know that path?" Nandi asked.

"Yes. It leads to the top of the waterfall."

"Looks steep. Why would they go there?"

"I guess they like nature. They are in good shape. They can make it."

"But at 4pm? They would not get back before sundown."

Nandi phoned William. "We found them!" she said excitedly. He woke Jayson who put him on speaker phone, ready to start the search and rescue. Darby Summer's helicopter pilot could search with floodlights immediately. Jayson asked if the path could be traversed at night. I said it was little used and required focus in daylight to stay on it, at night it would be impossible to traverse. He asked us to be at the trailhead by dawn. We could lead paramedics to the waterfall.

I lent Nandi a t-shirt and she slept over, so that we could start first thing in the morning. Nandi mused why Thad and Colleen could not spot them during their drone search.

"Two reasons," I said. "For one, Thad was probably blitzed. He couldn't see his hand in front of his face. Two, when it comes to a rainforest, aerial views are useless because of the tree canopy. It's too dense. Jayson sending the helicopter out at night was worthless."

We set out field gear for the morning. Only three hours before dawn, we could not resist each other especially since I offered her my bed and she insisted I sleep with her. This time I kept my eyes open, marveling her body, the way she moved over and under me, eventually coming home to her face, an intense serenity. Her dark eyes alternating from being closed, half-lidded and looking into mine. There was no hiding, no false pretense. We were connected, skin to skin, eyes seeing beyond our physical, primal thoughts. Naked.

I thought of Sierra. I felt guilty. Nandi saw the change, the drawing away. She wrapped her arms around my waist pulling me close

"This just is, Cody. We want it. No need to deny it. No past, no future, just now. Besides, my parents don't like you. They want me to leave the island, give university another crack."

The phone alarm buzzed. I felt rested even though we slept at the most two hours. It could have been the letting go. It was as if Nandi gave me permission to live for the moment. The past is done. More than the sex, I needed to connect to something, someone. Everything around me was spinning out of control. My mother had betrayed me. Sierra and her family were missing, most likely dead. The friction within our sick, little group, Christine's stealing from Thad's office and now Lois and Nigel missing tugged at what little footing I had in my life to a point of toppling. I could not give Nandi up.

We drank coffee and inhaled an energy bar and hurried out the door. Two paramedics were waiting at the trailhead. The sun had not yet risen, but the beginning of the trail was well traveled. A light rain began. As the trail steepened we lost footing several times. Rainwater poured off giant leaves as if they were mini waterfalls drenching us by the time we reached the trail to the top of the volcano. The rain became steady. My leg throbbed. Nandi saw me struggling and offered her hand several times to scale rocky segments of the path. Although it was midmorning as we climbed the trail, the overcast, and the rain caused poor visibility.

"We're the only creatures out. Even mosquitos are taking cover," Nandi grumbled.

It was true. The usual cacophonous chatter of songbirds in the rainforest was silenced by the heavy weather. Their absence was disturbing.

"This is not good," the paramedic said. "Why would two elderly people be out in this?"

The trail turned into a stream from the mountain rainwater runoff. We used sturdy tree limbs and flattened rocks to support treacherous footing. The paramedics showed their former inner-city selves with increased cursing with every slip or stumble. By the time we reached the top, we were out of breath. The mouth of the waterfall was deafening. The steady rain increased its volume gushing out in a ferocity I have not seen before. In the heavy mist we cautiously approached the ledge nearest the waterfall, barely able to see a few feet ahead. We crept slowly.

Through the mist, I saw it first; a light colored rectangular object atop the volcanic rock. Nandi volunteered to retrieve the object because the ledge was narrow, and she was smallest. The paramedic refused her help. On hands and knees, he gingerly made his way to the ledge, reached for the object, and backed his way off, not chancing to turn around. He stood holding the picnic basket Lois and Nigel were last seen carrying on the trail monitor footage.

"Recognize this?" he asked.

Nandi opened the basket. There was a drained bottle of red wine, two wine glasses and a plastic container with a cheese knife, soggy cracker crumbs and a sliver of remaining brie cheese. In a reusable sandwich bag was a cellphone. Nandi took the phone from the bag and tried to power it up. The battery was dead. She began to cry. I put my arm around her and made a feeble attempt to comfort her.

"It was an accident. They must have fallen," I said.

The paramedic spoiled my clumsy attempt to console Nandi.

"Or jumped," he said.

Chapter Eighteen

The rain continued as we descended. My feet went out from under me on an especially slick grade, landing fully on my right butt cheek. I slid several feet until a stone jutting from the trail stopped me. I absorbed a pound of mud with the skid. We finally reached the trail entrance late morning. The rain had eased. Small patches of blue with threads of sunlight poked through rapidly moving clouds. The paramedics left to report back to base while Nandi and I hurried to the consort with the basket and its contents.

I rushed into our office pod inserting a charger cord into Lois and Nigel's cellphone, while Nandi looked for Jayson and William. The cellphone battery was totally dead. I plugged an external USB cable into the phone connecting it with my pc monitor and collapsed into my swivel chair grateful to be off my feet and aching shin. "Come on," I uttered waiting for the phone to power up. Jayson swung open the door. Nandi was close behind.

"Thad is coming. We need him to crack the password code," Jayson said.

I had forgotten about the code to get into the phone. The phone charged to life. The screen saver pic was a selfie of Nigel and Lois smiling at the entry dock to Lemuria Down. We said nothing as we waited for Thad, anxious to see if there was a clue the phone might contain to explain why the couple hiked the narrow trail at sunset. It seemed like hours, but only a few minutes passed until Thad arrived. Now sober, he moved directly to the phone not making eye contact.

"This is a Droidkey," he said waving a slim black device with a jack that plugged into the phone.

In less than a minute the lock screen opened. Thad deftly picked up the phone inspecting text messages, calls, contact lists, and pictures.

"Christine is on their contacts," Thad pointed.

He searched the call history to Christine. There were a flurry of calls that began the previous week ending three days ago. Thad searched the text messages to Christine. There was only one, dated the day before Lois and Nigel's' disappearance. The message to Christine was a simple thank you to which she responded with a thumbs up. Thad then scanned their pictures. Then he found the video.

The frozen frame of the video was dark but discernible. Lois and Nigel were sitting on the ledge by the waterfall with wine glasses raised in a toast. They were smiling. It was dated the previous night. I shivered partly from being soaked to the bone but more in fear of what the video would reveal. Nandi grabbed my hand. Thad pressed the play arrow. The poorly lit grainy video began with Nigel and Lois standing together as she held the phone. His arm was around her waist as she spoke.

"This message is for anyone who might find our belongings. Firstly, Nigel and I apologize if we have caused any pain or worry to the good people of Lemuria Down. Our time here has been lovely, and we thank you all for your kindness and enthusiasm, but our time has run short. We kept from you that Nigel is dying. We wanted to spend his final days with other like-minded people in a beautiful environment, but now we have found a better place. We took a Heavenly Vacation, experienced for a few blissful minutes the afterlife, and could not wait to get back, together. Best wishes to you all!"

The couple raised their glasses in toast. She passed her glass to Nigel. Forgetting to stop her recording; the shaky images of her sealing the phone in the recyclable sandwich bag, placing it in the basket with the wine glasses and empty bottle in the basket, the lid closing, total darkness as the muffled audio continued. We heard the waterfall, snippets of their conversation, Nigel saying, "in our birthday suits?" Lois laughing, saying, "I love you," some scuffling and then only the waterfall roaring with a nearby cricket beginning its night song.

Thad fast forward the black screen video to see if any other image appeared. Nothing.

"Thad," said Jayson in the tone a father would address a mischievous child, "how was Lois and Nigel able to use Heavenly Vacation?"

Thad blankly stared at the monitor.

"I took both prescription bottles from you. I did not give any out. Christine stole the pills. She must have given them to Lois."

"Then why on earth did you steal those pills?"

"I was sick of being a sham my entire life. I wanted to see what it was like being dead, if there really was an afterlife. Turns out there is one after all."

"I thought you could only experience Heavenly Vacation by injection." I said.

Jayson explained in measured tones he kept secret his latest breakthrough to experiencing the afterlife. He developed an encapsulated pill that could stop brain function and send one to the afterlife while another pill taken simultaneously is a time released capsule designed to jump start the heart and bring the taker back to life. He kept the breakthrough secret because it could be self-administered while the injection method required a degree of medical knowledge.

"Why couldn't you have killed yourself instead of them!" Nandi shouted, shoving Thad into the monitor.

Thad jumped to his feet.

"I couldn't. I need to set things straight."

Thad ran out the door. Jayson's phone rang. He listened intently without saying a word. His face hardened.

"What?" Nandi asked.

"One of our captains found Nigel's body caught between two lava stones where the waterfall spills into the Pacific. Our small vessels are searching the area for Lois' body. I will have Thad direct the drones the entire length of the waterfall to see if Lois' body is caught among boulders."

Nandi hugged me. She began to weep. William put his hand on my shoulder.

"You two have done enough," he said. "Get a shower and rest, see you later today."

We took an autonomous vehicle to my place, put our wet clothes in the washer, showered, and crawled into bed. I held

Nandi until I could feel her body relax and heavy breathing took her to dreamland. I rolled to my side, our backs and butts touched. I couldn't sleep. I had too many questions tossing around my head. How did Christine meet Lois and Nigel? Did Christine sell Heavenly Vacation pills to others? What else is Thad hiding?

I called Lesmour against my better judgement. I told him about the finding of Lois and Nigel's cellphone then asked him if he knew how Christine and the couple might have met. He hesitated a moment until I became aggravated.

"I guess it doesn't matter now. They are dead," he sighed. "Christine helped them sneak into Lemuria Down just like she helped us. She knew a hacker like Thad that changed Nigel's medical records to make it look like he was healthy. Lois and Nigel were old hippies and grew pot on the big island. Christine helped distribute their weed. That's how they met. Like us, they changed their identities. Besides Nigel dying, they wanted to be here because the cops raided their farm. Christine made big bucks getting people into this place undercover."

"Some fucking utopia with tight security. Please tell me you knew nothing about the pills."

"I swear, Cody! I didn't! I feel like shit. Thad was right. She used me. She's making money off those pills."

Just then, Lesmour got a text from the harbor master telling him to do a shift searching the coastline. The harbor master said they found a small sized hiking boot at water's edge and the Hawaiian shirt Nigel was wearing on their last hike. Lesmour apologized saying he had to go.

I crawled back into bed, taking a peek at Nandi's body as I

raised the bed sheet. I was slightly disgusted with myself becoming aroused despite it all. Nandi woke up. She sleepily turned, reached for my penis. Without a word, we made love. We held each other afterward, still silent. Words would have ruined it. My phone alarm went off. It was time for the meeting with Darby Summers, creator of a phony paradise.

We met Jayson in his office. He was on the back patio, wistfully studying the ominous clouds. The rain had passed for the moment although another storm was rolling in. Jayson didn't even notice we arrived. I called his name. He started a bit then stepped in closing the slider.

"Quite the rainy weather," he stated. "Sparkling blue skies and then this. Makes one wonder. William is getting Thad. He has been hunkered in his cubicle for hours."

"When will she be here?" I asked.

"Shortly. Tomorrow she will address the community about Lois and Nigel's death, not the best first impression but necessary."

"Where is she staying?" Nandi asked.

"She has a mansion on the opposite end of the island with a helicopter pad. It is quite remote. An access road was built but is well concealed."

Thad and William arrived. Thad rushed to me, grabbing my shoulders.

"Cody, I am sorry. I thought it was best for us, for you!"

I pushed him away. The tone of his voice and panicked expression frightened me.

"What are you talking about?"

"I will fix it! I swear!"

"Fix what?," I asked.

Then we heard footsteps approaching from the reception area. One was heavy feet thudding across the floorboards while the other the unmistakable clicking of women's high heels.

"Ms. Summers," Jayson called out. "We are in here."

We all turned. They paused at the entryway of Jayson's office, a large man in black jeans, black tight-fitting t-shirt, and a revolver in a holster on his right hip, and Ms. Darby Summers. A shadow created by a reading lamp cast across the figures making it hard to see their faces. She took a step forward. She was wearing sunglasses on a rainy day, but I could tell by the tilt of her head she was staring at me. My hands trembled. My stomach tightened to a knot.

"Hello, Cody."

It couldn't be. Her voice gave her away.

"Mother?"

Chapter Nineteen

Darby Summers and Diedre Redman were one in the same. She removed her sunglasses exposing her familiar blue eyes examining me, as if I was a sample in a Petrie dish. Hair no longer blond but brunette. She looked thinner, her face tighter than before, maybe a face lift. Her thin lips and mouth seemed stretched, upturned, reminding me of a clown smile. My knees felt weak. I reached for the edge of Jayson's desk to steady myself.

Nandi pushed a chair to me so I could sit. I heard several voices excitedly speak, but I was so light-headed I could not focus. Nandi's voice came through the swirling din. "Are you, okay? Cody?" I nodded, dazed. The solidity of the chair helped. I buried my head against her chest.

"You must be mistaken." Nandi said, "She can't be your mother."

The click of high heels approached and stopped. She was near.

"But I am, dear," my mother said to Nandi. "I am not proud I left all those years ago, Cody, but it was best for us to part ways. You were growing up. Our revenue stream could no longer fuel the goals I set in life."

"Your goals?" I said. "I am your son."

"I know, Cody. I know I am not what a mother should be. I never have been. But look, in my defense, what I took from Sal Martino and Putz gave me the capital to begin my empire and the chance for you to have what you always wanted, a life of anonymity."

"That's not what I wanted." I said.

"Pity. We would never have met again if not for that girl in the bird sanctuary."

I looked up at her. Those ice eyes bore through me. The facelift with the lips upturned into a tight smirk was the sizzling fuse that ignited the bomb inside. I knew her voice, I recognized her eyes, but I did not know this woman. I bolted from the chair almost knocking Nandi to the floor.

"What did you do to her? Where is she, you fucking witch!"

My mother's bodyguard moved quickly to her side, placing a hand on the pistol. Nandi pulled me back. Darby Summers coolly addressed him.

"No need, he is harmless . . . like his father."

The man released his grip on the pistol. She then glanced over her shoulder. Jayson and William were speechless. Tears streamed down Thad's cheek.

"I would like to have a moment with my son. I will answer whatever questions you may have afterwards. We will deal later with the Lois and Nigel situation as well at the community meeting with the residents."

Jayson and William moved toward the door. Jayson suddenly stopped and blurted, "outrageous!" before leaving. William pantomimed a phone call pointing at me. He hissed, bitch in the direction of my mother. Thad didn't budge.

"Thad," said my mother. "Please leave. This is a family matter.

And you too, young lady, please go." She waved her hand in the direction of Nandi, as if she were brushing away a fly.

"Family?" said Thad. "How the fuck are you family? I am the closest thing he has to family. You've been gone for thirteen years. I'm staying."

"So am I!" Nandi said defiantly.

"Is Sierra alive?" It was difficult to repress my rage. Every nerve in my body tingled.

Mother turned to me. I fantasized wrapping my hands around her neck.

"I was aware of your trouble with the Martino's and ordered a liaison to get your girlfriend safely across the border providing her family enough money to reestablish their lives. They were in danger, so I planned for them to start anew. You can say thank you now."

I stared at her. This had not been my mother's decision to make.

"Sal knew you two were close. He threatened your girlfriend and her family. My liaison told your girlfriend she could no longer contact you. It would be your death if she did. That is why she never called." My mother eyed Nandi. "What a beautiful young woman," she said to me. "You should not be upset, considering your current situation."

"Why did you do that? To deprive me of any chance of happiness? You're a monster."

I didn't want to hurt Nandi. I hoped she understood. But it was not up to my mother to decide for me.

"I wanted to protect you," my mother said. "You needed to

stay on Lemuria Down for your own safety. Honestly, I never intended you to live here. This place is to be my legacy. I want to be immortalized for creating the building blocks for the future model society. But my hands were tied. I had no other choice but to bring you here."

"You didn't want to see me," I said foolishly. I was having trouble keeping up. I was a boy whose mother didn't love him.

"Bullshit," said Thad. "It was to protect your own identity first, save his life second. That's why you wanted to keep a tab on him and have me be his zookeeper. Keep him alive but never tell him where you are and who you are!"

"What? You knew all along?" I was knocked over by another tsunami of truth. I was drowning.

"She put me in a shitty spot, Cody! She said you needed protection. But I stayed with you because you are my friend. My best friend."

"Don't forget to mention you were paid handsomely," said my mother.

My mother paid him? Was his fake novel even a fake?

"You people are horrid!" Nandi took a step toward Thad. The bodyguard reached for his pistol. She held her ground.

"Cut the brit shit, Nandi," Thad said. "You are fucking horrid for taking advantage of Cody. You got what you wanted. A cheap lay."

"That's not true!" I shouted.

Nandi lunged at Thad, throwing him against the wall and then slapping him several times as he slumped to the floor, shielding his head. The bodyguard grabbed Nandi's mid-section, lifting her off the floor. "Calm down, little one," he said.

Nandi kicked wildly catching her heal in the bodyguard's groin. He fell backwards with Nandi landing on top, causing a loud crash rattling beakers on Jayson's desk. My mother calmly strode toward the door. She turned, dispassionately surveyed the tumult, while her bodyguard groaned, one hand on his nuts, the other on the back of his head. Nandi sat stunned.

The body guard's pistol had been flung across the floor. My mother stooped, picked it up and held it limply by her side.

"Come, Parker, I must talk to Doctor Robinette." My mother turned her icy glare to me. "We will talk more when cooler heads prevail."

The bodyguard rolled on his side and pushed himself up with a pained expression. Mother was almost out the door.

"Where is she?" I yelled.

My mother stopped. "Her family was enroute to Puerto Penasco," she said, without turning back to look at me. "That was the last communication I received from my liaison."

"Where's father!" I demanded. She stopped once more.

"Mexico City. Your girl asked for his whereabouts, so I told her. I suppose the poor thing thought he could save you. Seems all the ones you love go to Mexico."

Then she was gone. Thad scrambled to his feet.

"I swear I will fix this." He left, too.

I stood frozen in disbelief. There was too much to process. I couldn't form a thought. I was brought back by Nandi. "What do you need right now?" she asked, which was kind. I had just confronted my mother about taking Sierra from me, in front of her.

I could not think of a thing.

"I need to be alone for now," I said, wishing it wasn't true, "Sort things out."

"Of course," she said. "I better check in with my parents. Want me to come back?"

"Maybe. I don't know. Sorry."

She kissed my cheek and left. First my mother, than Thad. Now Nandi, even though I had basically sent her away.

Back in my little house, my first thought was to try calling Sierra. I dug out the last burner phone from a nightstand drawer. I dialed the number I had for her. My flame of hope was doused when it rang once followed by a no longer in service voice notification.

My second thought was to find a way off the island. I took a beer from the fridge and took a deep draw. I was about to settle into my couch when there was a knock on the door. It was Lesmour. I was so glad to see him. He opened his mouth, but I cut him off.

"Help me get off this island," I said.

"That's why I'm here. Thad told me. I can't believe Darby Summers is your mom! She has restricted travel, but Thad said he can help you leave. He sent me."

I laughed bitterly. The idea of Thad helping me was comical. Did he help me all the years he was my for-hire friend? I went to the fridge. Lesmour followed me like a hungry puppy. I passed him a beer and we sat on the couch. Lesmour was babbling about Thad being a good guy even though he was mostly an asshole. I ignored him. I weighed my options. I had none.

"Is he home?" I asked. Lesmour shook his head and pointed to my patio.

Thad stood on my patio peering in through the slider. It was dark but I could see the outline of his face from the kitchen lights. He looked like a kitten that was left outside in the rain waiting for its owner to let him in. I sighed, got another beer out of the fridge, and rolled back the slider handing him the bottle. We had a history. I shoved my way past him taking a seat on a lounge chair.

"I thought we were friends," I said.

"Dude, you are my best friend, my brother. You know that."

"Did he know about my mother hiring you?" I nodded to Lesmour.

"Of course not. He would have blabbed it years ago."

Lesmour angerly protested. This struck me immediately as true.

"You have to tell all, start to finish," I said, "The truth, and if you don't, I am done with you."

Lesmour sank in a chair by the table. Thad pulled up a chair. His expression changed. The signature smirk was gone. It was the three of us, like before, drinking slightly better beer, in Hawaii. But the person I knew for so long was not there. I did not know that Thad could lie to me like this.

"A week before your parents left, your mother stopped me on my way home from school. She insisted on giving me a ride. She said she needed to ask a favor. She and your dad were going out of town and could I ask my parents to take you in. I asked her where they were going. She told me they were in trouble, and no one could know their whereabouts, not even you. I was afraid you were in trouble, too, but she assured me you were safe for now. I knew my parents would take you in. I was afraid about my safety, too, but your mom was persuasive. Then she brought up my compensation. She paid me to keep you safe."

"How much?" I asked.

"Fifteen hundred a month plus fifty thousand upfront."

I felt my anger rise but held back.

"After graduation, she told me to change your identity and keep you out of the public eye. That's when we moved into The Oasis and lived in squalor, a place no one would think to find you. She checked in once in a while to make sure I was keeping my end of the bargain. When I told her about Gus and Sal's family wanting payback, she suggested we run off to Lemuria Down. You know the rest."

"We were hiding out?" I asked.

"Well, yes," Thad said. "I mean we were living our lives, and thought the people after your mom couldn't find us. So, yes, we hid out. Turns out Martino knew you never left. He chose not to look for you until his brother's lieutenant started snooping around and Gus recognized you."

"And you were in touch with my mom?"

"She kept in touch via email and poured money into my bank account. All those times you asked me to try to find them, I lied to you. I knew where they were"

"My Dad too? You knew he was in Mexico?"

"Mexico City, to be precise. He is part of a local theater group, he's typecast as either the ugly American or stupid gringo. Your mother has been bouncing around the globe making real estate investments, working to build the capital needed to create Lemuria Down."

This was too much. That this place, Lemuria Down was my mothers. And I was here. But not because she wanted me.

"Of course," Thad said. "She had to change her identity so Martino's family wouldn't come after her. She became Darby Summers, avoided the public eye. Cody, I am truly sorry. I thought it was the right thing to do."

"And what, this would go on forever, hiding in a miserable dump?"

"No. The deal was to wait until we turned thirty. She would throw us a bunch of money to fly the coop, go wherever we wanted. She thought we would be mature by then and probably Sal's family would have totally given up hunting her down."

I felt as if I was trapped in a fevered dream. Thad's earnest telling of a past I was totally oblivious to was shocking but not as disturbing as his demeanor. The Thad I knew was no longer there. This was a different Thad, soft spoken, devoid of arrogance and cynicism.

"You are acting strange," I said. "You are not acting like yourself."

"Actually I am. This is the real me. Don't you remember? I was a nice guy long ago."

I had to think back to when we first met. I had been ostracized when I first started public school. My grade school years were all homeschooled by tutors. That ended once the revenue stream from the Cody Redd Show dwindled. Public school was free. I was bullied by most boys because I was the sheltered child star. Thad had befriended me. He changed during the last year of high school, becoming more cynical and abrasive with each semester.

"I changed my act once your mother hired me. It was to keep you close. I wanted you to believe the outside world sucked. I knew how vulnerable you were when they left so I used that as a tool. Convincing you to hide out in that crummy apartment was the best way to keep us safe. I played the part of a recluse knowing you would follow my lead."

My temper flared.

"All this for fifty grand and fifteen hundred a month!"

"Yes and to keep you safe. It wasn't a total act. I really did think the world sucked. All three of our parents sucked and it was a dangerous place with clowns like Martino roaming around. Might as well be stoned hermits."

Lesmour went to the fridge returning with beer passing them to Thad and me while keeping one for himself. Lesmour paced a little then confronted Thad.

"So you being a dick all these years was an act?"

"Not so much with you, Pumpkin Head. You always annoyed me."

It was an effort to suppress my anger. I needed Thad in order to get off the island and find Sierra. I asked him if what my mother said was true, that Sierra might be in Puerto Penasco.

"It's true," he said. "All roads lead to Rocky Point, but that is a cold trail now."

"You said you can fix this."

"Your mother announced that stupid travel ban on the guise all watercraft is needed to search for Lois and Nigel but there really isn't anyone to enforce it. Tomorrow she is going to address the community and pretend they are still missing. She will not divulge what we already knows. She will intensify search and rescue to buy her time until she can figure out how to handle the PR blowback. My guess is she will say no evidence of them were ever found. It was just an unfortunate incident. She can't have people in her perfect wonderland offing themselves. Bad for business. People, out of civic duty will comply for now but I have an idea to end her travel ban immediately so we can get you off the island."

The Thad that I had grown accustomed to surfaced. His sneer appeared briefly.

"How about Martino?"

"He will not be a problem. I can book you a flight to Mexico from Los Angeles. Jeffery, my love, are you still in communique with Christine?"

Lesmour scowled.

"I told you she ghosted me, Thad!"

"Send me her number. I have an offer she can't refuse. She will respond if a gross amount of money is concerned."

Thad took from his shirt pocket a pipe and lighter. He lit it then passed it on. Lesmour went to his place bringing back left-over pizza. It was almost like our early days in Lemuria Down, the many nights on my back patio getting high, drinking, and eating. We did our best to keep the conversation light. At times I found myself wanting to scream at Thad while also feeling sorry for him. My mother used him just like she did me except he made a lot of money in the process. I did not. Lesmour was strangely a comfort. He was still Lesmour and always would be. He was the one, aggravating constant in our lives. Thad received a text notification. When he looked at the message he smiled.

"It's Colleen," he said. "We are madly in love. In a way I am glad this all came out. I don't have to pretend anymore."

Thad stood and stretched. Another text rang simultaneously on our phones. It was a message to the entire community announcing Darby Summers will speak 2pm tomorrow. It said she will give the latest update on Lois and Nigel's disappearance stating it was imperative to temporarily shut down travel to and from the island until the couple was found. The message encouraged residents to continue their search and rescue operations. Thad smirked.

"She is blowing smoke, just like I said. Good. I will have time to work before her meeting. I can even get some sleep. What I have in mind will not be too difficult."

I asked what did he have in mind. He smiled putting his finger to his lips.

"It's a secret. I am staying at Colleen's tonight but will get to the consort bright and early. Later gents."

Lesmour stayed a while longer. He was jabbering about a humpback whale he saw on one of his tourist fishing cruises. I was high and his non-stop stream of words had the effect of a white noise machine. I yawned several times then asked him to leave. I took a shower and swallowed two pain killers for my shin then kicked back in the recliner to elevate my legs. My cellphone rang. It was Nandi.

"I told my parents everything," she said.

"You weren't supposed to."

"Fuck your mother. I can't withhold that from them. They are ready to leave the island. We are moving back to London. But good news. They are horrified what your mother did and are now fine with me spending time with you. Should I come over? You want to see me, don't you?"

I hesitated responding, torn wanting her but feeling guilt knowing Sierra is most likely alive. She chided me.

"We are leaving on the first boat we can find. Don't be a wimp. I will be a memory in a few days."

This hit me, too. Nandi was leaving. Everybody leaves.

"I don't think we can be . . . intimate."

"Cody," Nandi said. "Get over yourself. I am leaving. We can snuggle. That's all."

"Ok, just snuggle."

I knew we were bullshitting.

Chapter Twenty

Our escapades under the sheets intensified, knowing they would end. Sunrise, we watched the morning news. We sat upright in bed, drinking coffee as the local station reported my mother's appearance would be televised so residents who cannot make the gathering will have a chance to view it. Darby Summers, my mother, had scheduled the community meeting at an open-air theater used for movies and live performances. It had plenty of seating including a canopied sound system and a large screen. According to the news, Lois and Nigel were still missing.

"Ha!" Nandi laughed. "Latest news my arse. She whipped up more lies."

I wondered if my mother would be able to conceal the bad press of a duo suicide. News of it leaking could shake confidence in her faux paradise, a blemish on her legacy. She would have to convince whoever found Nigel's body to remain silent, possibly pay him off. It occurred to me that we would all have to stay silent indefinitely. For once I had leverage on my mother. I thought it best not to do anything with this power, for the moment. Maybe my mother might come clean and tell the residents the truth knowing our group Parasites in Paradise and concerned friends will not stand for more lies. I thought it would be prudent to not take any action in case Thad's secret plan did work although I doubted his ability to make it right.

Lesmour called. Despite the nautical search, there was no sign of Lois. His boss was certain she was washed out to sea. Nandi put her coffee on the nightstand and grabbed my penis.

"Again?" she asked. I spilled my cup. There was a knock on the front door. I put on a bathrobe to see who it was.

It was William. He was upset. Another elderly couple were found dead in their home. A mutual friend went to check on them. The friend invited them for dinner, but they did not show or call to cancel. She went to check on them and when no one answered, she let herself in. The woman found them in bed. William was so excited he was practically shouting. Nandi heard it all.

"Is it for the same reason?" Nandi asked.

"They left a note on their nightstand stating they are going to a better place."

William went on to say the woman called island security and they informed my mother. She asked security and the friend of the couple to stay quiet until she could address the community that afternoon. I asked him how he learned about their deaths.

"Ms. Summers volunteered Thad to assist hacking their emails and phone in order to see if any foul play was involved. He told Jayson and I the couple were in contact with Christine. They transferred money into her bank account. Thad was sure it was compensation for Heavenly Vacation pills."

The day was a slow drip of minutes waiting until it was time for my mother to address all of Lemuria Down. Nandi and I killed time at the beach, laying out, listening to waves. It was quiet. We had an early lunch, my new favorite, a poke' and avocado bowl from Pig and Poi with mango juice instead of beer. Beer always tastes best on a beach, but we felt it wasn't the time to drink.

After eating I became drowsy. The waves soothed. My lids felt heavy. I woke to find Nandi not by my side. Sitting up I saw her squatting at the shoreline washing a shell she had found in the sand. I pushed myself up and joined her.

"You collect shells?" I asked.

"Just this one. It was sticking out of the sand. The surf unmasked it."

The shell was a large pink conch. Except for a small chip at the outer edge it was a perfect specimen.

"This will be my memento from my time here. My parents already secured a flat in London. We will be off to the U.K. on the first boat out."

She ran her index finger across the smooth pearl white underside of the conch to its pink interior. I didn't know what to say.

"Is Cody Redman going to miss me?"

"Of course."

She took her finger from the path to the inner part of the conch and ran it across my lips. It tickled slightly. I drew her close. We kissed. Nandi stepped back and smiled although a tear ran down her cheek.

"But not enough, luv. Come, it is time for your mother to spread her shite."

The amphitheater was overflowing. At the back of the stage the large projection screen used normally for movies displayed Welcome Darby Summers overlayed on an arial view of Lemuria

Down. I found Lesmour in the very last row. Colleen was beside him but not Thad. Colleen told us Thad volunteered to do the audio-visual part of the presentation. All the seats were taken so Nandi, and I rolled out our beach blanket on the crest of a hill. A buzz of excited voices pervaded while some musicians played tranquil island sounds infused with a jazz rhythm. It was weird not seeing Lois fluttering around the stage. She so enjoyed the community events. To the side of the stage I spotted Thad in the canopied booth studiously fiddling with equipment. William stepped on stage; Jayson was absent. He approached the band and spoke to a seated acoustic guitarist who nodded. William nervously waited while the band finished the song and exited the stage. William adjusted a cordless mic pinned on his button-down shirt tapping it to be sure it was on. He cleared his throat and spoke clearly although in a slightly surly manner.

"Although not in the best of circumstances," he began, and then glanced offstage. There stood my mother with her body-guard. "please welcome, the creator of Lemuria Down, Ms. Darby Summers."

Had the introduction been given a month earlier, my mother would have received thunderous applause, but her shine and luster was tarnished by the disappearance of Lois and Nigel. The applause was polite, maybe better defined as uncertain. It ended abruptly when she took the stage.

Overdressed for a tropical island, she wore a sleek blue dress that clung to her thin frame. Her hair pinned up and stiletto heels made her look taller than she was. She wore a lot of gold, gold necklace, bracelets, watch, earrings, the only exception two rings with large emerald stones all matched well with her air of detached dominance.

"I suppose it was presumptuous of me to attempt to create a utopian society," she began. "We are human not machine."

I laughed, thinking she was the closest person I had known to have more machine qualities than human.

"There are bound to be imperfections. I know you are all worried about the recent disappearance of Nigel and Lois Peters. We will get to the bottom of this to restore order and give confidence to the outside world that we truly have developed a society humanity may use as a template for peace and posterity. I am asking you, citizens of Lemuria Down, to use whatever sources necessary to help find our missing citizens."

A woman close to the stage shouted: "Admit it! They must be dead by now!"

The audience rumbled. Another voice shot out from the growing discontent, "We are not Guinea Pigs!" The bodyguard who was offstage moved two steps behind my mother. Lesmour bent near me and said above the din. "Wow they are pissed at your mother!" People near us eyed me suspiciously. I told him to shut up. My mother held up her hands to quell the crowd. Sunlight striking her bracelet and other jewelry flashed like lightning bolts as she waved her arms to lower the volume of the townspeople. She reminded me of Thor.

"We must remain calm and focused. We must hope for the best. For all we know . . ."

The image on the screen welcoming my mother suddenly went black. Video from the trail surveillance camera rolled showing the moment Lois and Nigel took the little used path to the top of the falls. It then cut to the final moments of Lois and Nigel before they put the camera in the basket and jumped. The townspeople at first were hushed, not sure of what they saw.

Then the friend of the other couple that perished stood, no longer wishing to remain silent.

"My friends committed suicide just like Lois and Nigel! She wants to cover it up!"

The crowd became a mob, raised fists, invectives, someone even ripped off a tiki torch from a nearby restaurant and charged the stage until the bodyguard pushed him with such force that he fell backwards striking the back of his head on the stage floor. The tiki torch man lay limp as a woman rushed to his aid. The bodyguard whisked my mother to an autonomous vehicle. They sped away swiping against an awning pole to a produce store spilling fruits and vegetables across the white roadway.

A new video on the outdoor screen appeared of Thad himself, a giant, imposing head shot. The volume was turned up high as he spoke which got the attention of his audience.

"People of Lemuria Down, you have been lied to," Thad spoke in a booming voice. It reminded me of the scene from *The Wizard of Oz* where the fake Wizard frightened the cowardly lion. Thad slouched behind the a/v panel under the canopy and took a long pull from his beer then continued. "Nigel's body has been found. Lois' body is still missing. It is clear they have committed suicide. Our utopian society is a sham created by Darby Summers to feed her own ego and greed. Darby Summers is a fraud. She is really Diedre Redman, producer of the once popular Cody Redd Show, a narcissistic mother who used her only son for profit and then abandoned him."

Thad inserted on the screen a current pic of my mother as Darby Summers next to an earlier one from an interview magazine cover with a younger version of me by her side. Besides the hair color, it was obvious they were the same person. Thad put the final nail in my mother's coffin.

"Citizens! You have been manipulated just like this innocent child! There is not a single altruistic bone in our leaders' body. Lemuria Down is also floundering! I have proof we are hemorrhaging money and will be bankrupt before the year is through! Our utopia is a farce!"

People jumped to their feet. The audience in sound and activity acted like a pot of water left to boil over on a stove. Amid the din I made out some individual shouts, people replicating Thad's last shrieking statement, "It is a lie!" while a smaller faction tried to restore order. Two older people climbed on stage as William made a hasty exit. They used an open mic to declare that Lemuria Down could still be a utopian society if the people wanted it to be, but they were roundly booed. The tiki torch guy that charged the stage earlier wobbled to his feet and yelled invectives at the couple until they retreated.

Colleen grabbed my arm.

"Thad's in trouble!"

Two men were in Thad's face arguing. One man chest bumped him, and Thad pushed him away. I dodged and darted to the outskirts of the fracas with Colleen, Nandi and Lesmour following. By the time we reached Thad, two more men were harassing him. Thad shouted, "I am just the messenger, man!" Lesmour and I got between Thad and the men while Colleen grabbed him by the waist attempting to pull him away. A muscular guy took a swing at me, grazing my shoulder. Nandi kicked the back of his knee with a tremendous force creating a sickening crack. The man fell to the ground wailing. It gave us the diversion needed to escape the chaos, piling in the nearest electric vehicle. Colleen sat on Thad's' lap in the front while Lesmour and I jumped in the back as Nandi sped through a winding residential area. Thad took a call from William. He called to make sure we were safe then told us to come to their house to discuss an exit strategy off the island. When sure no one was following; she drove to William and Jayson's house. William was waiting outside as we pulled up.

I confronted Thad as we left the electric vehicle.

"This is your idea on how to fix things? This will be all over! Martino will know who my mother is! He will figure out where I am too!"

Thad cackled. He shrugged his shoulders mockingly.

"This is what you wanted, Cody. You wanted the truth, so I put it to the good people of Lemuria Down. You wanted Sal off your back. He will soon know Darby Summers is your mom. He won't care about you anymore. He got what he wanted. You are off the hook and so is your girlfriend. I could have been killed back there. You should thank me."

Colleen was incensed.

"You could have been killed? You created a near riot! Anybody could have been killed! I loved this place, and you ruined it. Screw you!"

Before Thad could stop her, Colleen climbed in the autonomous vehicle and sped away. Thad was downcast for a moment mumbling, "Not the first time she told me to fuck off. She'll get over it," then walked the path to William and Jayson's front door.

Jayson was reclining in an easy chair, looking like a silent film damsel in a fit of melancholia on her bedroom settee. His eyes were closed and remained that way even after William had us sit. Lesmour asked for a beer like it was a social gathering. William glared at him.

"Jayson and I, as I am sure the rest of you, were blindsided by Thad's presentation. While we did not approve his method of delivery, we recognize it was best to tell the residents the truth.

That being said, we are not safe here. People know Jayson and I have been communicating with Darby Summers. By affiliation with us, you are also in danger. We must leave before it gets worse."

Nandi spoke up, insisting her parents must come. She also suggested that maybe people will calm themselves after the initial shock. Thad cleared his throat.

"I doubt that" he stated. "I did a deep dive on many residents and cherry picked the most reactionary personalities I could find to stir the pot. This morning I text seeded them dark truths about the island no one was privy to. The island really is going under financially. I wanted to create as much unrest as possible before I did the presentation. I uncovered a few people that snuck on the island under false pretenses like Cody, Lesmour, and me. One was even acquitted of a murder charge."

"My career is over," Jayson moaned softly, his eyes still closed in repose, "It will be forever tainted by this folly."

"I can steal a boat," Lesmour said.

Jayson snapped out of his melancholic pose, sat up with eyes wide open. I asked Lesmour how could he procure a boat when access to and from the island was prohibited. Lesmour said he padlocked to a dock the fishing boat he used in the search, so only he could use it. William suggested a sunset departure meeting at a remote location to avoid confrontation. It would give us time to pack, and the cover of a setting sun would be safer than broad daylight.

Lesmour sprung to his feet saying he better hurry. He had the keys, but he was afraid someone might cut the padlock and hot wire the craft. He would anchor it in a cove while the rest of us got ready then text us where we could meet at sundown. William and Jayson excused themselves to pack. Thad tried to get an autonomous vehicle for us, but none were available. It was an ominous sign that many people were moving about. Where they were going was uncertain and disturbing. Our only option was to walk home. Nandi called her parents to relay the plan. They were already packed. They had not attended the event because they were preparing for a catered afterglow of the presentation in honor of Darby Summers. It was in a park by the beach. People ransacked the place. They told Nandi it was too dangerous to come into town. Her parents would meet her at my house.

"Are they going to be ok?" I asked.

"My dad has a black belt," she said. "And my mum is not to be trifled with."

Walking downhill made my shin act up to the point I was limping by the time I reached my house. Thad veered off to his place to pack. We were all leaving. I wondered what my mother was up to. I gathered what I needed, clothes, toiletries, and the camera I used for nature photography then went to Lesmour's to pack his essential belongings while he got the boat. Nandi said her parents had her belongings ready as well as theirs. Through a text thread, Lesmour announced he swiped the fishing boat. Lesmour said his fellow captains were already taking passengers to Kauai in larger boats, damn the travel ban. He messaged us to meet at a tiny beach on the eastern part of the island. The trail in back of our homes would lead us there.

William replied on the thread saying he and Jayson were on their way to my place. Nandi messaged her parents to find out how close they were. When they did not reply she called. No answer. The local news station reported Darby Summers was a fraud and profiteer not a philanthropist, intent on making the world a better place. Overlaying video showed panic at the seaport as scores of people tried to leave. Lemuria Down had unraveled. Nandi called her parents again.

"Nearly there, luv," Nandi heard her father reply, panting.

Moments later they entered. They could not procure a vehicle, so they had to haul many bags with them. Nandi's mother had overpacked. Nandi offered them water. Her father drank half a glass then glowered at me.

"So you're Cody," he said. I nodded immediately on the defensive. "You've been playing with my little girl's affections. I don't like it."

He wiped perspiration off his brow then drank the rest. Nandi told his father to knock it off. He was athletic and large while his wife was short but wiry. With his size and a black belt he could have easily snapped me in half. My stomach fluttered and my groin tingled. I was too scared to reply.

"You get a mulligan given the circumstances," he continued. "First order of things is to get off this island."

Thad hurried through my patio slider, carrying a suitcase and an overstuffed backpack, followed by Jayson and William. He cheerfully announced he convinced Colleen to leave with him. She loved the concept of Lemuria Down, but she had to admit it was all a dream. Thad sweetened the pot by promising her a happy life on the Hawaiian Island of her choice. He divulged he made solid investments with the up-front money my mother gave him and amassed a small fortune. I shook my head in wonder.

By the time Colleen reached my house, all our suitcases and bags were stacked on the back patio. We took drinks and energy bars to pack in a small cooler. Thad made a point of scouring our homes for weed too. His only lament leaving Lemuria Down behind was the excellent weed grown locally. Hauling our belongings was difficult on the narrow trail. It ran in the opposite direction of the path to the volcano's waterfall, so it was little used and slightly overgrown. Backpacks and suitcases continually snagged on branches and vines. We were glad not to encounter anyone else. It was a good idea to exit through the back door so to speak because most residents evacuating were trying to leave by the port.

Late afternoon shadows draped over the mountainside by the time we reached the cove. The trail took us to the small beachhead where Lesmour moored the fishing boat twenty feet from shore. It was a neat and trim vessel, but I was uncertain if it would provide safe passage considering the number of passengers boarding. He raised the anchor upon seeing us and started its engine gesturing us to move to a natural jetty of lava stone. When we reached the spot he tossed two lines for Thad and me to tie onto kukui trees. On the starboard side rubber tires were attached so when Lesmour expertly chugged the boat to the edge of the lava jetty they provided a safe cushion. The waters were calm making it easy to board. Nandi and I were the last to board.

We untied the lines, tossed them to Lesmour and Thad then quickly hopped on. I lost my footing as I landed but Nandi's father caught me preventing a header against the portside gunwale.

I thanked him.

"Should have let you go," he said.

I was impressed how deftly Lesmour backed out of the cove and hit the open sea. If nothing else, he had found himself. He was a sea captain. He told everyone to stay seated, admitting the little fishing boat was not made to carry the number of passengers we had onboard. He stressed unexpected movements were not advised, stating as an example if we saw a whale on the portside and all moved to get a glimpse there was a fair chance we would capsize.

"Just point," he said. "Don't move."

Jayson and William sat at the stern in chairs designed for deep sea fishing. Nandi sat with her parents on a bench near Lesmour at the helm. I wanted to be with Nandi, but her father scared me. She picked up on my fear when I looked back at her. She winked at me devilishly before I sat with Thad and Colleen. Colleen's mood had changed since Thad told her they could live on any Hawaiian island of her choosing. He topped it off by saying she wouldn't have to deliver pizzas for the rest of her life. She had her arm locked with his and pecked him on the cheek. He smiled sheepishly.

"The Big Island," was all she said. Thad put his arm around her and laughed although it wasn't like his signature cackle. It was deep throated and warm. She sighed and closed her eyes. In minutes she was asleep basking in the warm sunset.

Thad and I were silent. The hum of the outboard and the waves smacking against the bow was soothing. Behind us, Lesmour jabbered Nandi's parents, hardly taking a breath. I couldn't make out what he was saying. Thankfully, the waves and motor drowned most of him out. It sounded like his typical boasting although this time I was sure none of it was bullshit.

"So the Big Island it is," I said to Thad. "Think your babysitting money investments will cover that?"

He smiled.

"I hit Bitcoin at the right time, got out at the right time. Played the stock market, did well. Your mother provided me some solid tips. She is evil but knows how to make a dollar, until her Lemuria Down fiasco. What's more, yesterday my parents told me they have been passing my unfinished manuscript around. Cody, they found an agent and the guy is certain he can find a publisher once it's done. He thinks I am the second coming of James Joyce. Can you believe that?"

His cackle laugh resurfaced. Colleen stirred, smiled then went back to sleep.

"You're full of shit."

"I kid you not. All I have to do is finish it using the asinine algorithm I came up with. I hope I don't have to do book tours because I don't know what the fuck it's about. I guess I could obfuscate then they will knock me off as an intellectual. You still going to track down Sierra?"

"Yep. Although her parents might want to kill me too for getting them mixed up in this."

"What about her?"

Thad motioned toward the stern. I turned around. I could only see the back of Nandi's head. She was looking out at the water. She was so beautiful. I felt so good around her.

"We had an agreement," I said. As if to convince myself. "It was just a casual thing."

Thad chortled.

"You had an agreement, but that ain't the truth, buddy boy. That girl loves you and you know it. Do you love her?"

I was nauseous but it wasn't from being at sea. Lemuria Down was almost out of sight. Kauai would not be in view for another couple of hours. I thought of Nandi and Sierra, thought of how only a small percentage of the ocean has been explored. Love was far more mystifying than the ocean.

"Is it possible to love two women at the same time?" I asked.

"Of course," Thad replied. "You just have to decide how to handle it."

"I made a promise to Sierra. I don't want to hurt, Nandi."

"Too late," Thad said, then stood, separating himself from sleeping Colleen and waved toward the bow shouting Nandi's name. She stood as he shouted, "Cody says hi!"

I shot a glance and saw Nandi laughing, while her father glowered. I quickly turned and punched Thad in the arm. He sat down as Colleen woke again puzzled by the commotion.

"Don't worry," he said to me. "She is strong as hell. Whatever happens, she will be fine."

The sun had set. Lesmour turned on only the cabin lights so we could admire the night sky teaming with stars. I was chilled by the spray from the bow. Colleen and Thad snuggled. I asked him about Christine and the Heavenly Vacation pills.

"I bribed her. I told her if she handed over the remaining pills she would not be charged with breaking and entering. Naturally she wanted compensation, so we made a deal. She gives me the pills; I give her a bank check. I have the money already wired to a bank on Kauai. When we get there I will go to her garbage scow and make the exchange."

The sway of the small fishing boat and the drone of its motor helped me drift off to sleep. I woke when the engine was cut, and the boat jerked slightly as we reached Kauai Harbor. Lesmour had the navigation lights on. As we approached, the dock was swarming with Lemuria Down refugees. Passengers from various crafts were milling about the dock toting luggage. Ubers and cabs rolled in and were immediately taken. Lesmour asked Thad and I to tie the boat down once we were near the dock. The water was choppy. Both Thad and I had to time our leaps so as not to take a spill. Wrapping the rope around the dock cleats someone noticed Thad.

"It's him! The one on the screen!"

Thad braced himself for invectives or worse. The man, with his wife and two adolescent daughters, ran up to Thad causing him to flinch. Instead of a punch the man grabbed Thad's hand and shook it.

"It took courage to speak the truth. I was able to get my old job back and take our house back home off the market. If we stayed on fantasy island any longer we would have lost everything. Thanks."

We made our way off the dock without further incident. The cover of darkness helped along with a crowd of fellow islanders who were more intent on securing a ride to their final destination. While waiting for an available Uber, Thad reserved a couple of rooms at Motel Lani while William and Jayson spent a fortune for a room at the Hilton. Nandi and her parents were invited to stay at a friend's house, a restaurant owner originally from the UK.

William and Jayson were the first to be picked up. The Hilton had their own shuttle service. We said our goodbyes. Jayson was still in a state of shock and was not very responsive. I said I was sorry for all that happened, although I had little to do with it.

"As William often says," replied Jayson, "Shit happens."

He gave a feeble wave and eased his tall frame into the shuttle. William drew near and whispered.

"This will make an excellent final chapter to my memoir..." Smiling, he squeezed my hand then joined his partner in the van.

Nandi tapped me on the shoulder.

"We have a flight out early morning," she said.

Nandi drew close, smiling sweetly, sadly. I glanced over her shoulder. Her parents were staring. I thought, "fuck it" then hugged her and gave a peck on the lips.

"Don't be a stranger, luv," Nandi said.

Her father called. Their friends were parked in a nearby lot waiting. I watched them make their way through the crowd until I lost sight. She was gone. I let her go. Months before I watched Sierra fade into the throng of people on Mill Avenue. I felt the same sense of panic and loss. I hated goodbyes. I had my parents to thank for that.

The Uber for Thad, Colleen, Lesmour and I arrived. After dropping bags in our rooms we found a small bar by Motel Lani where we had some mediocre food and cold beers. On the ride to the motel, Thad had already managed to find a VRBO on The Big Island for he and Colleen. It would give them time to house hunt. Despite the long day and tumultuous events, Colleen was ecstatic. Lesmour was uncharacteristically quiet. He poked at his hamburger and fries. Colleen was on her phone chattering to a real estate agent about different properties until he interrupted.

"Not that anyone cares," Lesmour said. "I'm staying here."

Colleen put down her phone. In all the excitement, we had ignored Lesmour. I felt a pang of guilt. We didn't even thank him for getting us out of Lemuria Down. It was surprising to hear he didn't want to tag along with Thad or me.

"What are you going to do?" I asked.

"A captain I worked with runs whale watches on Kauai. He offered me a job. He even has an efficiency apartment near the marina I can use until I find my own place. I love being on the ocean chasing whales."

As always, Lesmour left himself open for some classic barbs. Thad could have sarcastically compared the size of a whale to Lesmour's head, or if co-workers start calling him chum, don't assume they are being friendly, they could be short on shark bait. Instead Thad said something I thought I would never hear him say to Lesmour.

"I will miss you, buddy."

Lesmour's eyes reddened. He told Thad he could still visit him on The Big Island.

"Sure, just don't make a habit out of it."

Even Lesmour laughed at Thad's quip. Colleen chided Thad then told Lesmour and I the VRBO had three bedrooms, so guests were always welcome. We were the only people in the bar besides the staff except for a huge Hawaiian dude with a thick ponytail and tattoos covering his arms and legs. He grasped a half empty beer stein as he watched a crime show on a small TV over the bar. The kitchen staff was engaged in lively conversation. Dishes rattled while they cleaned up for the night. A bartender wiped down tables and flipped chairs on top so she could sweep the floor. She told us we could stay one more round if we wanted, no hurry. The big Hawaiian sat there as if he was invisible staring at a crime show without paying attention. He only needed a place to direct his eyes. Suddenly, I realized I was on my own.

All those years, growing up with my unfit parents in an isolated, sheltered life, then staying with Thad's family until our exodus to The Oasis, I have never been by myself. Many times I felt alone in my own misery, but there was always a human life form around until our brief stay in Lemuria Down. Even there, Lesmour and Thad were near. We hung out almost every day until the phony utopia revealed itself to be merely a mirage. I was going to search for Sierra, but there were no guarantees I would find her, and I would have to do it on my own. I panicked.

"Can I stay a couple of days? I need to chill and make plans on how to find Sierra."

"Take as long as you like," Colleen said.

Thad told me once they got to the VRBO he would see if he could find Sierra. I asked if he heard anything on mother. He told me before leaving Lemuria Down he leaked the location of Darby Summers secluded home via group text of his cherry picked agitators. Lemuria Down news reported several dissident residents invaded the home, but she and her bodyguard had already flown away via helicopter. The dissidents ransacked the place and set it on fire. Strong winds took the fire close to town. It was difficult to contain because a fair portion of the firefighters had already left.

"Do you think Sal will find her?" I asked.

"Martino and his family now have a lot of incentive, I'll say that. They know she accumulated a load of money on largely their dime. They will want it back and then some. I think we are off the hook."

"Yeah," Lesmour agreed. He had lightened up after confessing his future plans. "She is the big fish. We are minnows. When are you seeing Christine?"

"Tomorrow morning. Want to come?"

"Hell yeah, baby! I want to burn her ass!"

I offered to join them for moral support. Lesmour was thrilled saying it would be the "three amigos" hanging out one last time. It was so lame I almost gagged. Thad cackled sarcastically but said nothing.

We walked to Motel Lani, full and buzzed from beer and the pipe Thad packed. My sleep was troubled by a bizarre dream of me working in Jayson's office back on the island. I was pouring a dark liquid in a beaker when a blinding light emanated from the ceiling. It took the form of a bearded man in a red, flowing robe smoking a joint. It was supposed to be Jesus.

In a Californian surfer voice he told me it was uncool people were using a pill to check out heaven. He said he didn't run a tourist trap, and they were not welcome. He also said he didn't appreciate people dying and then coming back to life. Resurrection was his gig. I was about to explain I wasn't responsible, and he should speak to Christine or Jayson when he vanished up the beam of light through the ceiling.

I woke to harsh light. Forcing my eyes open I realized the blinding light was coming from the bathroom. In the middle of the night Lesmour was taking a dump.

Chapter Twenty-One

Everyone except Colleen slept in due to the thick motel curtains blotting out sunrays. We had a hasty continental breakfast at Motel Lani of coffee and pastries. Colleen stayed behind to search Zillow homes on The Big Island. Thad was able to find the hippie dude that rode us around after escaping Phoenix months before. He actually remembered us and passed a joint. It was a needed mellow. I was anxious about confronting Christine after all she did.

The private dock was north of the main harbor. It was part of a small community of neatly kept bungalows on a private street. We were dropped off in a visitor lot and walked to the dock while our hippy driver waited. At the end of the dock was Christine's boat. She was not onboard. Thad boarded the vessel and inspected the deck below to see if she was sleeping.

"You looking for Chris?"

Startled, we spun around to see a deeply tanned, wrinkled man in shorts, no shirt, and flip flops. Thad joined us and told the man we were supposed to meet Christine. He pointed up the hill to the bungalows.

"She lives in bungalow three. She might be out of town. Ursula hasn't left the dock in a while."

We ascended the hill to bungalow three, the smallest on the street. Lesmour walking briskly, reached the front door first charged that he would have a chance to confront the woman that used him. He banged on the door but no answer. After a few more knocks without a response Thad tried the doorknob. It was not locked so he went in. He called out as we hesitantly entered. Lesmour checked a back room with a screened porch that overlooked the ocean while Thad and I split up to check two bedrooms at the front of the house.

I picked the bedroom near the kitchen. I swung open the door. The room was dark. There was a banyan tree outside it's window that provided perpetual shade and the blinds were drawn. A figure laid on the bed. My eyes adjusted. Christine was lying on her stomach. When I went to wake her, I saw the revolver in her hand. Then I saw the bullet hole to her temple, a dark circle of blood on her pillow. Repulsed, I took a step back hooking my foot on a nightstand table leg and fell against the wall. Thad and Lesmour came running when they heard the ruckus.

"She's dead," I gasped.

Thad pushed past me and turned on the nightstand light. Lesmour shrieked and ran to the visitor parking where the hippy Uber guy waited. Thad placed his hand on her neck feeling for a pulse. He then dropped to his knees.

"What are you doing?" I asked.

"Picking up pills," he said.

By tripping on the nightstand leg, I spilt a glass of water and the Heavenly Vacation pills. Thad found the pharmacy containers under the bed. He stood up after collecting them.

"Asshole," he said, "She took a Heavenly Vacation then wasted herself. Even with all the money I was going to give her it wasn't enough. In a way she was like your mother. She always wanted more. She chose heaven over life."

The man from the dock came in the room. Thad deftly stashed the pill container in his pocket.

"Her body is cold," Thad said, "She's been dead a while."

"Better call the cops," he said and stepped outside to make the call.

I tried to calm Lesmour. We would have to give a statement. A cop came quickly. Thad told him we came to see what her rates were for a fishing excursion then found her body. He went back to his car to call in the suicide and get paperwork.

"Can't they trace her phone to you?" I asked Thad.

"I used one of your burner phones to message her, so I think we're good. She has a history anyway. They might think she offed herself because she got tangled in something she couldn't get out of."

The cop bought the crap. I was afraid Lesmour might crack and say something stupid, but he held up well. He was shaken badly seeing his ex-girlfriend with a bullet in her head. The cop left him alone because of his rattled state of mind. It was past noon by the time he let us leave after we each filled out statements, showing them our fake IDs for Lemuria Down. The Uber driver returned and was tripping over the morning events. He asked too many questions about the body, the bullet wound and if she had any drugs in the house. Thad pointedly said we didn't want to talk about it.

Thad broke the news with Colleen. He told us he had some things to get in town before they took the shuttle to The Big Island in the morning and suggested we meet at Dukes for dinner. Lesmour was in a fog. In our room, he sat on the bed staring into space. I booked the same flight Thad and Colleen had reserved, then sat next to him.

"We had sex. Now she's dead, killed herself. I can't live here."

I was so intent on making plans, I hadn't considered how Lesmour felt. It also occurred to me that since he was staying on the island, the police would come looking for him first if our story didn't hold up. I asked him when did he have to start his new job.

"A week."

"Talk to your captain buddy. He knows what happened on Lemuria Down. Maybe he can help."

He called the captain, while I checked flights to Mexico. I remembered Gus said Sierra wanted to find my father. I could get a flight from L.A. to Mexico City easily. I could also book one to Puerto Penasco where Sierra was last seen. I became excited making travel plans. The thought of finding her was part of the thrill. It was not like me to feel any sense of adventure. I wondered what Mexico would be like, the people, the food, the land. My time in the south Pacific had changed my perspective positively even though it ended in disaster.

Lesmour finished his call with the captain. His seafaring friend said he had a partner in Kona that also ran a whale watch operation. The captain would put in a good word for Lesmour. He was sure they could use him.

"I can live on the same island as Thad!"

I laughed, happy for Lesmour but also amused wondering how Thad would react to the "good" news. He was most likely looking forward to having Lesmour being buffered by a body of water. Thad messaged us saying that from now on we should use our real IDs in making travel arrangements and securing a residence. It would be more difficult for the police to track us down. He was no longer concerned about Martino since my mother had been uncovered. Fortunately I brought my passport. My parents and I went to Cabo San Lucus once for a Cody Redd special playing with beach toys. In retrospect, it was an excuse for my mother to have a paid vacation at Martino's expense. During the trip my father kept saying how relaxed and free he felt in Mexico. No wonder he fled there.

Lesmour waited until we went to Dukes to tell Thad the happy news. Colleen laughed knowing the news irked Thad and said he could stay with them until he found his own place. Thad forced a smile, holding back some nasty comment that he no longer felt he could voice. Thad had a girlfriend, lots of money, a possible book deal and would soon be a homeowner. It was time to grow up.

We shared a pupu platter, poke', and a wonderful macaroni salad with diced bits of pork belly then bought a six pack and hung out on the beach until nightfall. The light from the cruise ship shimmered. A few raindrops fell until the lone cloud drifted away by the constant, gentle breeze.

"Try Mexico City first," Thad said digging his feet in the sand. "I found your father's address. Maybe Sierra reached him."

The prospect of me seeing my father after all these years was strange. I no longer held anger towards him. There was more pity than anything. He was strung along like me. Both of us were pushovers although I don't know why he never tried to contact me.

"Did you find anything on Sierra in Puerto Penasco?"

"The problem is her last name. There are a shit load of people named Gonzalez. I was trying to find possible relatives, couldn't get anything concrete."

Colleen and Lesmour were wading in the waves.

"Think you can handle Pumpkin Head staying with you?"

"Once we get settled, Colleen will help him find a place. She likes doing that shit. I will pass him some bucks, so he won't complain about the expense. Which reminds me..."

He reached into his jacket pocket and pulled out an envelope handing it to me. The envelope was sealed.

"What's this?" I asked.

"The money I was going to pay Christine off with a bank check. I went to the bank and made a new one out to you."

"I don't know what to say."

"Consider it an apology. I shouldn't have taken the deal with your mother. I wasn't a good friend to you."

"Why do you say that?"

Thad laughed and tossed me the last beer.

I waited until I went back to Motel Lani to look at the bank check making sure Lesmour was snoring before sneaking into the bathroom and closing the door. I used my phone flashlight so as not to wake him with the bathroom's glaring light. I ripped open the envelope. The check was made out to Cody Redman for the sum of $50,000, the same amount my mother paid him in lump sum to watch over me. There was a note attached: "For travel expenses, if you need more, just ask. I love you."

Chapter Twenty-Two

The next morning Thad, Colleen and I took the shuttle to the Big Island. Lesmour had to wait for the next flight because ours was full. The next couple of days were a whirlwind for my friends. The rental Thad and Colleen chose was beautiful. It overlooked the ocean and sat on what used to be a banana plantation. Barely unpacked, they set out to hunt houses. I only saw them at dinnertime. Lesmour stopped at the marina before he even reached Thad's to meet the whale fleet owner. He was formally offered a job then found a rental that he could move into by the end of the week. He did complain about the price. As promised, Thad wrote him a check to help out. Lesmour was so overwhelmed by Thad's generosity he bear hugged him.

While everyone was out I took a picture of the bay and sent it to Nandi with the caption, "found another utopia." Within minutes she replied with a pic of her own, a selfie on a London street. She was under an umbrella amid a downpour. She wrote, "Me too, if you are a fish! Registering for university."

I made a call to Birds of a Feather in the hope of reaching Gus. I thought before I booked a flight to Mexico I would check in case he had any news of Sierra. I hoped by some miracle she made it back to the states. The phone rang a few times before a young guy answered. He said Gus was in the back then yelled for him. I heard Gus in the distance ask the young guy to find out who was calling and if he could call back. He was busy.

"Tell him it's Cody."

I heard Gus give out a hoot of joy. He told the young guy to finish up what he was doing then grabbed the phone.

"Kid! Glad you called. You are free as a bird!"

"Really? Did they get my mother?"

"Don't know and don't care to know. Sal told me if I spoke to you to say you and your pals are clear. He saw the clip of your buddy exposing her. It's all over the news. He says you guys were true to your word. He thinks you went to that scam paradise to uncover her. Come back and work here. I am in charge now!"

"No word on Sierra?"

The old man's excitement faded.

"No kid, sorry. You gonna look for her?"

"I have to. I got to know she's alright."

I promised Gus I would visit Birds of a Feather if I made it back to Phoenix. I had no idea where I would land, especially if I could not find her. I changed my mind about chilling out with my friends before leaving to find Sierra. I could not rest until I knew she was safe. I scheduled a flight to LA the next morning with a layover until the connecting flight scheduled landed in Mexico City at 10pm. Thad found a record of Russell Redman staying at Casa Roma in Mexico City. I reserved a room at a Holiday Inn by the airport and decided to figure out ground transportation after I landed. I knew nothing about Mexico City, so I searched attractions and dining. It was apparently a foodie heaven. I even found a local theater in which my father was billed for an upcoming show. It was written in Spanish, so I had no idea what it was about, but his name was listed as one of the players. There was a photo of him by his name. He was tan but aged by too many days in the sun.

By evening we gathered in Thad and Colleen's rental having pizza and beer. Thad rented a car to get around until they could buy one. He offered to drive me to the airport. It was our last night together. After several rounds of a pipe being passed we broke into fits of laughter. Even though paradise was lost, people died, and our lives had been at risk, we could not help to laugh at the absurdity. Indeed knowing the danger and loss had passed, the taboo of laughing at such things only made us laugh harder. It had been an adventure.

Colleen couldn't catch her breath between laughing fits. She ran outside to get away from the stream of ridiculous anecdotes. Above Thad's cackle, I heard her call. We went outside and found her lying on her back. The full moon gave a milky haze to the rolling hill the rental sat on all the way down across the main road to the shore. We joined her. The grass was soft and cool. I made the motions of a child creating a snow angel on a winter's day. My parents once took me to Flagstaff for a Christmas shoot. My father showed me how to make a snow angel. It was the closest I ever felt to him.

"Who needs Lemuria Down? We can make our own paradise," Colleen said.

The laughing had stopped. No one disagreed.

Chapter Twenty-Three

The next morning, Colleen slept in. Thad rented a Hyundai which was just big enough to fit my bags, and Lesmour who came for the ride. I slept well but was a little spacy from the massive quantity of weed smoked. I suspected my partners in crime felt the same because our conversation to the airport was muted and trite. We promised to keep in touch. Lesmour encouraged me to move to the Big Island whether I found Sierra or not. Thad harassed him saying I was an adult, and he was not my mother. This devolved into them falling into their old pattern of bickering. I commented how much we have grown because of our trials and tribulation. They both laughed and ceased the verbal foray.

Thad pulled up to the terminal. Even though I didn't need the help, they both got out to put my luggage on the curb. We hugged. "All shitting aside," Thad whispered into my ear. "Move here if you want. You are my family."

"I love you too," I said.

I quickly gathered my bags and kept it together until I got inside the terminal. I found a corner where no one was sitting, so I could cry in peace before going through security.

The rest of the day was spent in transit. I bought a self-help paperback in an LA terminal shop titled; Love Birds, How to Share

Your Nest. I thought it was ironic considering I was setting out to find the girl I loved while dreaming of a future life together and our connection with birds. I read twenty pages before boarding the flight to Mexico City, leaving it behind at the gate seating area in case someone else wanted to read bullshit.

Sitting in my aisle was a young Hispanic woman with her son. He was playing Roblox on his tablet. The child was very animated, totally absorbed in the game, his avatar bouncing around doing crazy shit. His mother fawned over him stopping him from his game at one point to snack on a homemade finger sandwich and cookies. Their interactions were in Spanish, not a lick of English but acts of love and caring never need translation.

It reminded me I might soon be seeing my father who was my main playmate during my early years. I was homeschooled until seventh grade. Because of that I barely interacted with other kids. My father was child-like. He enjoyed playing with me so in a way, I saw him more of a playmate than a father. I had an unspectacular epiphany; humans never stop playing games. The difference being adult games have bigger consequences.

The flight was smooth, the landing rough. I took a shuttle to the Holiday Inn, showered, and had a pedestrian hamburguesa with a Corona at the restaurant bar. The television over the bar broadcast news about Lemuria Down showed footage of people leaving the island. It was in Spanish, so I did not understand the commentary. It cut to a brief iPhone clip of the moment my mother fled the scene when all hell broke loose followed by Thad's image on the giant screen at the amphitheater. I wondered if my father knew. I wondered if he would recognize me. I made no attempt to find his phone number, intending to drop in unannounced, suspicious that if he knew I was coming he might run off.

Casa Roma, the apartment complex where my father was staying, was several blocks from the Holiday Inn, as was the little theater he was involved in. I took a walk after eating half the unsatisfactory hamburguesa. My destination was to find Casa Roma. I wasn't going to knock on his door late at night and say, "Hi dad, miss me?"

I was simply curious to see where he lived. I scuttled the idea after two blocks because the meal was sitting heavy in my stomach and the neighborhood to a gringo like me, seemed sketchy. In the hotel room, I drank bottled water and felt much better. I checked my phone. I had three new messages, one each from Thad and Lesmour asking if I had landed. The third was from Nandi asking where I was. I replied and got an immediate response.

"Good luck! I miss you!"

I missed her too.

I slept well and fortified myself the next morning with a very good continental breakfast of pancakes, chorizo, and fresh fruit. The walk to my father's was radically different from the previous night. The air was cool and breezy, the sun bright and the street scene was vibrant with pedestrians, people on bikes, dodging traffic. Nearing my father's, it turned into a more residential area filled with street vendors. Some sat quietly under umbrellas while others were very vocal trying their best to lure me from my destination.

Casa Roma was a small two story complex of only eight units, a white pueblo with bright red doors and to either side small elaborate gardens with benches and fountains. According to Thad's search, my father was on the ground floor, unit 103. I walked through the garden area, could smell lavender and thyme, and knocked on his door. My heart pounded. No answer. I peered through a kitchen window to the right of the front door. It was dark inside, but I could make out simple furnishings, a TV on a stand, one love seat, a recliner that had seen better days and a dining table with two wooden chairs near the kitchen. It was tidy and organized.

"Amigo, you looking for Russell?"

I spun around, startled by the Mexican man with a round face and neatly trimmed beard. I told him I was a friend so as not to arouse suspicion.

"He's at the theater, two blocks down. They have new play tonight, you see?"

I nodded, saying I would like to, thanking him as I left. Soto de Teatro was a small run down building with a steeple and concrete steps leading to the front door. I learned later it was an early schoolhouse converted to a theater named after an active person in the local art scene who championed bringing theater back to Mexico City. The front door was open. I heard a hammer pounding. As my eyes adjusted I saw several long rows of seats and a small stage. A man near the back was nailing a two by four across a stand of painted scenery of rolling countryside. I walked slowly toward the stage. My legs felt heavy. I almost turned away. The man stood to catch his breath. It was my father. He squinted trying to make out who the advancing figure was. I stood in the shadows of the audience.

"Can I help you? Do you need tickets?" he asked.

I took a deep breath.

"Dad, it's me, Cody."

The hammer fell from his side. It clattered striking the stage floor echoing throughout the building. He took a step toward me then stopped, bending forward trying to adjust to the light.

"Oh my God, son!"

He leapt from the stage and embraced me. I was limp at first. He smelled of sweat and lumber. I surrendered, hugging him back.

"How is this possible? I never thought I would see you again!"

"Especially since you never looked for me," I quipped, but instantly regretted. He sat in an aisle seat avoiding my stare.

"Your mother said it was not safe. You would be better off without us. I was fool enough to believe her. Are you well?"

I sat next to him and could not help to put my hand on his shoulder. He was a broken man. I said I was safe after leaving Lemuria Down now that Martino knew my mother was masquerading as Darcy Summers. He stared blankly. He knew nothing of what happened.

"Haven't you seen the news?" I asked incredulous.

"Son, not only did I leave you, I also left the rest of the world behind. I moved here and never looked back. Don't watch news, I get a local paper, that's it. This is my little world. I am clueless as to what goes on beyond Mexico City. You say your mother was discovered? Is she alright?"

I recounted a long narrative of my life from when he left until the most recent debacle involving my friends, Lemuria Down and my mother. My father was bewildered, kept saying, "Oh my, Oh my." I told him about Sierra, how my mother scared her off after she encountered Martino. Even though Sierra told Gus before leaving the states she wanted to find him, my father said she never came by.

We talked for hours trying to catch up on the past fifteen years. I felt conflicted, eager to engage in conversation, while dealing with the hurt and anger of his abandonment. He took me to lunch insisting on paying to his favorite taqueria down the block. It was nothing much to look at, open air seating that flowed onto the sidewalk, but the food was fantastic and cheap. Skirt steak, chicken and shrimp were skewered on a charcoal grill and tossed onto tortillas made on the spot with an array of garnishes. My father told me to try one of the many agua frescas drinks in big jugs lined on a table by the back wall. I tried cinnamon oats. It was delicious.

While eating we reminisced some good memories like the time my mother took what she called a business trip to Paris claiming she wanted to make The Cody Redd Show international. Of course it was another guise for her to vacation. It was fine with us, we stayed home, went to movies, and played video games. We both admitted how bummed we were when she came home and lamely proclaimed she couldn't work out a deal with an imagined French producer.

"She was sweet and supportive in college, you know," my father said. "I did love her, and I think she loved me and you, in her way.

But she loved money and power more. Unfortunately, she became her parents."

I nodded, choosing not to comment. I was about to lift the giant drink to wash down a last bite of skirt steak when my father grabbed my free hand.

"Now that you know where I am, don't be a stranger. We can make up for lost time. I was such a useless tool. You deserved . . ."

He couldn't finish his sentence. Tears streamed down his face. I put my drink on the table and covered his hand with mine.

"Stop. You are wetting your taco."

We both laughed as he stood.

"I have work yet to be done for tonight's performance. I did most of the stage construction on this one, but I also have a little part as an obnoxious tourist. It's a comic romp. Want to see the show? It's in Spanish, but there is plenty of slapstick."

I agreed and walked him to the theater steps. He hugged me tightly then ascended the steps to the theater in a trot. He was still my father, but he was different than the man I remembered. He seemed happy and confident.

In the motel room, I booked a flight to Puerto Penasco the next morning. I messaged Thad to let him know I found my father but not Sierra. He replied saying he spent much of the night trying to trace her but found nothing. He also said he and Colleen put a deposit on a secluded house on a hill overlooking Hilo Bay. In a few short months our lives had changed at a dizzying pace. Earlier in the year if a magical genie appeared in our Oasis hovel and foretold our fate we would have attributed it to a bad reaction from a bag of weed laced with a hallucinogen.

"And I finished my fake novel!"

Finding Sierra was unlikely but there was no way I could give up. I told Thad I was going to stay in Puerto Penasco until I found her even if it meant going door to door, shop to shop.

"Hell, anything is possible," he said. "Just be careful. I imagine a white guy looking for a young Latina might be taken the wrong way, especially since you don't speak the language."

Selfies of Sierra and I might dispel concerns to people I questioned in the touristy fishing village, but Thad was right. It was risky. Human trafficking was prevalent. I thought if I spent enough time there and got to know the locals, they would be more likely to trust me. I asked about Lesmour.

Thad said he was "happy as a pig in shit" and loved his new boss. Lesmour even saw an opportunity where he can start his own charter business. Thad offered to invest some of his money to kick start Lesmour's dream. He cut the call short saying Colleen was waiting to go furniture shopping telling me to call him once I got to Puerto Penasco.

I was groggy and took a nap before the show, feeling more a sensory overload of the last several days rather than a lack of sleep. I woke in a start noticing the sun was down, afraid I had missed the beginning of the show. The old digital clock on the nightstand showed I had fifteen minutes until curtain. I combed my hair and jogged to the theater.

The theater was packed. I found a seat in the last row on the left. Cast members were in costume as farmers conversing with the audience. There was much gaiety and familiarity between the cast and the audience. My father stuck his head out from behind a curtain. Apparently he was not in the mindset to mingle with the audience before a show. I stood and waved both my arms to get his attention. He smiled broadly, giving a thumbs up before receding behind the curtain.

Because of the language barrier I could not understand the play's storyline. By the actor's expressions and wildly dramatic physical gestures I could tell it was a farcical comedy. My father dressed gaudily as a tourist, receiving warm applause upon his entrance. He took notice, doing an exaggerated curtsy which triggered a huge laugh. It came as no surprise to the audience he stepped out of character, like it was a running joke. My father was correct about slapstick throughout the play, tripping, spilling, a fight scene with prop sugar bottles breaking over heads at a whirlwind pace. The energy and silliness made time fly.

The play ended with a standing ovation. Most of the actors mingled with the audience who stayed behind. My father sat at the edge of the stage, talking to a short middle-aged woman with wavy, shoulder length hair. She lightly touched his arm every time she spoke. I cut through the crowd to my father. He saw me and pantomimed a fisherman casting his line then reeling me in. The woman followed the imaginary cast to me. Her face was wide-eyed and beaming.

"Cody, this is my good friend, Luna. Luna, this is my son."

"I can see the resemblance! Both handsome men!"

He asked if I would like to join them for a late dinner. There was a restaurant three blocks away where the cast and much of the audience went after shows. It served the best sangria in Mexico, or so he claimed. Several high top tables were reserved for seating and a long table with taquitos, burritos, and other finger foods was set aside for the cast. The sangria was good, loaded with fresh fruit. I limited myself to two so my travel day would not include a hangover.

The joyous comradery of cast and community was uplifting. It was weird and wonderful to see my father at ease with these people though it also made me feel sad. He seemed like a lovely man, but he had chosen not to be part of my life. He spoke Spanish fluently, often serving as my interpreter when conversing with others, and telling everyone, with pride, that I was his son. His son. But it was getting late. I told him I had a flight out in the morning. He was momentarily disappointed but understood my urgency to find Sierra. He walked me out of the restaurant. Luna pecked me on the cheek saying that she was very happy my father and I reunited. "La Familia," she said, "is everything."

"Please visit again," he said on the street corner. "Or wherever you land, I will visit you."

"Sure," I said, not sure that I believed him. He was just letting me walk back out of his life. For all he knew, this would be the last time he ever saw me. "I am glad you are happy."

"Thank you, Cody. Thank you. I want you to be happy too. Are you?"

I had to think. The past months, I definitely had periods of happiness. Meeting Sierra was one those periods. It was an awakening for me because before her, my life was a meaningless string of highs from beer, weed and inane conversations with Thad and Lesmour. When Nandi was not kicking my fractured shin,

I reveled in her company, but to consider myself happy was too much of an ask. I would leave Mexico City, alone.

"I am getting there," was the best I could offer.

He hugged me.

"You have no idea how much we are alike. You will get there. I am sure of it. You are far stronger than me."

I held him for a long time. I wanted to feel his breath rise and fall to be assured he was really there. My father.

"Are you and Luna?"

"We are taking it slow. She has been widowed two years and then there is my baggage. It is all good, though."

On the walk back to the motel, the streets were still busy and brightly lit. There was an energy here. A vibrant heartbeat amid hard living. Homeless people huddled in shadows while others hopping to and from establishments with luminous colors full with pulsating music and animated voices. It was a clear night but difficult to see the sky in all its brilliance beyond the light and shadows of humanity.

Chapter Twenty-Four

My flight arrived in Puerto Penasco's Mar de Cortes International Airport shortly before noon. I took a cab to the Malecon, the center of town where fishing boats and many shops and restaurants spread along the seaside boardwalk adorned with statuary. It was warm. I booked a month at Casita en el Malecon since it was within walking distance of the busiest part of town. My mission was to make myself known by daily visiting shops, eateries, and bars. I thought locals would come to trust me believing I was a long term resident, rather than a weekend tourist.

The Malecon was packed with tourists being the middle of day on a Saturday. From Phoenix, it was only a four hour drive, and I wondered why I had never come before. Thad and I were too busy getting stoned, watching television, wasting our lives away. It was the closet beach to the water deprived desert. I put my luggage in what was to be my temporary rustic home then forced myself into the throng of tourists, searching for a place to eat. I scaled Whale Watch Road, climbing the steep hill from the Sea Of Cortez and found a restaurant. Its name, The Blue Marlin, was etched on a wooden sign above the door. The place was empty when I entered and took a table in the corner. I was about to leave thinking it was empty for a reason, that reason being it was not good, when a man wearing an apron appeared.

"Welcome home!" he said.

I smiled at the hospitality, wondering if he knew I was staying, telling him I just moved to Puerto Penasco upon the recommendation of a friend. He asked where did I live before. I told him Phoenix, omitting Lemuria Down because I didn't want to get into telling that sordid bit of my life. Odd the lowly years in Phoenix was preferable to convey. He handed me a menu, saying many people visit from Arizona and never leave. I couldn't decide what to have. The menu was mostly shrimp, octopus, flounder in various preparations. I told him there were too many choices, I couldn't decide. He asked how hungry I was and told him not starving. He laughed and recommended the smoked marlin appetizer. It was their specialty.

It became a meal I would order at least once a week, along with a cold Corona and lime. The waiter and owner, Ernesto, was to become a good friend during my stay in the seaside town. Every time I walked into The Blue Marlin he said to me and any other patron that entered, "welcome home." It was a great temporary home.

The best time to establish myself in the community was during the week when most of the tourists were gone. It was late October. The temperature cooled which eliminated much of the desire to escape southern Arizona summer heat. Daily, I meandered from shop to shop engaging in conversation getting to know people. Many of them spoke English. I started to pick up a couple of words by reading signs and listening intently but never enough to form a sentence. My favorite time of day was sunset when many working families casually strolled the boardwalk. It was serene. I was touched by how they treated their children. La Familia was no joke. They cared deeply about family. It showed in the attention paid to their kids. I chose not to immediately ask about Sierra hoping to first gain trust.

The second week, I was having a lunch of ceviche at The Blue Marlin when Thad called. He asked if I checked out the university to see if Sierra was attending, figuring she might have wanted to continue her studies after leaving ASU. I said I hadn't considered it because it was basically a business college. Her focus was getting a degree in Animal Health to become a veterinarian.

"It is worth a shot," he said. "She might be thinking of getting a business degree so she could run her own vet clinic. Hey, you want a visitor? We did a quick close on the house and Colleen is going apeshit decorating. I think she wants me out of the way."

"Sure. I got an extra bedroom. Just don't bring Lesmour," I kidded.

Thad said he hadn't spoken to Lesmour in several days. Our round-headed friend was engrossed in his new job. He ended the call saying he would book a flight as soon as we hung up and text the itinerary. The restaurant was nearly full, not saying much because it had six round top tables. Ernesto, after taking an order breezed by but not before I asked for another Corona. While waiting, I searched through photos on my phone stopping at a selfie Sierra and I took.

"Senor', you know Sierra?"

A thin, elderly man with greying, black hair was peering over my shoulder at the selfie. He and another older, thicker man was seated next to me shortly after I sat down.

"What? You know her?" I was startled.

He apologized for looking over my shoulder. He was going to the restroom, and the photo caught his eye.

"Si. I am friends with her uncle."

"Where does she live? I must see her!" So much for playing it cool.

He looked at me a long time. I felt slightly threatened.

"I don't know, senor'. She ran from Arizona. She was in trouble."

It was agonizing. Pure fortune the man saw my pic of Sierra and I, but what could I say to assure him I would not harm her? If I told the truth, it would only confirm I was the cause to her leaving the states. If I lied it would fuel more distrust once he told Sierra. Ernesto brought me the Corona. I begged him for a pen and paper scrawling my name, the address of my casita, and phone number on the paper then gave it to the gentleman.

"When you see her, please pass it on. I made a promise to her. She will want to know I am safe."

He stuffed the note in his jeans pocket and shuffled to the bathroom. Out of pure nervousness I guzzled the beer. The man's friend at the table locked eyes with mine until I turned away. When the elderly man came back, he paid Ernesto and signaled for his friend to leave. He turned to me.

"I will give her the note when she gets back. Her family is away."

I tried to reason with him.

"You can tell we are friends just by looking at the picture!"

"Si. You were friends but maybe not now."

"I miss her!"

His face softened.

"Don't follow me. Trust me. I will give her the note."

He turned and gingerly stepped out the door as his friend followed. Ernesto asked if I wanted anything else.

"Have you seen those two men before?" I asked.

"They come here sometimes, but I not know them."

I paid my tab and walked along the boardwalk until I came to The Point, a restaurant/bar propped on pylons in the ocean accessible by a long boardwalk. I found a table outside and stared at the Sea of Cortez until sundown drinking beer. Thad called saying his flight would be landing 6pm the next day. I shared my encounter with the elderly man at The Blue Marlin. He could tell how distraught I was and tried to put a positive spin to it.

"That's a good thing, Cody. You know for sure she is alive, and she lives there. You just have to wait until she gets back."

"What if the guy thinks I am suspicious and tosses my note never bothering to tell her?"

"Maybe but you don't know that for sure. In the meantime don't give up looking. We'll check out the university."

It was all I could do.

Thad flew in, getting a taxi from the airport to downtown Puerto Penasco. We reverted to our old selves drinking, getting high while bar crawling all along The Malecon finishing our night paying a driver to take us to The Lighthouse Restaurant up a steep, unpaved road that had a spectacular view of the Sea of Cortez. We caught the sunset on the huge patio perched precipitously on a rocky cliff. Far from shore we watched a pirate style party tour boat, its masts lit up like Christmas trees. When dark enough, a round of fireworks shot from the deck its' brief flashing lit the rolling sea in green glow.

It was a minor miracle to wake the next morning and not feel hungover. We had a truncated breakfast at a bakery with excellent coffee and a few too many conchas, a sweet bread roll with cinnamon and sugar shaped like a shell. I was so happy, to be in Mexico, with my friend, Thad. Then we got a driver for the day that took us to the university and even two vet clinics hoping to find Sierra. Thad, forever the expert liar and conjurer of alternate reality, came up with a story of why I was looking for Sierra so that I would not freak out locals thinking I was involved in human trafficking. I would show the selfie of Sierra and I and another picture Gus took of us at Birds of a Feather and tell them we had applied for a research grant at ASU to study nonnative birds in Arizona. We were a couple but had a spat and she moved to Mexico without telling me where. The grant came through. It was a once in a lifetime opportunity and I wanted to find her, make up with her, and fulfill our dreams in the field of study we love. He told me when I was doling out the crap to use my early years of acting skills to convey regret and despair to pull at their heartstrings.

It worked. The university searched their records but could not find Sierra in their database. The two vet clinics had the same result. We even stopped by a marine research facility which had a run-down aquarium for tourists to see if she volunteered but came up with nothing. Thad's time in Puerto Penasco ran out. I offered to ride with him to the airport, but he said he didn't like long goodbyes.

"If you strike out here, come back to Hawaii."

"Maybe. I don't know what to do right now."

He patted my back.

"You'll figure it out. By the way, my agent found a book publisher. The editor seems like a decent guy. I was telling him all the shit we went through, and he suggested that should be my next book . . . a tell all."

"You going to do it?" I asked.

"It's way more your story than mine."

He cackled while getting into the cab, waved in an exaggerated fashion as the cab chugged down the street.

I waited for Sierra. I booked two more months and spent my time roaming streets, shops and fish markets half living being, half boring apparition interacting with citizens, telling my phony story when opportunity presented itself to anyone who cared to listen. I bought some notepads and for lack of anything better to do, jotted down the bizarre events of the past year while having morning coffee. I eventually exhausted the recent past and continued to recount earlier years eventually putting my entire life on paper. It felt good to get it out of my head, a sort of purge, like when you get a migraine and the best way to relieve it is by throwing up.

One midweek blustery day when most residents sheltered home, I went to an alcove with my pilfered camera from Lemuria Down. The alcove was beyond the big docks where commercial fishing boats arrived. On the tiny beachhead locals docked motorboats used for their own fishing. It had a sandy area that some boats were dragged onto if there was not room on the crumbling dock. The sand relented to large obsidian boulders that continued into the shallow waters. Lounging on several black boulders were seals. I discovered the local beach a week before and felt the urge to return to capture a bit of wildlife. I was delighted to find a pelican floating on the waves, his long neck tucked against his body. I walked upon hundreds of shells cracking underfoot between the beached boulders to get better shots. Many were crab shells most likely their contents consumed by the seals. The thrill of nature and recording it had not left me.

My father had a break between productions and visited the first weekend in November. The acting troupe took a week off after every show to decompress. He was pleased to see I took up writing and encouraged my project, suggesting that if I chose to publish, it might provide closure. I said it already had. We watched the sunset each night at The Lighthouse Restaurant. He confided he loved Mexico, the people, the lifestyle. He wanted me to stay even if I did not find Sierra.

"You could move to Mexico City," he said. "Be near me."

By December, I had all but given up ever finding Sierra. My encounters with townspeople proved futile. There were plenty of people with her last name of Gonzalez, but none admitted being a relative. I began to wonder if anyone believed the story Thad came up with. Surely it held less credibility as time wore on. Grants offered by universities had to be plucked quickly or else they would rot and drop off the vine. I was certain the elderly man never passed the note to Sierra. She would have contacted me by now.

My only true friend in town, Ernesto, owner of The Blue Marlin, agreed.

"Cody, people are not as welcoming as me. We are good people but so many things happen. We protect each other, you understand."

Through my constant patronage we formed a trust. I told him the actual truth. He was amazed and said I should finish my tell all book. He said it would make an excellent adaptation to film. I had a few laughs to myself pondering who in Hollywood could play, me, Thad and Lesmour.

The first days of December tripped in with clouds, gusts, and sputtering bouts of rain. I felt I had run my course in Puerto Penasco. Tourist season was a memory. The town was quiet which became a good breeding ground for loneliness. I had run out of things to note about my life and had snapped way too many pictures of seals, pelicans, seagulls, and marlins pulled off fishing boats. I received Christmas invites from Thad and Colleen and my father, all tempting because I would have liked the company, but I was not a big fan of Christmas. Both my father and Thad understood, knowing the Redman family Christmas was just another vehicle for the Cody Redd Show. It was just another way my mother monetized me.

I wondered if my mother was still alive. Her hurried exit from the Lemuria Down amphitheater was the last anyone had seen of her. I could only assume Martino did make her disappear. Still, I would not be surprised if she someday resurfaced with a different identity besides Darby Summers. I sat at my laptop and googled Lemuria Down. Like my father, I now avoided world news. It seemed easy to ignore in Mexico. After our departure, the once vaunted utopian society continued with half the population at its height and much less ideological aspirations. Hawaii was in the process of claiming the island for itself and revisioning it as an exclusive resort for those with very deep pockets. The population that did not leave would be bought out, aka bribed to leave or retained if their services were required. Then I found in a recent article there were rumblings on the island but not rumblings by the residents.

When we first arrived, Jayson had mentioned a research team had begun a project to tap into the dormant volcano for thermal energy. According to the article, all involved in the research had left the island, and a core sample digger was accidently engaged by an unskilled maintenance man. Hurricane winds caused an island wide power outage. The maintenance man flicked on a power generator switch causing the core sampler switch to trip on. He then went to lunch as the sampler struck lava triggering the once dormant volcano back to life.

It was not a dramatic Pompei effect, just a steady flow from the top down to the valley where the town and port sat. The article said the Hawaiian government immediately cancelled plans to convert it into a luxury resort. The lava flow swept the fill that was used to make the entire town slough into the ocean returning the volcanic island much to its original state. I felt sorry for the oi' family and other creatures on the island, not so much for the inhabitants.

The winter sky opened. Rain pounded the roof of my casita as I stood, stretched, and poured another cup of coffee. Even though it was midday it felt like early morning as if an angry god had lowered a black curtain over the town. I had been meaning to call Grace for months to see how she was doing. She answered sounding annoyed until I told her it was me. She brightened and apologized saying she thought I was a telemarketer. I told her all that went down since we last talked. She knew some of it because she had become a news junkie. She had moved to Flagstaff securing a job as a motel manager. The motel was run down, but she liked the area and the job.

"I live at the motel rent free! You gotta come visit sometime!"

There was a knock on my door. I was shocked someone was out in the torrential rain. I promised to call Grace back, ended the call, and flicked on the outside lights. Peering through the kitchenette window, I saw a short figure holding an umbrella. The figure wore an oversized fisherman's raincoat with the hood up. I could not make out the face.

I swung open the door. Under the weak porch light of my bungalow huddled Sierra, shivering in the pouring rain.

"Oh my God!" I yelled. 'It's you! It's really you!"

She hurried inside. When I tried to embrace her, Sierra's umbrella poked my eye, and my sweatpants and t-shirt became soaked from the embrace. She said nothing. She did not return my embrace. I was unnerved. I took her umbrella and raincoat and hung them on the coatrack. I asked her to sit down.

"Where have you been? Did you get my note? I have been looking so long for you."

Sierra trembled. Was she shaking from the cold or was she crying? I wrapped the blanket on the loveseat around her. She took a couple of deep breaths.

"My uncle gave me your note a long time ago," she said, in a quavering voice. "I was afraid to tell you."

"Tell me what?" I said. "You have nothing to be afraid of. The danger is gone."

She covered her face with her hands and sobbed. I put my arm around her.

"I thought I would never see you again," Sierra said. "My parents hated you for upending our lives. Then you come here to Mexico and give a note to my uncle. What am I to do? I thought you would give up; you would go away, but you stayed!"

She cried like a microburst in the desert. Heavy downpour. The room seemed darker as if every light in the world had gone out. Innately, I sensed what was coming. My arm dropped from her like an autumn leaf releases from a branch. I knew what was coming. Winter.

"Every day you stayed made it harder and harder to tell you! You kept your promise. I didn't keep mine!"

I remembered our promise. I shivered. She hid her face in her hands, tried to speak but was overcome again with tears.

"It's ok," I said, "I understand."

She leaned against me, then I wrapped her in my arms. The rain was deafening on the roof. My little rental was dry. We were safe.

"You're not mad?" she said, taking a furtive glance at me.

"I can never be mad at you. Tell me this . . . is he less drama than me?"

She laughed through her tears. So did I.

Chapter Twenty-Five

I packed that night. I had a month left on my rental, but didn't care. I found a flight to Phoenix the following morning. I don't know why I chose Phoenix. Maybe, in my mind, it was the place that felt most like home. I could have stayed with Thad, Colleen and Lesmour. I know I wanted to get out of Mexico so staying with my dad was not an option. Phoenix was the earliest and shortest flight out. In my fragile state of being I guess that was reason enough.

On the short flight, I allowed myself to ruminate vowing to let it all go once the landing gear hit Sky Harbors' tarmac. This self-indulgence reminded me when Sierra allowed me to walk around the famous fountain in my hometown one time as I bitched about my miserable past. Back then, I was walking in circles. Now I was above it all flying in a straight line. Progress. Sierra and I had a dazzling, dramatic romance flare like a comet only to burn out once it hit the reality of our circumstances. The passion was there. It was real but not meant to last. If I never met her, I would still be in The Oasis with Thad and Lesmour. My life was caged before I met her. How could I ever regret loving her?

I rented a car at Sky Harbor and drove to downtown Scottsdale, getting a suite at Valley Ho, a retro hotel that looked like it was from the old Jetsons cartoon. I thought I should pamper myself since Christmas was nearing. It was a gift to me, from me. One day, I would have to get a job. Another sunny day in Arizona, temps in the seventies, best time of the year. The rains from Mexico extended to southern Arizona and had washed the skies clean of smog then moved on. It reminded me of perfect blue sky days in Fountain Hills when I was a child.

I ate at their Space Age restaurant, having an old-time meal of pork chops, mashed potatoes with gravy and a good sized salad. For a change I thought I would try an Old Fashioned, a drink that was popular in that time period. The waiter brought it spilling a little on the table for it was brimming over with booze. As I gingerly raised the potent drink to my lips I stopped and returned it to the table. I decided I would make a point of refraining from alcohol and weed for a while or at least curb the knee jerk consuming of mind altering substances. After eating, I went back to my room, drew the thick curtains, and slept soundly the entire night.

I had a crazy dream about Phoenix, the bird I had saved. In the dream, Phoenix was flitting about my head, swooping in a dive bomber attack, briefly landing on my shoulders and head then taking off all the while speaking a language I could not understand. I shouted, "speak English!" and woke with a start. I checked my phone. No one had called. I was alone.

At the restaurant, I had a breakfast of coffee and a Danish checking my phone to see if Birds of a Feather was open yet. By the time I could drive to Tempe, it would be. I finished my coffee, savoring even the last sip which had stray grounds. I let the bitterness of the grounds sit on my tongue before swallowing. I headed out.

As I pulled in to Birds of a Feather I saw the Spanish Mission front doors were swung open. I could hear the chorus of birds greeting the morning. I had missed that sound. It was a hopeful sound. In the backyard, I found Gus throwing out seed, a plethora of ground birds excitedly pecking away. I tapped him on the shoulder.

"Kid, you're back! You scared the bejesus out of me!"

"Sorry. Thought I'd surprise you."

"How'd it go, young man? You find her?"

"Yep."

He studied me trying to read my face. He shook his head and tsked.

"Women," was all he said, "You staying?"

"Don't know. Is Phoenix still here?"

Gus waved his arm for me to follow. There to the side of the yard, was the small aviary for all the broken birds where Sierra left him months before. We carefully eased in being sure not to let the several birds there to get out. Gus peered; his glassy eyes had a hard time adjusting to the shade of the huge acacia just beyond the yard. I picked out Phoenix quickly. I recognized the small tuft of feathers that jutted from his broken wing. I couldn't believe it. He was flying about without impediment. Even though his wing was slightly bent, his flightpath was straight and strong.

"He's healed," I said.

"Oh yeah, for a while now. You going to keep him?"

"No."

It took some doing but I coaxed him to land in my palm, baiting with a worm that Birds of a Feather harvested. I cupped him in my hands and slowly walked out the front door. Gus followed me asking if I was coming back inside.

"Nope."

Gus smiled broadly.

"Good boy," he waved then closed the door.

I could feel Phoenix's little heart pounding in my palm. I was afraid it might be too much for him. I spoke softly to the bird as I strode further from the place where it all began.

"It's ok. It's going to be ok."

When far enough away, I slowly opened my hands. He paused for a moment, scratched my lifeline, pecked at my pointing finger, then he soared. I watched him as long as I could until he became part of the unlimited sky.

I reached into my pocket and pulled out my phone. I found the number on my contact list.

"How's the weather," I asked.

"Dreary. Popping by for a visit?"

I booked a flight to London.

Acknowledgments

Thank you to Joyce Coyle Mohrer and Patricia Cowan, my first two editors and back slappers. To Marcy Dermansky, the editor who pushed, prodded, challenged and encouraged. To all friends and family who put up with me the past few years who listened to (or at least pretended to) the many incantations of this story while its feathers grew.

Thank you, Uncle Gus wherever you may be. Your soul lives within these pages.

www.ingramcontent.com/pod-product-compliance
Lightning Source LLC
Chambersburg PA
CBHW030125010826
48973CB00002B/423